The Opposite

of

Chance

Also by Margaret Hermes

The Phoenix Nest

Relative Strangers: Stories

The Opposite

of

Chance

a novel by

Margaret Hermes

Delphinium Books

THE OPPOSITE OF CHANCE

For information, address DELPHINIUM BOOKS, INC., 16350 Ventura Boulevard, Suite D
PO Box 803
Encino, CA 91436

Library of Congress Cataloging-in-Publication Data is available on request.
ISBN: 978-188328595-1
21 22 LSC 10 9 8 7 6 5 4 3 2 1

First Edition

Versions of several of the chapters in *The Opposite of Chance* appeared as short stories in various journals:

"All Roads Lead to Mekkah" was first published in the *Green Hills Literary Lantern*.

"Primo Class" appeared in *The South Carolina Review*.

"An Innocent/A Broad" first appeared in the *Owen Wister Review*.

"The Pensione Desirée" was published in the "Not Prepared for Adventure" issue of *Thema*.

For Ann Grace Hermes

Take Me to the War

1.

Betsy was not a complete idiot, though, once again, she felt like one. She had been grateful to the travel agent for securing a cheap fare from Montreal to Paris but now, waiting at Mirabel airport for her first transatlantic flight, each time she heard French spoken she thought reflexively that everyone around her was more cultured, except perhaps the young boy sandwiched between his parents who was energetically excavating his nose.

She had grown up in Milwaukee, gone to college in Milwaukee, married in Milwaukee, embarked on graduate school in Milwaukee. She had taken French classes in which she did reasonably well when tested on grammar or vocabulary, but in which her tongue—or arguably the vocal folds of her larynx?—led her to fail dismally in articulation, and therefore in confidence, hence fatally in conversation. "Like choking on your own tongue," her sister Gina, who had an obedient larynx, had supplied sympathetically.

She had chosen to pursue a graduate degree in anthropology in part because anthropologists seemed predestined to travel and in part because the study of kinship ties in tribal societies promised to be sparklingly devoid of the unbridled opportunities the Romance languages afforded to garble nasal vowels and the gargled R.

Not only was she unable to pronounce French, she couldn't *hear* the language. She had never overheard French outside a classroom in all her years in Milwaukee. German, *ja*. Polish, *tak*. Italian, *si*. Even Serbian, *da*. But never French, *jamais*. Her ear could not distinguish between war, *guerre*, and the train station, *gare*. The sounds were interchangeable when they were not indecipherable. This would be borne out for her explicitly some days later when she requested a taxi driver to take her to the train station and he replied that there was no war in France, she had missed it by four decades, *précisément*, by thirty-five years and three months. He would illustrate with hands grasping an invisible Thompson M1928 and saying, Ak-ak-ak, repeatedly, in the universal language of guns.

There were no open seats at her designated gate. That must mean the plane was oversold. She pictured herself discovering another passenger snug and smug in her assigned seat, his boarding pass identical to her own. Prior possession would be enough to ensure that he would go to Europe in her place. She wondered if she would ever get off the ground.

Betsy settled herself at the empty, opposing gate. She looked across the wide aisle nervously, speculating on the odds that her flight would be canceled or her backpack stolen. Her eyes dropped as a man in a rumpled suit approached. From a distance, he looked like a house detective in an old movie. She feared he was coming to chastise her, tell her she should not be seated there, but he walked past her to the large expanse of windows. He rustled through a creased duty-free bag and his dog-eared piece of carry-on luggage in their quiet corner. She watched through half-lidded eyes as he set a compass on the floor. He removed a folded, patterned orange and brown shawl from his carry-on, spread it on the floor, and knelt, his back to her, letting his shoes fall away from the heels of his feet. She noticed that the counters of his shoes folded inward, completely flat, allowing him to compromise with his faith, shoes half off, fitted only on his forefeet.

When he bent his forehead to the shawl she saw that his hair was dyed and the roots matched the gray in his mustache. Why would he dye his hair? This was the kind of question she believed she would be able to answer at the end of her travels.

The area around them started to fill: some families, several women with head scarves, one head wrapped in an improbable Burberry signature beige with red and black plaid. She wondered if she had chosen a gate set aside for Muslims. She had never seen any Muslims before, at least none she was aware of. She wondered if attending Catholic schools from kindergarten through grad school had isolated her more than the typical Milwaukeean, but then she thought, no, if anything, that marked her as a typical Milwaukeean.

The man sat back on his heels and refolded the shawl and retrieved his compass and tucked both into the shopping bag. When he turned away from the window, she was startled by how sensationally, almost aggressively, handsome he was, how refined his features. He looked like a movie star down on his luck, the suit in need of pressing, the hair dyed for his last role. Or a movie star *playing* someone down on his luck. The warm brown of his skin appeared no deeper than a perfect Hollywood tan.

Was there such a thing as a Muslim movie star? Wouldn't being a film idol be forbidden? Wasn't it akin to encouraging the worship of icons?

Whatever his career, she was certain of one thing: he was unmarried. A wife would not let him out into the world looking so at odds with himself. Betsy had spent the preceding decade—all of the 1970s—in the role of wife and so she knew.

*   *   *

Betsy and Greg had married while still in college. It had been like playing house. She pretended that she knew how to cook and mend. He pretended that reading the newspaper completely absorbed his attention, his purpose.

Before long, she was turning out tasty meals on a minuscule budget and turning remnants into curtains and floor cushions, and Greg had found other things to occupy his wandering attention.

They celebrated coupledom. Their friends, even the

determinedly, dedicatedly single ones, liked to while away the hours in their much cozier flat with its brick-and-board bookcase and orange-crate end tables and couch of cinderblocks topped by a sheet of plywood and littered with pillows. They all entertained each other, occasionally vaulting into the world outside from this central location. Ruth and Paul were their tennis partners and were ushers alongside them one night of each production at the Milwaukee Rep so they could see theater for free. Caroline and Leo scrounged bikes at yard sales and the four made forays on county roads. Every week Alan and Marilyn and Jan came faithfully to watch *Saturday Night Live* on Betsy and Greg's flickering screen. There was a constant parade of companions in and out of their apartment, most of whom seemed to aspire to be just like them someday.

Nine and a half years would expire before she tumbled into the real world: a disproportionate number (disproportionate given that nearly half were male) of the fellow undergrads, later anthropology and philosophy grad students, still later Greg's colleagues in the philosophy department, who joined them at their table had been auditioning for the part of Greg's lover. So many of those young women who sipped his Almaden and swallowed her home-baked Swedish rye while circled round an enormous cable spool of rough wood rescued from a construction site proved to be ripe for an extramarital adventure. And continued to sup with them at the thrift store replacement with peeling painted legs but a top scoured down to bare oak. And stayed on at the formal mahogany—bestowed upon her by her warmhearted, white-haired neighbor on Kilbourn who had taught Betsy to crochet before being scuttled off to a nursing home—after making the transition to "just friends."

She had been stunned to learn that her dinner parties consisted so lopsidedly of Greg's former/current/prospective bed partners. These were her friends. In some cases, so were their husbands or boyfriends. If they were not her friends, then who were? And who was *she* exactly? And what was she to them?

She saw what she was to him. A comfort. A convenience. A wife.

*　　*　　*

Betsy had learned the excruciating subtext of her marriage from biking buddy Leo whose sweetheart Caroline had enjoyed not one but two separate affairs with Greg. During the last, Leo came to the realization that he was no longer content to be on standby. More than that, he decided he had always been more drawn to steadfast Betsy than to flighty Caroline. His mission was to convince Betsy that she ought to feel the same, so he was obliged to expose Greg's past/present/probable future.

At first, Betsy didn't believe Leo. Oh, she believed that Leo had become awkwardly, desperately infatuated with her. She came to think he would do or say any outrageous thing in his campaign to secure her affections. She tolerated—and admitted to herself that she was flattered by—his persistence. It seemed like an eternity since anyone had paid her that kind of attention. She and Greg were long settled into their husband-and-wife roles, so she let Leo wax on about her glossy hair, her liquid eyes, her milky skin, but she drew the line at his talking about Greg.

She remained full of faith in her husband, who could not manage to be faithful for a week at a time, until the afternoon Leo engineered a restaurant lunch with their mutual friend Ruth. Leo alluded to Ruth's relationship with Greg, and Ruth took issue with his verb tense. "Oh, stop it, Leo. Greg and I haven't slept together in at least four years."

Betsy actually fell off her chair. Later, she wondered if one or the other of her two close friends had pulled the chair out from under her literally as well as figuratively.

Ruth had been distressed by Betsy's tumble, by her spiraling down. "Oh, God," she said, her face as white as the restaurant's bleached table linen, "I always thought you knew. I thought it didn't matter to you. You seemed to genuinely like Caroline and Jan and the others. And me. I thought you were cool with it. Like Paul was. We all thought you knew." Ruth didn't mean to be cruel. There was no mistaking it: she was genuinely stricken, the more so because she could witness the immediate effect the words "the others" and "we all" had just had upon her friend.

"It's the '70s," Ruth said, as though the decade just ending explained or excused everything. "Everybody's doing it."

"Not everybody," Leo said, laying his broad hand over Betsy's delicate one that was gripping and bunching the tablecloth.

"Was everybody lying about it, too?" Betsy asked. "Or was everybody just lying to me?" She reimagined her dinner parties as complex conclaves of intrigue and lust. She wondered if it was lust or boredom that propelled Greg. She remembered that when she had expressed disapproval of their friends and acquaintances who hopped from one bed to another, Greg would cluck his tongue in accord. She had said that it wasn't so much that their promiscuity meant they were immoral as that they were unmoored. Greg had agreed, declaring himself lucky to have fastened onto her as his anchorage. *Right here*, she told herself, *sitting in this restaurant, hunched over a plate of shrimp Newburg gone cold, everything changes.*

At first Greg resisted the divorce. But then he came to understand Betsy was done with housekeeping.

Betsy moved out of their flat and into the house of her sister and her sister's husband and their twin boys. Gina and Matt lived in the suburb of Waukesha, where residents had safely eluded the 1970s. They managed to bypass the lanky era of bell-bottoms and long, straight hair and march directly into the puffy decade of shoulder pads and big hair.

Betsy shed her old life and her old friends. She didn't take anything with her except some of her clothes and all of her books and half of their record albums. She didn't even take the beloved mahogany table. Especially not that.

She had been struggling with her dissertation. Now she decided she didn't want to pursue a doctorate in anthropology after all. She didn't want to resume any part of the life she had shared with Greg or cross paths with any of the people she used to know. Half of them were women and she would be wondering darkly about all of those. She told her sister that she wouldn't have made a very good anthropologist anyway. Clearly, the study of mating habits was beyond her.

As though she had always had a backup plan, she enrolled at the University of Wisconsin in Milwaukee, emerging two years later with a Master's of Library Science. Tired of going to school—she been doing that for twenty-seven of her thirty-two years—she opted to take the proficiency exam rather than undertake a master's thesis.

She wondered if she had elected an emphasis in children's and young adult literature because or in spite of her inability to conceive. Her periods had never been regular. Gina, whose bad cramps arrived every twenty-eight days, a finely timed affliction, always told her sister she envied her—Betsy could go months without even spotting. At her weakest moment, Betsy asked herself if Greg had sought fulfillment elsewhere because she couldn't bear him children. Perhaps his straying was a form of loyalty, his way of not abandoning her and her barren womb. Perhaps he had been accommodating his disappointment and sparing them both the constant, nagging sorrow of it. When she voiced this to her sister, Gina found a therapist who disabused Betsy of that notion. "Worth her weight in gold, frankincense, or myrrh," Gina patted herself on the back.

*   *   *

Betsy clutched the fake leather arms of her seat as she saw the sign behind the desk at her designated gate change first in French then in English. Her flight would be delayed for two hours. Two additional hours of speculating on the pitfalls awaiting her if she ever actually boarded and if her seat turned out to be unoccupied.

Betsy followed the unsettlingly handsome middle-aged Muslim with her eyes as he walked away from the gate. Then she followed him with her feet.

He made his way to the food court on their concourse and stood, weary, bags suspended from both arms, like a dusty traveler from the past. She thought of caravans and the Silk Road. After three full minutes of indecision, he stepped up to one of the counters. Betsy got into line at a kiosk that sold coffee and croissants. She wondered if Muslims were permitted to drink coffee or if they were forbidden not just alcohol but all stimulants as well. Or was she confusing them with Mormons? Could either of their tribes enjoy a Coke? When she turned around with her paper cup of steaming *café au lait*, her Muslim was nowhere to be seen.

The extent of her disappointment surprised her, especially since she had no intention of trying to make contact. She had wanted just to observe him, in part for something to fill the time and in part because looking at him was its own reward. She found an empty seat at one of the scattered tables and stared despondently into the oily swirl of coffee and milk.

"Pardon me. May I join you?"

She looked up to find him—him!—standing awkwardly, his bags hanging by their straps from his forearms, his hands balancing a tray. She nodded dumbly and he set the tray down very slowly, so that the bags would not swing forward and jostle the soup and—aha!—the coffee on his tray, and then he sat opposite her. She was pleasantly conscious of heads turning in their direction.

"In my country," he explained, "meals are taken in common. A solitary meal is"—he extended his hands, palms up, as if holding the concept out between them—"indigestible." He shrugged.

"Where is your country?" she managed, despite his eyes, which were an unexpected green. She couldn't believe that she was sitting across from him, talking to him. Rather, she couldn't believe he had chosen her.

"Oh," he blinked, his long lashes brushing his cheeks, "my country would be Canada now. But I was speaking of Lebanon."

"You're Lebanese." She wanted to keep him talking. She found his accent—which she could only describe as "French"—improved her outlook, even her posture.

"I am afraid there is no such identity."

She looked her puzzlement back at him.

"There are Phalangists and Palestinians and Kurds and Armenians in the country of my birth. There are Muslims and Jews and a dozen different flavors of Christians. There are the various Syrian forces—Saheka, Yarmouk, As Sai'qa. If we are not talking about political factions or religious faiths or the sects within them, then we are talking about partisans fighting in the name of their town. We are Zghortiotes or Tripolitans, but we are not Lebanese. And every group has their own fighting force. That is civil war in Lebanon."

"I'm sorry," she said, feeling that she was getting tutored in both politics and perspective and extending her regrets for her deficits in both. Her own worries were trifling, his profound.

He smiled at her, and for a moment, she stopped breathing. He was more beautiful than Robert Redford or Richard Chamberlain. Yes, but that was apples to oranges. He was more beautiful than Warren Beatty or Sean Connery. Still not right. Omar Sharif. He was more beautiful than any of them and their more handsome brothers.

"I'm exposing my ignorance," she said when she resumed breathing, "but I'm really confused by your war. It's called a civil war, but on the news it sounds more like a war between Lebanon and Syria. And I know there's been bombing by Israel. But I'm not sure who their target is."

"It is confusing even for those fighting in it. According to the president of Syria, Lebanon itself does not exist. Or should not. He has said that Lebanon and Syria are one country and one people. He thinks they should have one government."

"His."

"Already you understand more than most."

They talked for another hour, Betsy asking him about the city of Beirut, where he had been raised, and he reciprocated by questioning her about growing up in Milwaukee. He told her that she would have found much of the Beirut of his childhood indistinguishable from Europe. "The architecture, the automobiles. Even the clothing. Except for what men wore on their heads. In the 1930s a man living in the city might wear a fedora or straw boater with his suit and tie or he might wear a tarboosh or a turban."

Betsy described running in the streets of the North Side of Milwaukee with her playmates in the 1950s behind trucks that sprayed entire neighborhoods with DDT. "An enormous traveling cloud of thick white mist. My sister and I used to run with our arms outstretched, as if we were trying to embrace it. The thrill was that you couldn't see. You were in the cloud and you were running blindly to stay inside it. We were more than blind, we were oblivious to any danger. And so, I guess, were our parents. I am amazed at all the things parents didn't worry about back then."

He told her that his parents were accomplished worriers and that they had successfully passed this skill on down to their son. "It was my mother's worry that finally got me to leave our country, taking the family with me, of course."

"When did you leave?"

"Three years ago. In '78. Not as soon as my mother would have liked. But I am being unfair. Not as soon as I should have. Everything that wasn't being destroyed by the war was being transformed by it, including my job."

At last she could ask, "And what was that?" She had developed a practice since her divorce of assessing male character traits and manners: *Like Greg* and *Not like Greg*. She was certain (though she recognized she had a poor track record in judging such matters) that the man sitting opposite her was not a womanizer. At any rate, he wasn't womanizing her.

Which made her all the more curious about the dyed hair. She felt his profession would finally explain this incongruity.

"I had been the assistant director of antiquities at the National Museum. When the fighting broke out, we took measures to protect the museum collections. I supervised the removal of our most vulnerable objects into storerooms below ground. Then we walled up the openings, so that there was no longer any access to the lower floors." He produced a rueful smile, "No longer any suggestion that there were any lower floors."

"Like the tombs of the pharaohs," she said.

"Yes," he sighed. "Very much like that. On the street level, all the mosaics laid into the floor were covered over with concrete. Those things that could not be moved—large statues and sarcophagi—were surrounded with sandbags until we could replace the sandbags with shielding made from formed concrete. Even thus, so many rare, even peerless, artifacts have been shattered. And the fighting goes on." He shook his head. "My entire professional life had been spent bringing antiquities before the public. Now instead of researching and cataloging artifacts for display, I was overseeing their being removed from view. Of course I wanted to preserve the museum's collections, but I felt much saddened. We all did. We closed the doors to the museum in 1975. After we finished protecting the collections as best we could, I had no real work. And of course there was the danger. It was better to go elsewhere," he sighed again.

"Why Montreal?"

"I had completed two years of study here as a young man. I remembered the city fondly."

"Is that when you learned French and English?"

"French was the first language of our household when I was a child. In my country, people who live in the cities typically speak Arabic, French, and English."

Betsy flushed. She didn't say that in her country people native to the cities often fail to master English; instead, she changed the subject. "Are you working at a museum in Montreal?" she asked.

"Yes," he said. "I am working at a museum in Montreal." He looked at his watch and stood abruptly. "I must leave you. Thank you for letting me share your table and your company. I find it"—he smiled—"unpalatable to eat alone."

"I very much enjoyed talking with you."

He bowed slightly.

"Where is it you're going?" she called after his retreating form. She had assumed he was visiting Lebanon but now worried that he would.

"To Saudi Arabia," he said, turning, his face all at once suffused with a light that made him, impossibly, still more handsome. He raised his hand, not quite a salute, not quite a wave.

Heading back to her gate, Betsy discovered she was no longer anxious about boarding the plane for Paris. If not this plane, then another. If not this day, then the next.

Already she had made it out of the United States onto foreign soil and into her first adventure. Savoring the jangle of languages in the air, she congratulated herself on having begun her journey with not just small talk but meaningful conversation with very possibly the most piercingly handsome man on the planet. That would be something to write to her sister about.

* * *

Four days later, Betsy climbed into a taxi, the first she had permitted herself since arriving on the continent. The driver surveyed her and said "Where to?" in English. She decided that he was extending a courtesy, addressing her in what he had deduced was her mother tongue, and she would do the same. She requested, in French, *s'il vous plaît*, that he take her to the train station. Her words—her pronunciation—unleashed the monster (or *monstre*) in him. When he'd finished ranting in the vernacular that there was no war in his country save the war she and those like her were waging against the

French language, Betsy checked her watch. She had ample time to make her train. She waited until he had lowered his invisible submachine gun, then she hoisted her backpack off the seat beside her and opened the taxi door. "I was talking about the war in Lebanon," she said in English. "But never mind. I think I'll walk."

All Roads Lead to Mekkah

2.

Kassim wished, devoutly, that he could have put off his journey until Dhu al-Hijjah, the last month in the Islamic calendar. Only then could a hajj be made. He longed to be addressed respectfully as hajji, as one who has completed the pilgrimage to Mekkah required of all who are able to make the journey. But his hajj must be delayed indefinitely because his petition to Allah could not wait.

His mother insisted that he could not afford to put off his journey for even a few months. "You cannot wait for the seasons to change, my son. It is always winter in your wife's heart." Financially, he couldn't afford to make the journey at all. His mother, Azar, had solicited funds from her two brothers to supplement their dwindling reserves. Najwa, his wife, resented that their savings were being exhausted by a pilgrimage that did not even fulfill her husband's obligation, but of late Najwa resented everything to do either with money or with her husband.

When the family had lived in Beirut, they'd employed four servants, three in the house and one who tended the grounds and the automobile. Now Najwa was expected to do the work of all those, not that they any longer had a house or grounds or automobile to tend. All six of them—Najwa, her husband, their three daughters, and Kassim's mother—shared a two-bedroom third-floor walk-up in the Mile End neighborhood of Montreal, "the End of the World neighborhood," according to his daughter Hala. Kassim's mother and youngest daughter shared the second bedroom while the two teenagers unrolled a mattress that was used for seating in the living room during the day and fell asleep each night to a soundless flickering TV screen.

When Kassim had shepherded his family out of Lebanon in 1978, everyone agreed there were many more reasons to leave than to stay, but the reason that dwarfed all others was unambiguous, they had lost so many: Kassim's father to a sniper's bullet, Najwa's brother and cousin to a suicide bomber, other relations listed as *casualties*—their deaths so insignificant—of the fighting between Israel and the PLO. Leaving Beirut had been wrenching—they mourned their old life—but not only was that way of living already lost to them, they feared the loss of their very lives each day. Kassim's family, what remained of it, had regarded him as their savior. Back then they blessed this man who brought them to a land of peace, of unbroken buildings and empty skies, but now fear for their lives had been supplanted by fear for his livelihood, the cataclysmic eclipsed by the everyday.

At home, Kassim had been the Assistant Director of Antiquities at the National Museum of Beirut. In Montreal the best he could find was work as a security guard at the Redpath Museum at McGill with its extensive natural history collections and relatively modest accumulation of archaeological and ethnological artifacts. Kassim was baffled by his failure. He had nineteen years of experience acquiring, cataloging, and displaying significant archaeological treasures and supervising those who handled them. He spoke a more refined French and polished English than many of his Canadian counterparts. He assumed that his fluency in Arabic along with his deep knowledge of the gilded votive statuettes and other finds from the Obelisk Temple of Byblos, not to mention his paper establishing the sarcophagus of Ahiram with the oldest text written in the Phoenician alphabet as belonging to the Iron Age rather than his own Bronze Age, would make him valuable in the museum marketplace.

His mother was known for saying that it was fitting that Kassim should work in a museum as he himself was a work of art. Saying so did not endear her to her daughter-in-law.

Najwa was keenly aware of her husband's exceptional good looks and Azar's remarks suggested that her mother-in-law did not find his wife worthy of her beautiful son. Azar and Najwa had kept an uneasy peace between them, one that had been buoyed up by the charged air that had buffeted them in Lebanon and was in danger of complete collapse in enervating Canada.

After nearly five decades of futile appeals, Kassim had almost given up asking his mother to stop drawing attention to his appearance. He found the unsolicited attention others paid to be disturbing enough without her reminding him that he was sought after and singled out for his looks rather than the things a man hoped to be remembered for. As a small child, Azar had dressed him in lace and skirts in the European manner. He had been as pretty—more pretty!—than any little girl. As a schoolboy he had been thought shy. He had kept his gaze downcast, not just because he was self-conscious but because he wanted to veil his green eyes, a gift from his Persian great-grandmother.

His first stay in Montreal, as a young man doing postgraduate studies, had inspired open, aggressive declarations by both women and men. He was approached with offers of a cruise to the Bahamas, an engraved Swiss watch, a gold and onyx ring with a ruby winking in its center (that for a single afternoon tryst with a commodities broker), as well as modeling jobs and party invitations. When he declined, as he always did, Kassim became still more desirable.

As an object of intense interest, it was not so surprising that he became interested in objects rather than people. He chose as his companions dusty artifacts so long buried that they carried no imprint of the hands that made them.

When he returned to Beirut, a marriage was arranged, and despite his travels and time away from the traditions and conventions he had grown up with, the marriage suited him. Najwa had been a dutiful wife during their years in Lebanon and Kassim was not the sort of husband who was aggrieved at being presented with daughters. Secretly, he felt relief that he was not responsible for fathering a painfully handsome son. Such a boy would either suffer, as he had, or glory in his looks, a prospect surely as repugnant to Allah as it was to Kassim. The daughters looked well enough, but none had the haunting, harrowing good looks of their father.

The youngest, Reem, whose name meant "white antelope," had a bend in her nose that grew more pronounced with each passing year. This attribute was pointed out by her unremarkable older sisters and appreciated by her father, who felt it saved her from being perfect. Reem was the daughter of Kassim's heart.

When, in their cramped apartment in Mile End, Hala and Leila conspired with their mother in their grand scheme to ignore Kassim, to converse around him as though he weren't there, to show him of what little consequence he had become, Reem would appear at her father's side and slip her hand into his. Her sisters picked on her for her devotion to him, and for her independence from them. Kassim was pierced by the aptness of her name: a white antelope was an easy target as well as a symbol of purity.

Surprised at first by her disloyalty and then bewildered by her distance, he had admonished his wife to praise Allah for their deliverance. "You cannot wish our daughters back in that house, huddling against the stray bomb, the intentional bullet, unable to go to school in safety." When that failed to arouse Najwa's finer feelings, he would remind her that it wasn't just the bombs and gunfire that had driven them from their home: the National Museum had closed and the cost of living had tripled in the three years before their departure. But she could no longer see where they had been, nor could she see where they would be now had they stayed, only where they were at that moment. He had brought her to this.

His pride was the first victim of his family's disdain, followed shortly by his pleasure. Gregarious by nature and more at ease with the intimacy of females than most of his countrymen, Kassim missed the interactions that family life should have afforded him. He was already bereft of the recognition and rapport that workplace relations had once furnished.

Though as disrespected as her son, Azar felt his disgrace more acutely. When Kassim's employment prospects proved meager, Azar cursed the Canadians. "Spite and jealousy," she spat. "These pasty cold blood pashas cannot bear to work around someone so much more distinguished than themselves." In their third year in Montreal she decided that Kassim was unable to get a better position because only young men, or at least more youthful-looking men, were getting hired to fill the most important posts. Now she blamed both his good looks and the deterioration of his looks. "All eyes would turn to you. Now they look away." Kassim ignored her for months, but when she pointed out that the disregard of his wife and older daughters coincided with the advent of his gray hairs, he thought perhaps his mother was right. He let Azar color his hair with the same potion she used on her own. He should have realized that every strand on his head would be painted the same flat, false color. He might as well have used boot black. He recognized the extent of his mistake when his daughter Hala laughed openly and his wife shook her head in disgust. "Now you look like a security guard who is chasing after the young girls." So he felt the fool as well as a failure. Waiting for the hair to grow out and reading the scorn on the faces of his wife and daughters would only destroy the remains of his confidence.

Despairing of all else, Azar began prodding him to make an *'Umrah*, the lesser pilgrimage to Mekkah that could be undertaken at any time of year, to appeal to Allah for His aid in once again achieving prosperity. "All will be better after your return, *inshallah*." Kassim did not need much prodding. Once Azar had secured the needed extra funds from her brothers, whom Kassim had helped settle in Montreal, he contacted a Lebanese travel agent (who had once been a surgeon in Beirut) and two weeks later found himself on the first of three flights that would take him to Saudi Arabia.

*   *   *

When Kassim arrived at the Meeqaat, he bathed and assumed his *Ihraam*. Before leaving Montreal, he had practiced wrapping himself in the two pieces of white sheeting, one for the top of the body, the other for the lower half. No other clothing was permitted during *Ihraam*. Kassim rejoiced in what was much more than a ritual: the visual acknowledgment that, stripped of their possessions, all stood equal in the eyes of Allah. He left behind, in the pockets of his now shabby suit, his grief and his failures. Mingling with the other pilgrims, he discovered what it meant to be faceless in a crowd.

He entered the state of *Ihraam* by making his intention in his heart while reciting the opening *Talbiyyah*. His heart brimmed with prayer and hopefulness as he passed through the mammoth doorway and crossed the threshold of the sacred mosque, careful to set out on his right foot across the cool marble. "O Allah! Forgive me my sins, and open the gates of your mercy for me," he pleaded. All around him pilgrims were studying or praying from the *Qu'ran*. He felt the peace of the mosque and the honor of their intentions.

Even though not yet the season of the *hajj*, the sight of the multitude in the roofless courtyard surrounding the *Kaaba* caused Kassim to gasp. Then his eyes fixed on the *Kaaba* itself, the structure of stones brought from the hills surrounding Mekkah, the holy structure that had been ordained by Allah, constructed by Adam, rebuilt by Ibrahim and his son Ismael, rebuilt again by the later prophets, and finally by the Prophet Muhammad. Kassim knew that at the east corner, five feet above ground, he would find the most sacred Black Stone. The Stone that had been white when given to Adam on his fall from Paradise, the Stone that had turned black from absorbing all the sins of the millions of pilgrims who had grazed it with outstretched fingers. Dazed, he watched the blur of bodies swirling around the structure tautly enshrouded in black fabric covered with Qur'anic text, a black as deep as faith against the radiant sun-illuminated whiteness of the marble floor of the courtyard there in the center of the Grand Mosque—that center toward which he had pointed his whole being in prayer five times each day of his life.

Kassim was propelled forward by a surge of pilgrims into the vast open area. He joined the mottled whirlpool composed of streaks of brown and yellow and pink and black bodies draped in white. He was one of thousands at that moment performing a *Tawaaf*—"around the House"— the counterclockwise circling of the Kaaba seven times. As Kassim strode, each circle converging more nearly on the black edifice, he meditated upon his own name, which meant "dispenser of food and goods" and prayed that Allah would again make him worthy of it. It was said that every prayer recited within the Grand Mosque was of one hundred thousand times more worth than any spoken outside it.

A part of the swirling mass of humanity—a particle of it—Kassim felt that he no longer existed as a separate entity. His spirit flowed alongside and through his brethren.

As he neared the Kaaba on his seventh round, he ached with joy, his fingers stiff with anticipation. "*Allahu Akbar,*" he whispered as the palm of his right hand brushed the Black Stone in the eastern corner. "Allah is the Greatest." Suddenly he was alone with Allah in a sea of a million people.

When Kassim left the mosque, he was torn, both reluctant to turn away from the *Kaaba* and eager to complete the *'Umrah*. He fell into a procession heading for Mount Safaa to perform the *Sa'y*. He climbed Safaa until the Kaaba became again visible, and he recited, "Allah is the Greatest, Allah is the Greatest, Allah is the Greatest. None has the right to be worshipped except Allah alone, Who has no partner. To Him belongs the dominion, to Him belongs all praise, and He has the power over everything." He repeated the prayer twice more, inserting his own petition between the repetitions. His imam back in Montreal had laid a firm hand upon his shoulder, "Make supplication from your heart for that which will benefit you. Whatever it is you need. Do not be reluctant to ask. Do not hesitate. You cannot be embarrassed before Allah. You cannot bring false pride with you on this journey. For your petition to be granted, you must ask."

Kassim descended and trotted to Mount Marwah, ascended that, and then returned to Safaa. Given the 107-degree heat that day in June, he was relieved that the Mounts were mounds rather than mountains and that the distance between the Mounts was a matter of meters rather than kilometers. He made the prescribed seven circuits, completing the reenactment of Hajar's frantic search for water to keep her son Ismael alive in the desert until Ibrahim's return. He was never struck by the irony that men were expected to jog the *Sa'y* while women were cautioned to proceed with a measured decorum, yet all were replicating the desperate ordeal of a woman. Hajar herself could not have been more uplifted when the Well of Zamzam miraculously appeared than Kassim when he drank from the sacred well. He could feel the water of the Zamzam Spring, a tributary of the Waters of Paradise, flow through him like grace.

The *Sa'y* complete, Kassim submitted to the final ritual of the *'Umrah*, the *halq*, the shaving of the head. Now he was ready to go out of *Ihraam*, out from being a pilgrim, a searcher, and return to the known world.

He exchanged the two panels of white sheeting for the white shirt and discreetly pinstriped suit that had seen better days. They seemed like the clothes of a past life, as indeed they were. For him, the *halq* was transformative. Shaved bald and beardless, he felt fresh, newborn. This exhilaration of rebirth would carry him through the long days of travel overland and by air, across continents and across oceans. It carried him almost as far as the door of the flat in Mile End.

He had not let the family know when to expect him.

Overseas calls were prohibitively expensive. An unjustifiable indulgence after all his other expenses.

His wife and daughters might be at the shopping mall gazing at all the things he could not buy for them. Reem might be playing in the first-floor apartment of her little friend. His mother could be at the Halal Meat & Grocery rejecting cuts of lamb as not good enough for the celebration of her son's return, expected one day very soon.

When he inserted his key in the lock of the door, he stood frozen for fully three minutes. Then he removed the key and slid it back into the pocket of his suit coat and turned and walked softly down the stairs.

Back on the street, he couldn't help but contrast this neighborhood—its jangle of voices, the shabby residential and commercial buildings and abandoned warehouses—with the dignity and splendor of the Grand Mosque. But both were peopled by seekers from elsewhere, he reminded himself as he passed the Greek restaurant with its Mediterranean blue and white walls and the little Portuguese grocery and the squat brick building—was it a temple? a school?—with its Hebrew inscription over the double doors.

What was he expecting from his family? He asked himself this question as he circled the block for the sixth time. It was on the last circle that he told himself that the answer was that he should not expect anything from his family, but he should expect much from himself. After all, it was he alone who had made the journey. Only he could be expected to have been changed.

As he completed his seventh circuit, he paused to inhale outside the steamy café where the old Italian men hunched over their playing cards and their *espressos*. He thought of the *kahva* that his mother would prepare for him, even thicker and stronger than *espresso*, made from finely ground beans with pinches of sugar and cardamom dropped into the boiling pot.

The stairs to the third-floor apartment did not seem so

steep as he climbed. He turned the key decisively in the lock. When the door fell open he was surprised to see all three of his daughters, his wife, and his mother gathered in the living room, as though waiting for him. Except for meals, he couldn't remember the last time he had seen them seated all together. They stared at him but no one spoke.

"I have not been gone so long that I should be a stranger to you," he smiled.

Still they were silent. His daughter Hala, who was never at a loss for words, leaned forward, her mouth gaping.

"Is it my baldness that alarms you?" He brushed his palm over his scalp. "Already the hair is growing back."

Still nothing from them.

"I have been reborn in the love of Allah, but I am still your father, husband, son," he said, nodding around the room at each of his daughters perched along the rolled-up mattress draped with carpeting and at his wife and mother sitting stiffly on the brocade couch. "When I change from these much-traveled clothes and shave the stubble from my face, I hope you will then at least be able to recognize me."

Still no one spoke. Kassim wondered if something terrible had happened in his absence. If another family member had been killed. Or if Allah had sent a plague to their small flat that had left his women dumb. For a fleeting moment, he pictured a future with no nagging, no scorn, no conversations that excluded him, but then shook off the vision as unworthy of a returning pilgrim. Later Najwa would confess that she and their middle daughter had both heard his footsteps stop at their door, heard his key in the lock, and then heard the footsteps that could only have been his retreat and had been paralyzed with fear. They had told the others and, for the time it took Kassim to complete his circles around their neighborhood, they had huddled together in the windowless living room thinking the unspeakable: that Kassim had abandoned them. And they thought of all the reasons why he should have done so.

While he stood puzzling, Reem ran into the bedroom he shared with Najwa and came out carrying the hand mirror that lay on their dresser. Seeing that cheap plastic mirror that Najwa had picked up at a flea market reminded Kassim of all that had been lost. Throughout their time in Lebanon, his wife had used the heavy, gold-encrusted vanity set that had been a wedding gift from her aunt and uncle. Najwa had personally packed the set into one of the crates that had accompanied them to Canada but it was missing when the crate was opened. Azar cursed the Customs officials, but Najwa blamed the housemaid whom she had long suspected of coveting the set when she brushed her mistress's hair. Kassim resolved that he would buy his wife a new vanity set, one suited to their renewed life together.

He wondered why Reem saw fit to bring him the looking glass. Because he was not comfortable with his looks, Kassim had learned to avoid glancing in mirrors. He didn't want to see himself, nor see others looking at him. He even managed to be oblivious of his image in windows and, most recently, the mirrors in airport bathrooms.

Reem held the streaked glass up to her father's face and he saw what they had seen when he came through the door, what they could not stop looking at. There was only a short growth to be sure, but there was no denying the evidence of one's eyes. All the hair on his scalp and cheeks and cleft chin and along the plane of his upper lip was growing back in the luxuriant dark brown of his youth.

Body Language

3.

She had an idea that riding *en couchette* would be like a slumber party: four women, complete strangers, from the earth's four corners, thrown together for one cozy night. Betsy envisioned a kind of *esprit de cot* inspiring the air in their small cabin, producing a chorus of *"Frère Jacques"* followed by several rounds of *"Bruder Jacob"* in a burst of international harmony.

She had spent the afternoon and evening on a train from Tours and an eternity in the station at Lyon. She began a postcard to her sister in minuscule script: *A place not to be is the train station at Lyon. The time not to be here is night.* A convention of jackals, she shivered as she looked around. Every breed of miscreant had at least one voting representative present. She affixed a stamp to the card picturing the overwrought gothic *Cathédrale Saint-Gatien* she had visited in Tours and set off in search of a postal box.

When a patron of a bar in the station lurched out into the night and nearly collided with Betsy, he seized the situation as an opportunity. As he curled his fingers around her hip from behind, her first thought was what Greg would have done to him. She didn't wait for a second thought. Fellow lechers, she shuddered, and gave the local one a backward jab with her elbow into his ribs. She left him wheezing as she headed for an empty platform to contemplate just how sheltered she had been, maybe not in every way, but in many.

She had gone from the confinement of her parents' house to her dollhouse of a marriage, then fled that for the refuge of her sister's home. Being a "townie," she hadn't even experienced the measured liberation of a Jesuit college dormitory with strict curfews. Her parents had paid her and her sister's tuitions but declared dorm room-and-board not in the family budget, and her summer earnings were never enough to permit her to live on campus. Betsy supposed the apartment on Kilbourn was one reason she had jumped at marrying Greg even before she completed her undergraduate degree. She realized with a jolt that this trip was really her first time being on her own in all of her thirty-two years.

Shortly after midnight, she sought to board her sleeping car for Nice. The numbers outside of the cars were confusing—one single digit and below that five digits, nothing to correspond to the *Voiture 44* printed on her ticket. She stopped a conductor, literally translating *I go to car 44* and relying on inflection to turn the statement into a plea for help. He answered her over his shoulder and left her to salvage meaning from the scant phrases she understood. She thought she had puzzled out his instructions but would never trust her ear. Just the night before as she went out to dinner from the small hotel in Tours, a woman in the lobby sought Betsy's confirmation of the beauty of her baby. Betsy was pleased to be consulted and assented heartily, heaping all her small vocabulary of admiration on the sleeping child's head. Only later, reviewing the woman's increasingly appalled expression and slowly replaying their exchange, did Betsy realize that she had fervently joined in complimenting herself on her own appearance, her *charmante robe*, her *joli visage*. She had walked the streets of Tours until she was confident that any of the hotel guests who had overheard her would be settled into their beds for the night.

So, every five yards, she would stop a conductor or another traveler to confirm that she was headed in the right direction, that these cars were the *wagon lits*, that this was the train to Nice.

It was inside a car that she found the elusive 44 posted. She arrived at the berth assigned to her, an upper, and was dismayed to see it barren not only of linens but of mattress as well. A finely made, finely dressed man entered the dim compartment carrying a thin suitcase and a still thinner attaché case. He looked like she imagined a member of the diplomatic corps would, with even the imagined tidy moustache.

Betsy realized that the unfurnished berth could not be hers after all. Again she had made a mistake; some small error in translation had turned each step into a misstep. Perhaps there were two cars numbered 44, this for men and the other for women. She begged the man's pardon and showed him her ticket. He nodded politely.

"*Non, Monsieur,*" she insisted. "*Où est la voiture quarante-quatre? Je vais où?*" He frowned. She hoped she'd made something like sentences. She hoped he wasn't nauseated by her vowel sounds.

"*Ici, Madame.*"

Here. Together with him and God knew who else. Betsy felt herself flush to the roots of her hair. Despite the fact that she was one full week out of Milwaukee, seven days of traveling abroad on her own, her expectations had remained steadfastly midwestern. It had not occurred to her that sleeping quarters could be shared by unrelated travelers of both sexes. It became a point of American honor that this man never be permitted to grasp what struck her now as a fatally telling presumption on her part.

"*Mais, ma couchette—voilà!*" She extended her arm to illustrate this passable explanation for her confusion. He looked up and then over at his own upper birth and mumbled what Betsy was sure could be characterized as "a mild oath." His bunk, too, was devoid of bedding.

He instructed her to wait there, to do nothing, that he would assume responsibility for her comfort as well as his own. Betsy was relieved that, if she must pass the night in male company, at least this particular specimen seemed to be a gentleman. She wondered what their other two sleeping car companions would be like. When she had been certain of females, she had imagined chatter followed by easy sleep.

Now she supposed she ought to prepare herself for silence preceding a symphony of snores.

He came back with a porter, who fled, throwing his hands into the air, denying any accountability. Next her gentleman expressed their combined indignation to the conductor, who reassigned to them the outfitted bottom berths and gave them the entire compartment to themselves. Betsy felt it unlikely that her sole companion was a snorer.

When they were alone, she asked in a combination of broken French and pantomime where she should change into her bedclothes. He raised his hands, palms up, and bowed his head at the same time, making a present to her of the privacy of the compartment, then stood sentry outside the door until she emerged in her embroidered Indian cotton gown to take his place. Betsy blinked at the framed pictures flashing past the window until he reappeared in the corridor, dapper in his creased pajamas, navy blue trousers and complementary but not matching shirt. His sandy hair was short and wavy and coarse, the only thing coarse about him, Betsy felt sure. An odd thought came to her: he will never go bald. There was something almost too fastidious about him. Maybe it was his moustache. It looked like it might have been penciled in above his lip. Without the camouflage of suit and tie, she saw that he was not as old as she had first assumed, perhaps only a few years older, not yet forty.

The compartment was stifling. He apologized on behalf of his nation for the failure of the air conditioning. They eased themselves onto their respective pallets and lay looking out through the open window at periodic bursts of light, like camera flashes in the night.

Twice, farther down the line, other passengers tried to enter the compartment. Holders of the reservations for the two lower berths, no doubt. In the first instance, Betsy's companion politely directed the intruder to the conductor as the proper repository for his wrath. He then locked the door and on the subsequent attempt responded not at all, except to smile at Betsy. She imagined him accustomed to telling others what to do, heading a company or a consulate.

It was only then that she recognized the conspiracy of circumstances and vented a nervous giggle. As she prepared for this trip, she had tantalized herself with the prospect of international alliances, international dalliances. After all, she was a thirty-two-year-old woman traveling alone, not looking for love, not even for companionship—she had brought the last volume of *The Alexandria Quartet* along for company. (It was Durrell who had said, "Travel can be one of the most rewarding forms of introspection.")

She had lusted after Europe when an ocean away but had found nothing enticing about the males thus far, certainly not the scruffy teenager who had followed her out of the Louvre or the white-suited man in the Tuileries who offered to buy her an aperitif, and especially not the fat-fingered patron of the bar back in the station at Lyon.

And now here she was alone with an impeccable Frenchman, sealed in until morning. Fate had thrown them together and locked the door. She shifted on her bunk and he made an identical movement. She sat up to unravel the cocoon of sheeting from about her feet and moments later he did the same.

It was a dance.

She glanced over and found him staring at her.

After a few minutes, he let his hand loll out into the space between them. She considered his hand, considered reaching out to it. It fingered the air and then retreated, scurried back under the sheet like a frightened squirrel. Suited up and carrying the slimmest of monogrammed attaché cases, he had struck her as a paragon of efficiency and composure; now in pajamas and struggling with wadded sheeting, he seemed vulnerable. It was all too much like a vintage movie, more slapstick than romance. Betsy redoubled her efforts toward sleep.

Twenty minutes clacked by.

Something hurtled in through the open window. The fluttering noises caused Betsy and her fellow traveler to sit upright at the same moment. "A bird!" Betsy exclaimed in wonder.

"*C'est impossible!*" The man reached out and flicked the light switch by the locked door. "*Mon Dieu,*" he cursed while a small scream escaped from Betsy's throat as a bat dove kamikaze-like from point to point in the compartment, veering off just short of the walls.

She watched the man lie back and fumble under his cot until he found his shoe. Then he lay still and gestured to her to do the same. She tried to flatten herself against her mattress, briefly raising a hand only to twist her hair beneath her head so no loose tendril could ensnare the creature as it skimmed over her. The humans lay frozen while the other mammal chased through the air as though shot from a miniature cannon, darting in straight, short lines. Tense minutes ticked by before the bat settled on the floor between the cots. The Frenchman raised his shoe and brought it down swiftly.

"No!" Betsy shouted. Then she saw that he had not brought the sole of his shoe down upon the bat but the opening, which he held firmly in place, unable to move lest the captive escape.

Betsy sat up, looking around the compartment for something, but she didn't know what. She reached for her backpack and took from it the box of Belin crackers she'd bought in the train station.

She pulled out the cellophane liner with the crackers and then separated the cardboard at its seams. Holding her breath, she carefully slid the flattened cardboard along the floor and under the man's shoe. He swung his legs off his cot and together they lifted the makeshift cage and thrust it out the window. He raised the shoe and they waited more than two minutes, giving the bat ample time to make its escape into the dark night. Then they drew their arms back inside and turned to face each other in the narrow passage between the cots and erupted into laughter.

Each babbled over the other in their own language, reliving the entrance and maneuvers of their bat and the expressions on the other's face, and then both cracked up again at the sheer improbability of the intrusion as well as the absurdity of their recounting it to themselves.

As she lowered herself back onto her cot, he extended a hand above her head, protecting her from bumping into the frame of the upper berth.

"*Merci,*" she said.

"*Pas du tout,*" he returned with a slight bow.

And then both collapsed onto their mattresses, laughing all the way down. Betsy thought this was not so unlike a slumber party after all.

Once they had regained control of themselves, they spoke slowly, haltingly, both confessing to only two years adolescent instruction in the other's tongue, though he professed fluency in German and admitted to a passing familiarity with Japanese. His work as an economics consultant had taken him through Europe and Asia—he was just now returning from a business trip to Switzerland—but never, to his regret, to the United States.

They closed the window in the compartment to prevent their voices from being sucked out into the hot night. They found they could make jokes together. Betsy felt the anxiety of travel melt away.

She told him how in a café in Tours she had serenely ordered a bottle of *rouge blanc*, thinking she'd asked for red wine. She had at first been baffled by the waiter who, taking the middle ground, delivered a bottle of rosé to her table.

Her gentleman apologized for any lashings she had suffered at the tongues of his countrymen while she declared the mistreatment of Americans by the French to be a myth: she had received nothing but kindness. (Betsy had conveniently erased the Paris taxi driver from her memory.)

Instead, she told him about splurging on a dinner cruise

along the Seine and regretting her decision almost as soon as she had boarded as every person on the boat, with the exception of their guide and the crew, was half of a couple. "I am traveling alone," she explained, as though he hadn't noticed. She told him how, as the remnants of their meal had been cleared away, the guide became a crooner, singing *a cappella* in a low, sweet voice. When he had finished to warm applause, he proffered his microphone to an elderly gentleman at a nearby table, who rose to the occasion and, facing his companion, sang to her what was surely a love song—no translation was necessary. Then the guide crossed the deck and, to Betsy's horror, held out the microphone to her. She shook her head but still he extended his arm. "*Je suis américaine*," she apologized. "Do not Americans sing?" he asked, entertaining the assemblage. So Betsy accepted the microphone to a smattering of encouragement from her fellow diners. But nothing came out of her mouth. She did not want to sing anything in English before this gathering and she would not sing *Frère Jacques*. The first seemed shabby and the other pathetic. So she stood and sang the only other French song she knew. She got as far as *Allons, enfants de la patrie, Le jour de gloire est arrivé* when all the other passengers stood and joined in, thank God, because she wasn't sure of remembering all the words and was sure she would be garbling most of them. When they had finished singing, everyone applauded her as though she had performed an aria and they had been her rapt audience. And then her glass was filled from the bottle at an adjoining table and a young couple joined her at her table and others came over to toast her. And when the boat docked, she was the recipient of many kisses on both cheeks.

Betsy and her gentleman laughed again, but this time it was the laughter of comrades rather than two strangers thrown together in an absurd situation.

Betsy told him she had to give credit to the nun who had taught her high school French for opening class each morning with the *Marseillaise* rather than a prayer. She confessed she also had to give most of the credit for their ability to communicate to that same perpetually disappointed Sister Jean Louise, who had cringed at Betsy's rendition of vowel sounds, a little credit to her own interest in etymology, and some to the church Latin of her youth. She was surprised at how much could be conveyed with a very limited vocabulary and, as the conversation continued, at how much more could be left unsaid.

He reached across and tentatively touched her shoulder as he spoke of the cities he attributed to her. "Milwaukee is on a lake, yes?" So close to Chicago? He hadn't realized.

His hand rested long enough to telegraph another message.

Betsy asked if he had always lived in Nice and he laughed, this time at her notion of him as an urbanite. "*You* are the *citadine*," he said. He had grown up in the countryside, where his parents bred rabbits and daughters: he had five sisters. His childhood had been both rich and impoverished and neither had anything to do with his family's modest accumulation of francs.

With eight females in the house, including his widowed aunt and paternal grandmother, he emerged the family pet. The women and girls coddled him. "They feed me cakes."

"*Gâteaux*," she confirmed, nodding. She pictured him: eyes large and luminous, thin then as now, his mouth opening and closing birdlike as each sister vied to stuff him with sugared treats and honeyed words.

He reached across the small space between them and laced his fingers through hers. A small flutter of disappointment rippled through her—it felt as though he were trying to draw her into his memories, not seduce her.

He confided that, as full as his childhood was of female affection, it was equally bereft of male companionship. His eternally disappointed father expected him to be manlier, to casually break the necks of rabbits—with his free hand he sliced a karate chop in the air—and cheerfully skin them after. Neighboring boys sought him out not for his own sterling qualities but for his proximity to his sisters, all uniformly blonde, beautiful, and buxom. This time with his free hand he pantomimed shielding his eyes from the light of the sun.

"Dazzling," she provided the word he was seeking. She struggled to reconcile his soft hands with those of a farmboy.

He tasted the word: "Dazzling."

So his friends were never really his friends but rather his sisters' suitors. Only after his sisters were wed did he acquire true friends in the shapes of his brothers-in-law.

"*Pauvre petit garçon*," she patted the hand that still held hers.

He told her that a "peculiar" thing happened (he grinned at the surfacing of the English "peculiar"). He said that, after their weddings, each of the four of his sisters who married let go of their looks. He believed that being beautiful had been a burden to them "no less than the pack a donkey carries." His theory was that, once married, they had no more need of beauty. He was sure it was a conscious choice. And—he offered as proof—only his spinster sister remained dazzling. It still hurt to look at her.

Betsy told him this was the perfect bedtime story, a fairy tale to dream on.

He started to say something but stopped. She could feel the uncertainty telegraphed through his fingertips. W-H-A-T (tap-tap-tap-tap) N-E-X-T (tap-tap-tap-tap)? He released her hand to drink from the water bottle she had set on the floor between them. He was buying time, gauging her responsiveness to his words, his touch.

He was utterly transparent. She marveled that she'd been fooled by the tailored suit and his manicured fingernails into supposing him austere and superior. She thought about his dapper pajamas, his orderly cases, his guarded smile. She saw a wife waiting in the distance. When they arrived in Nice, he would find his breakfast table laid, his morning paper folded beside the plate.

He set the bottle back down and leaned over, his finger following the curve of her arm. "*Vous êtes très douce.*"

"*Je ne comprends pas,*" she said in all sincerity. Did he say she was very two?

"*Tu es très jolie aussi.*"

This time Betsy recognized that she, not a babe in arms, was the subject of honeyed words. And she noticed his slide from the formal to the familiar *tu*.

He leaned into the space between their cots and kissed her hand. Then he turned her hand over and pressed his mouth into her palm.

The sensation of his lips on her skin surged through her like an electric current. Involuntarily, her hand trembled in his. There was no mistaking his intention now.

Betsy supposed that even if he had kept his vows until now, he couldn't evade the claim of national honor, international ardor, that called upon his manhood. At last fate had chosen her to be the one in the right place at the right time. Or was it that fate had chosen him to be there, for her? He was an elegant gift that destiny had bestowed upon her, one that she deserved.

"I was very young when I married," Betsy said slowly. "Only twenty. *Vingt ans,*" she confirmed. She said nothing about her divorce.

"*Non!*" he exclaimed, taken unawares and, then, after a pause, "*Moi aussi.* I, too, only twenty." Relief and disappointment struggled in his voice. "*C'est ça,*" he sighed, more to himself than to her. He withdrew his limbs to the island of his berth, relaxing finally.

Idiot! she congratulated herself. Lauren Bacall would never have released him like that.

Betsy smoldered in the breathless compartment. She had wanted him to turn heedless, ruthless, to sweep her away as all the women in those movies had been swept. She was furious with herself for saving him and was tempted now to seduce him. She was angry that it was *her* marriage that had made him safe: always the gentleman.

She saw now that she had miscast herself. This was not a romantic screwball comedy; this was a television sit-com. She was Mary Tyler Moore playing Mary Rogers, a character to whom things almost happened.

Suddenly the smell of armpits and feet and bad digestion closed in upon her from the walls and floor and ceiling of the sleeping compartment, as though she were sharing the cabin with all the bodies that had ever steeped there in their own juices. Opening the window as far as it permitted, she delivered a curt *"Bonne nuit"* and hardened herself against the bewilderment in the economic consultant's face.

Sleep eluded Betsy for the brief remainder of the night.

In the early light, he began to organize his things. Behind half-closed eyes, she watched him sort through his case and tried to think of the word she would use to describe him to her sister. His nose was perhaps too long and his moustache too thin to qualify as "cute." There was some kind of gunk in his hair, and he wore cologne—she hadn't noticed that before—so she wouldn't label him clean-cut. *Dapper*, she supposed, described more than his pajamas—a word she'd never had any use for until now.

As he bent to retrieve his shoes, the bat emerged and shot out the open window.

He yelped in surprise, then shook his head and grinned at Betsy. She merely shrugged in reply.

They took turns dressing a few stations outside Nice and then stood side by side in the corridor while he offered commentary on the passing sights. He told Betsy he was worried about her. He feared she would not find a place to stay in his tourist-strewn city. Forehead furrowed with the effort to construct a proper sentence, she said, "There's always a room for me: *Il y a une chambre pour moi toujours.*"

They left the sleeping car together, walking the long platform, descending stairs, passing through a tunnel, then the station proper, emerging at last into daylight. Betsy stopped as if to get her bearings. He, too, stopped. Setting down his two slender cases, he took her hands in both of his. His polished nails gleamed with the sun. She looked at them and felt a flash of sympathy with his farmer father and then looked away, ashamed that he might see this in her.

His was a long and wistful speech. It was only after she had said goodbye—in English, no *au revoir* for him—and was heading in the opposite, unknown direction that she realized she hadn't understood a word he'd spoken since their arrival at the station in Nice.

Rabbit Punch

4.

Christian waved away a taxi outside the station and began the short walk home in the first light of an already sultry morning. Élodie had offered last evening to pick him up when he phoned before boarding the train, but he had told her to sleep in. One of the great conveniences of living in the *Quartier Musiciens* was its proximity to the station. Another was that their apartment had been a gift from Élodie's father, Gustave, who also lived in *Musiciens*. Christian made good money, but not enough yet to afford their princely rooms on Boulevard Victor Hugo.

Christian had long benefited from Gustave's intent to keep his little family close. When Christian was growing up, that resolve meant that at least twice yearly he would have the company of Élodie. They met when they were both twelve years old during one of her family's vacations at their estate not far from his family's rabbit farm. Wherever else they might travel, Gustave brought his wife and daughter to their property on the outskirts of Gémozac for the Christmas holidays and for the first two weeks of every August.

Élodie liked Christian from the time of her family's initial excursion to the rabbit farm. Élodie's mother had been drawn to the farm's hygienic display of fresh meat at the Friday market as well as the *cassolette de lapin* prepared and individually packaged in a red-and-white-striped serving cloth by Christian's older sisters. That was the last time Madame Rochefort was pleased by anything to do with Christian or his family, but it had been she who had suggested to her husband the visit to the farm as a family outing.

Gustave Rochefort, like his daughter, admired Christian from that first visit. He watched the boy guide his only child through the two long, narrow barns and listened as he explicated the care and feeding of the stock.

"Right now we have sixty-three does and twelve bucks for breeding." Having grown up with five sisters, he was not shy with girls.

"What do you call the babies?" she asked.

"Kittens," he said, shrugging.

"What is this one's name?" Élodie swirled the fur of a brown-and-white with her fingertips through the cage wire as though dipping into a pond.

"These are livestock, not pets," he replied soberly, quoting someone. "You don't name livestock."

"You don't? Really?"

"Well, you shouldn't. Anyway, that's not one that I've named."

"Then I will call him Bernard."

"Bernard is a girl." Christian explained that with an immature rabbit you couldn't tell gender by looking. He opened a cage further down the row and told Élodie to take the trembling creature by the scruff and slowly run the fingers of her other hand—the hand that had rippled the fur—down the animal's belly. "If it's very smooth, like...like a fur jacket, then you are holding a doe. If you feel tassels under the fur, then you have a buck." He waited. As she maneuvered to corral the young rabbit, he took a step back and appraised her. The girl struck him as alien. At first he thought this a distinction conferred by wealth. Christian was certain he would have known she came from money even had he not witnessed the gleaming Jaguar MK II the trio arrived in. Then, with a sudden insight sophisticated for both his years and circumstances, though he would not have been able to put the notion into words, he understood that he had been accustomed to an antagonistic standard of beauty. His flaxen, earthbound sisters were opulent in their golden looks, a different kind of wealth. Élodie's short bob, arched brows, and deep-set eyes were more than dark—they were austere. Even at that tender age, her finely chiseled features made an imprint on the beholder. If he had been asked to describe Élodie's appearance, he would have said *not blonde* but meant a sort of stunning photographic negative of what he had been used to regarding as the feminine ideal. This foreignness initially intrigued him and, eventually, enthralled him. "Well?" he said when her lips parted in surprise.

"A buck," she announced, startled that she had successfully followed his directions.

Gustave marveled that neither of these pretty children seemed self-conscious in this talk and touch of sex. He thought that had they met a year or two later, this earnest tutelage would never have taken place. As it was, two years later they became sweethearts.

"*Amour de l'adolescence*," Élodie's mother dismissed. "Puppy love," she added in English with a sneer. "Bunny love," Gustave smilingly corrected, also in English. "The babies are called kittens," she said, reminding her husband that she never forgot or forgave anything.

Élodie worked harder during her vacations than in any other setting. Not, Gustave was confident, because she was enamored of rabbits, though she even helped Christian rake the droppings out from under the cages and bag for sale at the Friday market the prized fertilizer that wasn't used on the farm gardens. Christian would try to time the replacement of rusting water and feed pans with her arrival. Using tin snips, he would curve down the sides of empty large tomato cans and roll the sharp edges which Élodie would pound flat with a hammer and then nail to the wooden supports inside each pen. Élodie loved to wield the hammer, but she absented herself from the farm on the days when stock was slaughtered and skinned.

When she was fourteen, conscious of the ache Christian suffered in his right hand from cutting down the metal cans (though he didn't complain but rather thrust his fist into a can of ice at the end of the day), Élodie spent months collecting empty plastic bleach containers from the mothers of her classmates, or from their housekeepers. Her urbane schoolmates swooned at the episodic fairy tale of the country boy tending a flock of fluffy rabbits between visitations by the damsel who resided in a distant palace.

She and her friends cut the containers into the shape Christian rendered the tomato cans, trimming down the sides and front and leaving a wide neck at the back for nailing to a post. Élodie was delighted with herself as she anticipated Christian's appreciation of her efforts and his admiration of her cleverness. Gustave was amused by her project; Madame Rochefort was not. She was annoyed at having to share their apartment and finally their car with the enormous stack of nested bleach containers and she was more than annoyed that her daughter persisted in this childish infatuation with that unsuitable boy. "The farmhand," she called him, "*l'ouvrier agricole*."

Poor Christian wanted very much to praise Élodie's handiwork. He thanked her but she knew that something was wrong. "What?" she demanded. "We washed out all the bottles with soap, and after we cut them, I dried them in the sun on the balcony. There's no bleach in them anymore. And they'll never rust. What is it? Tell me."

"There can be no plastic in the hutches," he said regretfully. "'Plastic and rabbits do not go together.'"

"But why?" she tried not to whine.

"That's one of my father's rules." He shrugged.

"But why?" she repeated, this time with tears of frustration.

"He only says, 'Because,' but I think it is that they would eat the plastic and the meat would be poisoned. I'm sorry, Élodie."

When Élodie, this time without tears, reported the results of her grand project to her father, Gustave said, "And there you have the difference between the father and the son. One declaims; the other explains." As much as Gustave had grown fond of Christian, just that much had he become disenchanted with the boy's father.

Gustave took it upon himself to see to Christian's education. He was unsurprised yet disappointed when Christian's father didn't object. And again unsurprised and disappointed when his own wife did object. He said, "Our daughter doesn't seem inclined to give him up despite the parade of boys you invite to the apartment and to the country. So we might as well see to it that he is made 'suitable.'" But Gustave was not just grooming Christian to make him more acceptable to his wife or a better provider for his daughter. Perhaps unconsciously, he was recruiting a son for himself. It never occurred to Gustave to worry that he might be taking Christian out of his element. Nor did it occur to Christian. The only elemental consideration the boy recognized was his determination not to be separated from Élodie. He would become whatever he must in order to secure her. His gratitude, respect, and affection for Gustave, who didn't stand in his way, who in fact made everything possible, were uncomplicated.

When Élodie's mother protested at the pair's announcement of their intention to wed at age twenty, Gustave said, "Can't you see that waiting won't change their minds? So why make them unhappy? Why not enjoy their happiness? You know, we are lucky. Christian is smart and kind and he loves our daughter. He will never do anything to hurt her."

Even after Christian had been taken under the wing of one of Gustave's friends in finance and then emerged to start a small firm of his own, his mother-in-law persisted in thinking of him as a *former* farmhand. When Élodie and Christian still joined her parents for their vacations near Gémozac, Madame Rochefort felt that he ought to be staying at the rabbit farm. Perhaps she would have come round eventually had the young couple given her grandchildren, but the fact of their barrenness juxtaposed with the thought of breeding rabbits caused explosions of bitterness in her brain.

*　　*　　*

For the Christmas after they declared their love to each other, Christian gave Élodie one of Bernard's paws on a necklace he had made from a pull chain. "You know what they say," her mother shook her head at Élodie. "'That foot did not succeed in bringing luck to its original owner.'"

For her fifteenth Christmas, Christian gave her a muff he had made from pure white skins. Every Christmas after that, he gave her a book carefully chosen. Gustave approved of each of these gifts and of the sensibilities of the giver. The year of the muff, Madame Rochefort asked Élodie if she really wanted such a cheapskate, *un rapiat*, for a boyfriend. "His family sells the meat and he gives you the discarded skins instead of throwing them into the waste bin."

But Élodie knew that Christian had skinned the rabbits himself and tanned the pelts and worked them until they were supple and then painstakingly sewn the muff under the tutelage of one of his sisters so that the stitching could be neither seen nor felt. She knew that the record album she had given him was nowhere near so fine a gift. When she was not proudly wearing it, she slept cradling the muff like a stuffed animal.

*　　*　　*

Christian barely noticed where he stepped as he looked back to check the time on the ornate clock on the façade of the Nice Ville Train Station. It was dangerous to be preoccupied while walking about in Nice in 1981—the sidewalks were paved in dog shit—but his thoughts were fixed on the woman who had shared his sleeping compartment. She was an American and she was charming, two adjectives he would not have previously linked together.

He would have made love to her—he had thought they were going to have sex until she brought up her husband. He couldn't believe he had so misread the cues. But one doesn't bring up a husband on the brink of lovemaking. The fact of the husband had made Christian sad out of all proportion to a missed misadventure. He'd felt an urge to stop the train. Their destination meant an ending. A death.

He was in mourning for what was not to be.

And he was confused. Surely, he loved Élodie, had loved her for all the years before and since their marriage. He had never been either scandalized or envious of friends and colleagues who had strayed from their vows of fidelity; he had just felt lucky by comparison. He wondered how it was possible that Élodie and all they had shared could seem irrelevant now.

What had it been about the woman on the train? Was it the laughter? He could not remember laughing so much, not ever, not with anyone. He was stunned to realize he didn't know her name. He had learned so much else.

In all fairness, Élodie was the more beautiful, certainly more striking in appearance than his American. Perhaps the explanation was that he was accustomed to his wife, that there was no longer anything alien about her to keep him enthralled. But he could not rid himself of the feeling that he had missed his last chance. Not just for something—someone—new and surely not just for the opportunity for sex without attachment—that is always available if one really wants it. What he wanted was to be attached to the woman on the train, to laugh with her. Every day. With her he'd been able to shed the snakeskin of sophistication. He felt he could be himself instead of the person others had needed him to become.

It seemed to Christian that if she had not set her husband between them, the two of them would at this moment be plotting the gentlest way to abandon their respective spouses, their homes, perhaps even their countries. He wondered if it all seemed so plausible because neither of them had children to abandon. He pictured them learning a new, shared language together in a tropical setting. "*Merde!*" he cursed appropriately as he stepped into a smear of dog shit. "*Merde!*" again for his failure to insist on escorting her to a hotel, to arrange another meeting, to acquire any information whereby he could find her again. What had he done? With each step homeward, he grew lonelier, more bereaved.

He reached the Art Deco building where he and Élodie had spent the last fourteen years. Where he had been content, he reminded himself. He wondered if he would be content again, if the interlude on the train had been a mere ephemeron or if his life had been altered, had come undone. He adjusted his features, erased his frown. None of this was the fault of Élodie. She would be unchanged when he walked through the door; he would try to appear the same.

His key in the lock must have summoned Élodie for she stood just inside the doorway, looking at him, unblinking. Her stare recalled how she had reacted all those years ago when she first witnessed the birth of a litter on the farm. "They are born with their eyes open!" she'd whispered, astonished and disturbed. "They see everything!"

Christian barely had time to set his cases down before she fell into his arms. He felt a surge of panic rising in his chest. They had been so close for so long—had Élodie sensed some alteration in their marriage even before he entered? He experienced a small thrill, followed by relief: he had needed things to be different and somehow they were.

Élodie buried her face in his shirt. "*Papa*," she said, her voice unsteady. "*Il est mort.*"

So this was the death that had been coming. Gustave had died in the night while Christian was with the woman on the train. Now he noticed his mother-in-law, sitting in the next room, smoking a cigarette and staring at a blank space on the wall.

Had he been a different sort of man, say a man who had grown up with brothers instead of sisters, Christian could have convinced himself that he had remained faithful to Élodie, had never actually strayed, that ultimately nothing of consequence had occurred. But the death rattling his bones said this was not so. He had betrayed Gustave. And he would atone for that.

He kissed Élodie's forehead and, a supporting arm around her waist, guided her into the next room, where he placed his free hand on the cold shoulder of Madame Rochefort. As there were no children taking up the extra bedrooms, spilling over into the shared space, there was ample room in their apartment to welcome Gustave's widow.

Primo Class

5.

Had Hester Prynne lived in Nice, Betsy theorized, she would have had no convenient site upon which to stitch her scarlet letter. Betsy was everywhere confronted by bare breasts: on billboards advertising fashion magazines, on posters in bus kiosks heralding rock concerts, in pharmacy windows promoting skin care, and in heaving mosaics of salmon, coral, sepia, maroon, and walnut nipples burnishing in the sun upon the sand beaches.

Eager to put Nice behind her, Betsy paid the surcharge for a reservation in a first-class coach. She had tried to purchase a second-class Eurail pass in Milwaukee but Dottie, her slightly dotty travel agent, had said, "You can't send a blouse to your sister for the book rate, dear." Deciphered, this turned out to mean that the second-class pass that was available for purchase in the States was only for students and Betsy was finally finished with all that.

That evening, she walked beside the track, checking and rechecking her ticket against the flaking black numbers painted on the outside of the coaches and then against the raised, once gilded numbers over the compartment doors. Unable to rely on her understanding of the words trumpeting out of the loudspeaker, she found herself doubting her ability to read numbers as well, as though 7 properly translated might yield a 2.

Her compartment was already overflowing with only one passenger. His suitcase occupied one of the seats next to the door; his briefcase another; a folded newspaper took up a third; his madras jacket was sitting in the fourth; and he himself was seated in the fifth. Betsy took the only remaining seat before he could rest his feet on it.

"*Bonjour,*" she nodded curtly.

He looked so blond and hearty she supposed he was another of the ubiquitous Germans until he drawled, "Same to you, honey."

Betsy shivered at the prospect of fending off conversations about the arrogance of French waiters or the foulness of un-American tap water until she feigned sleep. "*Pardon, monsieur?*" she said after a moment's hesitation, trusting he didn't have enough French to expose her.

"Forget it," he shook his head elaborately. "It was nothing. *Nada.*"

She gave him the brief shrug that signals the end of unsuccessful communication.

"Roger," he responded. "Over and out."

She settled into her seat, allowing herself a self-satisfied smile, which was sure to be taken as further evidence that she was French.

A small, dark young man with eyes flattered by thick lashes slipped into the compartment but remained by the door looking at the littered seats.

"You've got a first-class reservation, pal?" Betsy's well-muscled compatriot flexed.

The other pulled a ticket from the breast pocket of his white cotton shirt.

"No offense," the blond said. "No harm in checking, right? Name's Bradshaw. Last name. First name Kelby."

"How do you do?" the other said with an enunciation that reminded Betsy of *Masterpiece Theatre.* "My name is Winston."

"First or last?" Kelby hoisted his suitcase up onto the overhead rack.

"First. My last name is difficult to spell, impossible to remember," Winston apologized as he brought his battered, soft-sided suitcase in from the corridor and placed it on the opposite rack.

"So where are you from, Winston?"

"Pakistan." He looked over at Betsy, offering her a small,

impeccable smile.

"A foreigner," Kelby explained to him. "Doesn't speak English. So, you came over here to get a job?"

"I came to study. I am between classes and so have opportunity for travel."

Betsy wondered what kind of student would be traveling first class. She was beginning to regret that she had renounced English.

"Well, I'm an attorney, Winston. From Tampa. That's in Florida. Where we have plenty of sun and great beaches, but nothing that can compare with Nice," he shook his head.

"No?" the Pakistani said.

"Hell no. Three days I went without lunch, but between breakfast and dinner I made a meal of all those boobs. A picnic. A banquet. The beach was so crowded, you could barely move without brushing against one. You must have seen it: acres of sun-kissed nipples puckering on the sand— and then when they would sit up and rub themselves with oil: Christ. Nothing like that back home. But then everyone there except me is over sixty-five so I guess it's just as well." He inclined his head toward Betsy. "You know, I think that little lady over there looks more and more familiar. If we could get her to take her blouse off—I'm not very good with faces, Winston, but I never forget a boob."

Betsy's eyes flashed at the scenery that had begun flashing past the window when the Pakistani entered the compartment. *Bas-tard, bas-tard, bas-tard,* she counted the telephone poles as they clicked by.

She stood and lifted her borrowed canvas backpack toward the overhead rack. Carrying it was one thing, lifting another. Three quarters of the way up, her arms began to tremble and the Pakistani student silently rose to brace the backpack. Suddenly the powerful smell of leather and juniper encircled them and the backpack was removed from both their grasps. "No problemo," the lawyer said as he swung it up onto the rack.

"*Merci,*" Betsy said crisply to the sun-darkened lawyer,

then, "*Merci,*" more feelingly to the darker student.

"This is your first time abroad?" the Pakistani asked after a short silence.

She almost answered him without thinking, grateful for his redirection of the conversation, but the lawyer saved her. "Yeah, I'm on my honeymoon."

The Pakistani put his fingertips together and bowed his head slightly. "Then congratulations are in order."

"Thanks," said the Floridian while Betsy tensed, waiting for the student to ask all the obvious questions, but he only unfolded his copy of the *International Herald Tribune.*

Maybe the bride was traveling in a sleeping compartment while he preferred to travel upright. Maybe she didn't like trains and was flying to meet him in Rome. He couldn't have invented the honeymoon to lure Betsy into English. Kelby didn't have it in him, she was sure.

When the lawyer picked up his copy of the *Herald Tribune,* she pulled a bottle of mineral water and *her* copy of the *Tribune* from her oversized, shopping-bag sort of purse. At the station her glance had landed on a reprint from the *New York Times* with the headline "Rare Cancer Seen in 41 Homosexuals." She started to read about Gay Related Immune Disorder, or GRID as they had titled it, then realizing her blunder, quickly stuffed the English language newspaper back into the bag.

She wondered what her parents would think of the *Messieurs* Kelby and Winston. It was her parents' gift of money when she finished her master's that had augmented her travel fund enough to launch her trip, so she found herself frequently wondering if they would approve her choice of cities, her choice of hotels, her choice of dinner entrées. She was confident they would approve of her wordlessness; they set great store by reticence and even more by reserve.

After her divorce, Betsy had plunged into therapy until she decided she couldn't afford both her therapist and anything else. She banked her "therapy money" in a separate account and it accumulated faster than the insights ever had. Europe was only fourteen unattended therapy sessions away when her parents gave her a check for a thousand dollars and told her she'd better get going.

Betsy felt a little trapped by their check: it seemed less a gift than a challenge. She always suspected that her parents didn't expect much from her, though they would never say. They had seemed surprised when she enrolled in a doctoral program in anthropology, impassive when she abandoned her dissertation, and surprised again when she went back for a master's in library science. But nothing had surprised them more than when she had married at age twenty. Her father said she was setting a bad example for her younger sister. Her mother asked her if she was pregnant.

As she waited in the long line at the railroad station in Nice, it had struck Betsy that they had hardly raised an eyebrow between them when she told them about the divorce. She shuddered at the thought that perhaps they had been among the legions who were aware of Greg's unbridled unfaithfulness.

*   *   *

At the border crossing of Ventimiglia, the coach instantly filled, the passengers materializing in mid-sentence. Bodies burst into the musty, upholstered compartment and were fended off by the booming young lawyer from Florida. "Taken," he would growl, indicating the three unreserved and vacant seats menacingly. "*No comprendo*," he was adamant. He explained to Winston that in Italy whole families, the generations layered— "you know, like lasagna"—rode the rails in the dead of night.

An hour past the border and the first tide of unseated, the lawyer rose to make the perilous journey to the WC. He instructed the Pakistani student not to admit anyone into the compartment in his absence. He repeated his instructions to Betsy very slowly, but she shook her head. She was searching for enough words to make a speech. *C'est impossible,* it would begin.

"Look, none of them have paid for first class," he tried again, enunciating each word with care, pantomiming a ticket purchase. "We did *and* stood in line for reservations. No reason we should be crowded and miserable all night. See, these seats can be pushed down to meet across the aisle," he demonstrated for her. "We'll each have a bed to ourselves if you two don't blow it."

The Pakistani arranged his features into those of a deaf-mute. Communication with him would prove impossible. Satisfied, the lawyer nodded in his direction.

Betsy colored and said, "If someone asks me if there's a vacant seat, I won't say no."

The lawyer's back stiffened at the English words. He whistled softly, "Don't say anything then, *mademoiselle*. Say you don't spreckenzee or whatever. 'No savvy.' For you, as easy as stepping on a bug." He pivoted hard on his right foot and removed a roll of toilet paper from his suitcase before looking once more at his two first-class companions.

The Pakistani sat looking at his shoes, discreetly oblivious to their exchange.

"You won't worry if I leave you alone with Winston, will you ma'am?" The lawyer snorted and pulled the heavy curtain across the glass of the compartment that faced the aisle. "It'll be hot as hell with everything closed up, but it's just for a few minutes. Until I get back. There," he congratulated himself, "that says 'don't fuck with this compartment' in any language."

Moments after his departure, a small dark woman slid the door open and threw aside the curtain, surveying the chamber.

"*Libero?*" she demanded, pointing to the seat that the lawyer had just vacated. Her left eyebrow arced across her forehead like black lightning.

"*Non parlo Italiano,*" Betsy returned faintly but with scrupulous adherence to the truth. Her practiced Gallic shrug would do no good here.

The woman's voice rose in a crescendo of abuse. Betsy wished herself back in Nice where invective would not continue to be showered upon an uncomprehending ear. She waited for the stream of words to empty the woman's mouth, then realized that the flow had only begun, that the woman, all umber and umbrage, was just now warming to her subject.

Betsy held up her hand. "*Scusi*," she said. She pointed to the lawyer's seat. "*Non libero*," she said. Then she pointed to each of the remaining empty seats. "*Libero. Libero. Libero.*"

The woman clasped her hands together before her face, giving thanks to the *madonna*, or in a salute to Betsy as a *madonna*. She disappeared after the rigorous exercise of imparting to Betsy and the Pakistani instructions to advise any other comers that the seats were now all *non libero*."

She returned with five suitcases, one at a time. The Pakistani student turned to Betsy with both palms up and said, "But where are the chickens?"

The woman trailed back with a saucy girl of eighteen and a sullen boy of twelve. Her offspring carried the two remaining bundles before them—massive sprays of flowers, at least four feet in length, wrapped in varied swatches of colored paper and bound by string. The luggage was wedged in here and there, displacing the air that had made the hot, tiny compartment bearable. Betsy rested the lawyer's briefcase on top of the student's suitcase and the madras jacket on his seat. She watched as the enormous parcels of flowers were laid reverently across the top of her canvas backpack and the lawyer's creamy, butter-yellow leather suitcase in the overhead racks.

Suddenly the light from the aisle began to flicker like an old film. The regularly exercised frame of the lawyer filled the doorway as he slowly shook his head. "Christ," he said.

"No chickens," Betsy said humbly, sending a small smile to the Pakistani.

The conductor arrived to collect the increase in the fares of the *signora* and her children. The daughter's eyes hibernated, cold and unanimated, beneath half-closed lids, while the conductor spoke in a hushed voice, but her short yellow skirt moved several inches up her thighs, snaked its way, as though the conductor's voice had charmed the skirt quite apart from his failure to charm the girl.

"Now me," said the lawyer to the Pakistani, "you've probably guessed I've never been a leg man myself. Just between the two of us, what's your preference, Winston? White meat or dark meat? Breast or thigh?"

The Pakistani smiled.

This little *senorita* is pretty flat, what you might call titless, but then so's her old lady."

"For God's sake," Betsy said.

"*Que pasa?*" the lawyer turned an innocent face to Betsy. She stared at the lines etched into both sides of his mouth and the faded scars on his forehead—perhaps left by childhood chicken pox.

The *signora* perched alert and quiet as a cat, as a *duenna*, until the conductor left. Betsy waited for her to address her daughter, but instead the *signora* stood up and closed the window with great satisfaction.

"No," said Betsy firmly, "no, *signora*," confident the lawyer had her pegged as the type to be cowed by foreign bullies and domestic welfare cheats.

"*Per favore*," said the *signora*. "*Un momento.*" She left an opening of a few inches at the top of the window.

Betsy pushed down on the upper pane until there were ten inches of air coming into the compartment. She was pleased with her no-nonsense manner.

The Pakistani was writing a letter on his lap. The lawyer was watching Betsy noncommittally. He made her think of her parents.

A few minutes later, the *signora* got up and closed the window another two inches.

"No," said Betsy on the edge of her seat.

"*Per favore*," the *signora* pleaded, her raised thumb and forefinger separated by the tiniest space to show how little she deprived them. Betsy turned away and the woman closed the window another inch before settling back into her seat.

Betsy picked up her newspaper but her eyes wouldn't focus on the print. Fifteen minutes later, the *signora* stood and subtracted another four inches from the open space.

When Betsy said, "No, *signora*," the woman produced a cough of consumptive proportions. Defeated, Betsy sat back in the stifling compartment. The boy, embarrassed, was staring out the streaked window while the girl chipped away at her painted nails. The Pakistani slowly added words to the paper in front of him.

When the *signora* took a blue-flowered handkerchief from her dress pocket and held it to her lips as she rose toward the window, the lawyer crossed the compartment with one stride. He jammed his tightly rolled *Herald Tribune* between the top of the glass and the frame. Looking at neither the *signora* nor Betsy, the lawyer said, "You heard of John Kenneth Galbraith?" He took the Pakistani's newspaper and opened it and stabbed with his forefinger. "He says, 'The happiest time in any man's life is just after his first divorce.'"

Betsy struggled with her newspaper, trying to appear absorbed in each page, until she found the Galbraith quote. Maybe the lawyer and his wife had begun their marriage with a trial separation.

After another uncomfortable hour, Betsy caught herself slapping at her arm. Seconds later an identical gesture came from the lawyer.

Betsy examined her fingers. "Ants," she diagnosed, puzzled.

The student pointed above their heads to the bundled bouquets.

"Oh no!" the lawyer roared. "No livestock in first class, lady!"

The woman was all incomprehension. Betsy displayed on her palm another ant, then pointed to the flowers. The woman replied in obdurate pantomime that the ants came through the small opening at the top of the window.

"No," Betsy said resolutely. "The window stays open. *Les*

flora avanti," she insisted, though not at all confident she had said anything in any language.

The lawyer jerked his thumb up at the flowers and then in the direction of the corridor.

"No, no," wailed the *signora.* Words frothed and bubbled at the woman's lips, now beseeching Betsy, now bemoaning all the injustices that had befallen her in life. Her daughter said something low, cold, and knifelike, but though the woman paused for half a heartbeat, upsetting her rhythm, the barb did not stop her. The boy turned his face against the window.

"Let's pitch the damn things," the lawyer said.

Betsy said nothing, knowing he didn't expect her to reply.

"We can at least put them out of the compartment, can't we?"

"Where?" Betsy said.

They kept their eyes from the corridor, where people now stood as cattle, as people traveling as cattle. "Christ," he submitted. Betsy almost liked him at that weakened moment.

She spent the rest of the night slapping at ants and keeping her face averted from the malodorous stockinged feet of the slumbering *signora,* which somehow came to rest on the edge of Betsy's seat from across the narrow aisle. Then the train broke down, or the track needed to be repaired—she could only salvage the word "broken" from the conductor when he looked in on the *signora's* daughter.

Betsy fretted about being late for her four-thirty a.m. connection in Pisa. Overtired, hemmed in by the bodies of the student, the *signora,* and her children, all floating in sleep, she felt like she was underwater. Only the lawyer was awake to throw her a line of conversation, but she knew she had cut off any hope of rescue from that quarter.

They were delayed an hour and a half somewhere between stations, but even, so the train for Florence had not yet departed. She could see it across the train yard from the compartment window. Betsy stood and set the bundle of flowers upright on her seat. She eased the heavy pack down from the rack and then replaced the flowers. All eyes were shut in the dim compartment: there was no one to take leave of. But Betsy knew the lawyer was playing possum.

She scattered "*scusi*"s all over the corridor like rose petals and still could not find a path through the tangled, drowsy mass of travelers. As she stepped over bodies, Betsy wondered suddenly what the lawyer's bride had been doing while he was surveying the beaches of Nice.

Finally out on the platform, she saw she must scrabble across lines of empty, forbidden tracks—there was no telling when her train would leave—but she stopped outside the coach and pulled a map of Nice from her capacious purse. With a felt-tipped pen, she quickly printed KELBY! in large block letters across the diagram of the city. She counted the windows to their compartment and held the map to the glass above her head. Seconds later he was at the window looking down at her.

She glanced over her shoulder toward the other train but her overstuffed backpack curtained her view of the station. "Where's your wife?" she whispered.

A long, pale pink spiky bloom spiraled down from his fingers and hit the platform near her feet. "No capish, sugar," he said before he disappeared from the window, taking his rolled-up newspaper with him.

Thick and Thin

6.

Winston Mansukhani was the shame of his father. Or he would have been, had anyone in the family or among their acquaintance in Hyderabad known of his true occupation.

Father and son both continued to wrap him in the camouflage of a student. But Winston had not been that for some time. "Not even a student of human nature," his father thought sadly.

Already now his "studies" exceeded the norm in duration and his father was running short of explanations. "Even graduate students would have graduated by now," his father wrote with some bitterness. "And loving sons would not let so much time pass without a visit home to their mother." Or their father, Winston read between the lines. But he was even worse at dissembling than his father, so he stayed away.

The truth was that Winston had withdrawn from Trinity College. Sanjib Mansukhani could not understand how a boy who had worked so diligently in school and achieved top A-Levels in Maths, Chemistry, and Classical Civilization could throw his education away. This came close to breaking Sanjib's heart.

Sanjib would have been so proud to have a medical doctor—which Winston had talked of becoming—in the family, or a chemist. A chemist would have brought him exquisite joy.

Sanjib's own father had aspired to be a chemist but was unable to complete his education due to ill health. He had been severely beaten in an anti-Hindu riot two years after his son was born. Both his legs had been fractured and his left lung punctured by a broken rib. By the mercy of Vishnu, he had been carried to the doorstep of a Muslim physician, who took him in and tended to him. The doctor had plunged a needle attached to an empty syringe into his chest. Sanjib's father was ashamed to report that he had thought the man was trying to finish him off, injecting air into his Hindu heart, but the doctor was just letting the air around the collapsed lung escape without allowing any external air back in. "He was not killing me. He was saving my life, even while he could see I thought the worst of him." He had wanted to resume his night-school education when his strength returned, but he never fully recovered. As he grew older, his legs gave him enough trouble that merely walking any distance caused him to have difficulty breathing. When his own doctor warned that he must not exert himself or he could bring on repeated incidents of pneumothorax, he retired to his bed in despair.

His disability necessitated that Sanjib forgo his own dreams of a university education and go to work for his father's brother in the umbrella trade. Not only did they manufacture umbrellas for personal use—"the best bumbershoots in Pakistan," the uncle persisted in calling them—they also made kaleidoscopic accordion umbrellas for shading pedicabs and cycle rickshaws and shipped those around the globe. At first Sanjib had hated his job but felt that this abhorrence was tantamount to hating the uncle who employed him, so he squelched the discontent in himself and cultivated gratitude instead. He was very glad he conquered those unworthy feelings for it made him a happier person and a more effective businessman.

Not only had Sanjib been able to support his parents, but in time, he had managed to provide a costly education for his son, both in Pakistan and later in England. Now, with the money Winston was posting home, Sanjib was even able to send his daughters to university and perhaps eventually on for postgraduate degrees. He tried to be happy about that, but it was proving very awkward.

People were talking. Not just the neighbors, but the

family too. After so many years of being trusted, it pained him to see the glint of suspicion in his uncle's eye. But he understood. Where was all this money coming from that went to educate Winston and his three younger sisters? His uncle didn't want to believe him guilty of embezzlement, but Sanjib's explanation that he had carefully invested his savings and they had grown exponentially was less plausible. Especially since, upon questioning, he did not seem to know much about the entities he had invested in.

In the beginning, Winston did not reveal the source of his income to his father. He said only that he had come by his earnings honestly. His secretiveness combined with the sheer improbability of a university student sending money home caused his father to write, "Everyone knows that university students are careless spendthrifts. They are always asking their parents for money. They do not send large sums home to the parents. It is against the order of things. I am sorry to say this, my son, but I cannot believe in my heart that you have truly come by this money in an honorable way. I am thinking many fearful things. Please tell me the nature of your good fortune so that I can put these worries aside." So Winston finally telephoned from London, a complicated business made more complicated by the content of the conversation. "That is not coming by money in an honorable way!" the father cried. "'Legally' does not mean 'honorably,'" he fretted.

Sanjib was troubled and conflicted. He wanted to assure his aging uncle that the increase in his own fortunes had been honestly obtained. Or to confess that it had at least been legally obtained, but he couldn't bring himself to reveal that his pre-med son whom all admired was a dropout and a professional gambler. And he couldn't bring himself to refuse the bank drafts Winston deposited in his account.

* * *

Winston was awakened by the *signora* and her two children gathering their belongings in preparation for exiting the train. The brazen, painted daughter loaded parcels onto the arms of her sullen younger brother, her sherpa. The mother wordlessly thrust the enormous bundles of spiky flowers at Winston, who managed to hold them and shield his face from them at the same time, while she arranged herself and her packages for departure.

When the *signora* threw back the curtain covering the door of the compartment, he saw that the corridor had emptied. The American, sitting opposite him, noticed as well and collapsed back into his seat with a deep sigh.

The *signora* and her feral offspring gone, Winston cast an eye over the luggage racks, taking inventory.

"She left in the middle of the night," Kelby Bradshaw said of the young American woman who had occupied the sixth seat in their compartment. "Good riddance, I say. She was even more of a pain in the ass than that mamamia." He jerked his head in the direction of the corridor, where petals from the floral spears littered the floor, "With any luck it will be just the two of us from here on."

Winston nodded. He watched as the lawyer opened his briefcase, which held little in the way of papers and much in the form of foodstuffs. Kelby set a half-baguette, a wrapped wedge of cheese, a small jar of olives, a bag of granola, and two bottles of beer on the seat next to him. He snapped the case closed and set it across their knees like a dining table. "Breakfast," he said.

"One moment." Winston slid out from under and stood to remove a plastic sleeve of shortbread biscuits and an orange from his bag. "A modest contribution," he said, settling himself back into place.

Kelby produced a Swiss Army Knife and set about slicing cheese, loosening the lid on the olive jar, popping the caps on the beer bottles. They took turns sampling from the spread, their makeshift table too small to accommodate both pairs of hands. "So, where are you headed?"

Winston was silent for a long while, perhaps because he was clearing his mouth of food, perhaps because he was considering. Then he said, "To the next casino."

Kelby's eyebrows climbed up his face. "No shit?"

"No," said Winston. "No shit whatsoever."

"A job?" Kelby ventured. He studied the circumspect demeanor, the white shirt tucked into black pants, the meticulously trimmed fingernails. "You a dealer?"

"No," Winston took a swig of the warm beer and felt his face flush, "I am a player."

"You're shitting me, Winston."

"I assure you I am not."

Kelby laughed with his whole body, threatening the jar of olives. "This meal may turn out to be the most interesting part of my entire trip."

It was Winston's turn to register surprise. Before they had been invaded by the *signora* and her family, Kelby had announced that he was traveling on his honeymoon. Both Winston and the American woman had refrained from question or comment, but both, Winston was confident, had turned the remark over in their minds, examining it, speculating on the whereabouts of the bride.

"Spill," Kelby said.

Winston checked the surface of the briefcase, then his pant legs, and looked up questioningly.

"Not noun. Verb. As in 'talk.'" Kelby said.

"Ah," Winston said, "as in 'spill your guts.'"

"Exactly."

"Where do I start?"

"In the middle. Beginnings are always boring."

Winston pondered what of his history constituted the beginning. Was it the circumstances of his birth, being the oldest and the only son of a father who worked to support three generations? Was it wanting to protect his family from the anti-Hindu rage that still erupted without warning in the province of Sindh? Was it the nights at Trinity where he learned the game of blackjack and learned that he could outplay any of his opponents? Was it realizing that what he had regarded as companionship had been mere proximity, and that even that was lost when it became apparent that he always emerged the winner?

"I was a student," he said. "At Cambridge," he added, knowing this would impress his listener.

It did. Kelby whistled.

"I was doing well enough in my course work, but I was doing even better at blackjack. I decided to postpone my education. It was a good time for me to leave the school. The blokes I had thought were my friends were starting to put it around that I had been cheating them. That was not so, but you cannot convince a loser of his incompetence. Bad luck, yes; bad play, no. And I was winning too much for them to see it as a matter of luck. Which, of course, it was not. At least they were correct in that. So I took off with their money, my winnings, as my stake."

"How much?"

"Seven thousand pounds. A little over."

Kelby whistled again. "No wonder you weren't popular on campus."

"Yes."

"And how long did it take before you blew that?"

"I have not lost my stake."

Kelby tried to estimate Winston's age. His face was so unlined as to look blank. The perfect poker face, Kelby thought to himself. "So, you're off on a grand tour of casinos? Are you going to set a limit on how much you can lose each time? I hear that's maybe the most important rule, or else you lose your shirt fast."

"That is important. It is as important as setting a limit on how much you can win." Winston fell silent long enough for Kelby to register that, then, "I am starting my sixth year of play."

"I guess the artificial light in casinos helps preserve youth. No sunshine wrinkling the skin." Kelby tossed an olive into the air and caught it in his mouth. "Maybe good for keeping the brain young too. You must have a great memory."

"Not particularly."

"But everyone knows you have to count cards if you're going to beat the house with any consistency."

"Do you play cards?"

"Bridge. A little poker with the guys. The times I've gone to casinos, I would play a couple hands of poker—more like *lose* a couple hands of poker—and then dump some quarters in the slots. Nothing in your league. Truth is I don't like to gamble."

"Neither do I."

"So what's your racket?"

"You make it sound like you suppose I am engaged in something nefarious. I am surprised to hear myself saying this," Winston smiled, "but you are reminding me of my father. I did not expect disapproval from you."

"Okay then, I should have said what's your strategy? Wait. If you tell me, will you have to kill me?"

"No killing necessary."

"Don't you want to swear me to secrecy?"

"Also not necessary. Are you finished with your breakfast? Let us clear the 'table' for a demonstration." Kelby packed their breakfast remains into the briefcase while Winston rummaged among his things until he came up with a deck of playing cards.

Winston dealt four pairs of cards face up. "When you play bridge, you have to keep track of what has been played. Not just the cards themselves and which face cards have fallen in play, but also the number of cards remaining in each suit."

"Only if you care about winning." Kelby fiddled with the corner of a jack, flicking it. "And you have to remember who played what, and the bidding, of course, so you can figure out who's likely to hold what's still out there."

"Yes. Very complicated. And in the poker variations there is some of that as well. Figuring out the percentages. Suits matter because of flushes. I play only blackjack. Suits do not matter; the ranking within a suit does not matter; only the value of a card matters."

"Still, you have to remember how many cards with the different values have been played."

"Actually, no." Winston was enjoying himself. He realized he hadn't really enjoyed himself in a long while. He also realized he hadn't talked to anyone this much in a long while as well. "Did you know that the shoe the dealer uses customarily holds six decks?"

Kelby whistled a third time.

"At some establishments, as many as eight." Winston put the tips of his fingers together, tenting his hands. "Consider how difficult it would be to keep track of 312 cards or more."

"Impossible."

"Perhaps not. But impossible for me and for most people. And of course that is why so many decks are used. My system is simple. First, I play by the suggested best practices. If you play by these, you will not do very badly, as these are determined by the odds. A novice can ask the dealer what to do. He will tell you if the odds dictate that you should take a hit. A gambler relies on instinct or some other foolishness. I rely on the odds."

"But if the odds favor the house, even if only slightly, how do you make money by following the odds?"

"Because I bet more money when the odds shift in my favor."

"And how do you know when that happens?"

"By keeping track of the value of the cards that have been played."

"Counting."

"No. Not the face value of the cards. Not the number of them played. The assigned value."

"Okay, Winston, I'm in the dark. Enlighten me. Dazzle me."

"I assign a value to each card in the deck. Ace, king, queen, jack, ten—they all have the value of minus one. The low cards, deuce through six, are plus one. The middle cards—seven, eight, nine—they have a value of zero. So I watch and add as the cards are revealed." Winston pointed to the first pair, an ace with a deuce. "The ace has a value of minus one, the deuce is plus one, so their sum is zero." He gestured to the next pair, a three and a jack. "Three is plus one, jack minus one, total zero." Of the third pair, he said, "An eight and a seven are both zero." The last pair consisted of two face cards. "Both minus one. So the total for the deal is minus two. Zero plus zero plus zero minus two.

"I don't have to remember what was played, only the sum of the values. I add or subtract to that sum with each deal. What is left in the shoe, the positive or negative value, determines how I bet. Or if I walk away from that table."

"Okay, I'm beginning to get the idea. So you know when to make the really big bets."

Winston shook his head. "I know to never make really big bets."

Kelby looked his question.

"For two reasons. One is that a big bet can mean a big loss. 'Always avoid the big loss.' That is a lesson I learned from one of your fellow countrymen, Casey Maguire, in Las Vegas. The second reason is that you want also to avoid the big win. He taught me that as well."

Kelby kept his eyes on Winston, waiting, knowing that the answer was coming at him with the certainty of a train moving along a track.

"It is not good for a player to draw attention to himself. Before I learned that, I was banned from two casinos. Also I was robbed once. You are familiar with the saying the father gives his son when he goes out on a hot date with a young lady? 'If you cannot be good, be careful.' My father said much the same thing to me, but about playing blackjack. If I could not be a good son and stop playing, then he asked that I should be a careful one. So I am that. I play quietly. When I am doing well, I endeavor to appear mildly surprised by my good fortune. And I place all my winnings, except for modest tips to the dealer, to the servers, and the cage worker, in the safe-deposit boxes of the casinos.

"The only time I draw attention to myself is when I make it obvious that I am not carrying any cash beyond the equivalent of twenty dollars American on my person. The days on which I withdraw my winnings from the safe-deposit boxes are not the days when I spend time at the tables, often not the same weeks. So it is not just a game of odds, it is also a game of cat and mouse."

"But *not* a game of chance," Kelby nodded. "I'd like to see you in action."

"I am afraid that if you were watching, you would give me away."

"Probably right. I'm not known for my subtlety."

Winston smiled. "I think I understood this when you spoke so extensively about female breasts."

"Hey, I didn't know that prissy bitch could understand what I was saying. Serves her right, though. I like thinking of her having to sit there and not being able to say a word because of that bullshit, pretending she couldn't speak English."

"I am sure there were things she would have liked to say." Winston lowered his eyes. "I, too."

"Like?"

"Not about the breasts. I think that subject was fully examined." He allowed himself a smile before he pressed on. "Excuse me, but you said you are on your honeymoon?"

"Yeah."

"Then it is your turn to spill."

"Use your imagination."

Winston shrugged. "I am not a very imaginative person."

"Doesn't take much to figure this one out. She dumped me. Two days before the wedding. At least it wasn't one of those at-the-altar-in-front-of-everyone-you-know jobs. Nina was engaged once before. She didn't show up at the church for that one."

Winston nodded. "Yes, that would be worse. But how do you tell people, the relatives who have come from far away?" He immediately regretted letting the question escape, leak out of him. He was rubbing salt in a too fresh wound.

"*You* don't. That's what parents are for. My mother never liked Nina, so sharing the news was its own reward. I can imagine how she phrased it." He shook his mother's words out of his head. "What *you* do is go on a three-day bender and then you leave on the flight for Paris with an empty seat beside you."

A flyspeck of an idea became trapped in the web of Winston's thoughts. He leaned forward. "What is your itinerary?"

"I don't have one. Nina and I were going to spend the better part of a month touring around France. She's fluent in jilting and in French." Kelby gestured to the Italian countryside passing in the window, "Here you see me bailing on France. I don't speak *foie gras* and there's no reason for me to wander around the Frog pond solo. Hey," he said, registering the shift in Winston's posture, "what would you say to me riding on your coattails? You could set the itinerary. I don't care where I go, except I'm determined not to go home until this honeymoon is over. We could take in the sights by day, do some meals together, and then you could hit the casinos at night while I hit the bars."

"Customarily, it is during the day that I visit the casinos."

Kelby felt the rejection like a body blow. "Sure. No problemo. Dumb idea."

"Not a dumb idea," Winston said. "Not at all. But I think I have a better one."

Kelby spread his hands wide over his thighs, his arms tensed, as though ready to spring up and exit the compartment, waiting for the right or wrong word to set him off.

"I am thinking we should go someplace that is so unlike France that you will have things other than the missing Nina to occupy your mind."

"We should?"

"Yes."

"Crap. Now you're feeling sorry for me."

"Of course. Only a person completely devoid of feeling would not feel sorry for you. You have had a terrible blow. You are dealing with it most admirably, but, like you, I think companionship would be beneficial to you at this time. I know companionship would be of particular help to me. There is something I would like to do, someplace I need to go, and I would be grateful if you would go with me. I am confident that if we go to this place together, you will forget your pain."

"Are we talking brothel?"

"No. I hope that does not disappoint you." Winston frowned, finally looking of an age to place a bet. "I propose that we travel to Pakistan. More particularly to the city of Hyderabad. Most particularly to the home of my family."

Kelby whistled. "Seriously?"

"Most definitely seriously. I would pay for your transportation. Once we arrive in Hyderabad, my family will take care of everything."

Kelby's eyes widened, reflecting the scope of the generosity of the offer and of the distance to be covered. "Thanks—money is not my problem but, come on, Winston —Pakistan? How about we get off at Venice? That would be un-French enough for me. Or maybe go to one of those Greek islands. They're a lot closer. Why Pakistan all of a sudden?"

"Such a dramatic change would be good for you. You would see everything with different eyes, I promise. And my eyes have not seen my parents or my sisters in six years. You would be rendering me a service." He lifted his hands, palms up, into the space between them. "I cannot face them alone. And perhaps my family could come to view me through the eyes of my friend."

"I guess it would be a dramatic change in itself to render a service to someone that wasn't billable by the hour. My *pro bono* for the quarter." Kelby sat back in his seat and exhaled.

"Hell, I'll never get to Pakistan any other way."
  Being men of resolve and best friends, they shook on it.

The Pensione Désirée

7.

Betsy started down the hall of the Pensione Désirée slowly, touching her fingertips to the wall every few feet, as though steadying herself at sea.

"*Dove?*" she said to a young man leaning against an open doorway. "*Scuse. Dove gabinetti, per favore?*" She heard the words hum in the back of her head so she knew she had spoken.

"Sorry," he said with a distinctly American twang. "Don't speak Italian."

"*Bravo.* Me either. Where can I find the toilet, please?"

"Second door on the right."

When she emerged from the amber-and-white-tiled room that also held a bidet, a footed tub, and a marble sink, she felt comforted by the amenities, felt that life was less impossible.

She tapped at the frame of the doorway where her countryman had stood.

"Come in," commanded a female voice, a hostess.

"I'm hoping," Betsy said as she took in the engaging portrait of reclining woman and hovering man, "I am desperately hoping you might have a bottle of mineral water you'd be willing to sell."

"Have a glass on us," the young woman said. "I'm Helena."

"Betsy. Thanks, but I'm afraid a glass won't be enough. I must be dehydrated—'thirsty' doesn't come close—and I just can't manage the streets tonight."

"You wouldn't find anything open now anyway. We have some extra water, don't we, Stephen? Give Betsy the bottle over there on the desk. Will that work?"

"Better than a wonder drug. Let me pay you."

"Don't be silly."

"I feel like you've saved my life, but that's possibly an overstatement. Thanks. Good night."

She was offered three good nights in return and pivoted slowly to see the third person, a sandy-haired man wearing wire-rim glasses and a correspondingly intent expression. He sat antagonistically erect on a straightback chair in a corner formed by one wall and a massive armoire.

The next morning, fortified by two rolls, apricot preserves, and several cups of *caffè latte*, Betsy tapped at the door of her rescuers. The voices intersecting on the other side stopped abruptly. "Come in," Helena called, bright as the Florentine sunshine.

"Good morning," Betsy curtsied.

"Morning," the one called Stephen smiled at her. He was serving breakfast from a tray.

Her body's needs taken care of, Betsy was able to turn her attention to the couple. She hadn't been in a noticing frame of mind the night before. Lanky and alert, Stephen struck her now as catlike, a painter perhaps, visiting this city of painters. Even if he were not an artist, his wife would still seem the ideal artist's model. "I'm disturbing you," Betsy said.

"Not at all. Sit," Helena patted the bed beside her. Betsy noticed for the first time that her left foot was encased in a thick white sock and elevated on one of the *pensione*'s unimpressionable, boulder-like pillows. "Ridiculous, isn't it?" Helena had followed her gaze. "Only an idiot would cripple herself on vacation."

"But what happened?"

"Actually, *I* happened," Stephen said. "Helena's taking too much credit—merely a matter of her being in the right place at the right time. I got myself entangled in the cord of the traveling iron, which was sitting on top of the wardrobe. So I've given her a broken toe as a souvenir of our trip."

"A *memento mori*." Betsy was pleased with herself until she saw the blank faces. "A reminder of mortality," she shrugged.

"Well, anyway, it's transformed him into the most

attentive of husbands: he can't do enough for me. I spent one day out on crutches. Never to be repeated. My arms ached and I kept bumping my foot," she shook her head. "I decided I'd rather lie here and be waited on."

"But then you're stuck in the *pensione*?" Betsy raised her eyebrows: "A prisoner of your own Désirée."

This time the couple laughed and Helena said, "Are you by yourself? Good. Then there's no one to object to your spending time with us."

Having resolved to take up with no Americans during her travels, Betsy had remained resolute and lonely. She decided she had earned a vacation from her vacation. "Sounds good. Turns out I brought along something that might help you pass the time, Helena. *Tar Baby*."

Helena looked blankly back.

"The latest Toni Morrison," she said, handing over the book. "In return for the water. I finished it on the train so it's really dead weight. But I couldn't just abandon it."

"Perfect. I've been trying to force myself through *Anna Karenina* but it's impossible to care what happens to her. I'll start your book this morning."

The man with the eyeglasses came through the open door. "Good morning," he spoke into his collar. His greeting didn't take any of them in.

"Paul, you remember Betsy from last night. We've recruited her."

Paul nodded in her direction and the very act of recognition seemed to exclude her. Not much for women, Betsy concluded.

"Now, what have you seen already?" Helena grilled her. "If I have to lie here, I at least get to direct traffic."

"Nothing yet, really. I only arrived yesterday and then I just wandered around trying to find a place out of the sun. I didn't really see anything. When I couldn't go another step, I stumbled in here. I was so tired I even agreed to take a triple room. Mostly I've slept."

"You and Stephen," Helena clucked. "He's been nursing me so faithfully—guiltily—that he hasn't taken in a single museum or church—nothing."

"And you?" Betsy sympathized.

"It's shitty luck but it could be worse. I was in Florence six years ago, as a student."

"Her junior year abroad, lah-de-dah," Stephen raised the tip of his nose with his index finger.

"At least I have my memories." She put the back of her hand to her forehead.

"What about you, Paul?" Betsy asked to show she wasn't edging him out of the circle.

"What? Oh, it's my first time here but I arrived four days before Helena and Steve. I thought I might as well come on ahead when they called the strike."

"What strike?" Betsy thought she might have heard something about a railway workers strike happening somewhere, maybe England.

He looked at her as though she had confirmed his suspicions about her IQ. "The Major League baseball strike. With any luck it'll be over by the time we get home. Anyway, I've seen everything here I want to see. And more."

"Paul's impatient to leave," Helena confided as though he weren't present. "He thinks Florence is hot and dirty and crowded."

So it had seemed to Betsy as she tried to find a cool and clean and open space the day before. Still, Paul's dismissal irked her, precisely because it resonated.

"I have a plan," Helena announced, hands folded clerically across her chest. "Stephen and Betsy go off to the museums and Paul stays and keeps me company. He can read aloud while I languish—doesn't that sound romantic? Betsy has even supplied the book and Stephen needs a break. He won't leave unless there's someone to watch over me. So, Paul, if after all your whining about this city, we find you prefer it to me, Stephen and I will both be deeply offended."

"I'll be happy to stay," Paul said, "but I'm afraid I'll bore you."

Betsy examined Paul's face and found him in earnest. This trace of humility elevated him a notch.

"We can bore each other. So," Helena turned to Stephen and Betsy, "where are you two off to?"

Stephen made a deferential bow to Betsy.

"I guess I'd like to start with Michelangelo's *David*."

"Agreed," he said. "Anything you want, Helena, before we abandon you?"

Stephen and Betsy walked to the Galleria dell'Accademia. "It's at 60 via Ricasoli," he said. "Ricasoli. Everything in Italy sounds like something to eat."

Stephen questioned Betsy about her travels. He was easy to talk to—partly, she supposed, because he was unavailable. Betsy found herself, quite unexpectedly, telling him about her divorce.

They saw the *David*, instinctively separating when they arrived at the great hall, each viewing from their chosen vantage points. Afterwards they stopped at one of the outdoor cafés and Stephen resumed, as though following a momentary interruption, "So you came to Europe for romance. A new love to erase the old."

"No," she was surprised to be so misunderstood. "I came to be alone really."

He raised an eyebrow quizzically.

"You can't be more alone than in a crowd of strangers. I figured that not only would I not know anyone—not even the mailman—but I'd be isolated by language. I can't speak anything but English, except the standard travelers' phrases I try to memorize while I'm riding on the trains. Anyway, it's worked. I've been thoroughly alone." After all, the people she'd met in airports and on trains couldn't be counted as traveling companions. "Until today."

"And tomorrow? Where are you headed after Florence?"

"Not sure. I don't have an itinerary exactly. Just a return

plane ticket. I thought I might brave Venice next."

"Why 'brave' Venice? Helena said she'd like to move on to Venice as soon as her foot is better. We should go together: safety in numbers."

"It's not that I'm afraid of being alone in Venice. I guess I'm afraid of being in Venice at all."

"Is this a mystery?"

"More a superstition. A sort of morbidity, I suppose. When I think of Venice, I think of death and decay. It's the idea of elegance and decadence intertwined that unnerves me. You know—an ornate gondola skimming above a fetid canal. Somehow I don't think I expect to escape from Venice intact."

"Well, I don't know about elegant decadence—I'm just a country boy—but I do know I'm glad I'm not doing Florence by myself. Helena has good instincts."

"*Grazie*. And I'm pleased to have your company. Helena also has good taste."

As they walked back to the Désirée, Stephen said, "What made you decide to come off your retreat and take up with us?"

She laughed. "I think your wife did the deciding. But I must have been ready."

When they returned, Helena's voice spilled out the perpetually open doorway. "You're back," she burbled, shifting gears as soon as they appeared. "Well? What do you have to say for yourselves? For *it*?"

Betsy realized that she and Stephen had not once discussed the statue though they had toured the rest of the gallery together, a comfortable flow of words passing between them. She was conscious of being slightly if inexplicably embarrassed. "It was—what's the word I want?—not powerful exactly—affecting."

"Maybe you were carried away by the worshipping throngs," Paul said.

She was startled by the hostility.

"People draping themselves around the base, getting

their pictures taken," he continued.

Despite recalling her own shudder of distaste at precisely the scene Paul described, she was angry. "I didn't expect to be moved, not after a lifetime of photographs and reproductions, but there was something extraordinary—I don't know—some cruelty in the face, something heartless, and yet at the same time this utter innocence."

"Don't apologize," Stephen said. "I felt the same."

"Ah, *simpatico*," Helena smiled. "Enough talk. I'm starving. How about you, Betsy? I say we send the men out to forage. We'll picnic here."

"If I can pay my share."

"We know you're no freeloader. Toni Morrison for water, wasn't it?"

When the men left on their assignment, Helena tugged on Betsy's arm. "You mustn't mind Paul. It has nothing to do with you. He's just like that."

"Like what exactly?"

"Oh, always complaining." She laughed. "I'm sure he thinks Europe is a cliché because he's seen everything in the art history books."

"Sounds impossible to please."

"He likes you, though."

"Does he?" Betsy's eyes widened. "That's a surprise."

"Really?" Helena said vaguely as she chewed on her bottom lip, her thoughts somewhere else.

"How's your foot?" Betsy asked with a guilty start, fixing, she was sure, on the cause of Helena's distraction.

"Better, thanks. No more throbbing. Just plain hurts now."

"I'm sorry."

"No, really, I meant it when I said it was better."

"Have you seen a doctor?"

"Enough about my malingering. I'm becoming disgusted with myself. Let's talk about you and the wonderful Fates that brought you to us. Stephen was in need of somebody to do the tourist things with and I'm thrilled to have a woman to talk to, but I think it's especially good for Paul that you're here. He can be painfully serious, and we know him so well that with us he doesn't feel the need to make an effort."

"I'm supposed to be a good influence?"

"You'll hardly notice."

By the time Stephen and Paul had returned, balancing three bottles of wine and plastic-foam dishes rim upon rim filled with tortellini and scallopini, and a napkin of sliced bread, and slabs of watermelon, Helena and Betsy had revealed enough of their pasts to share a flushed, conspiratorial ease. Betsy had related to Helena much of what she'd told Stephen about her divorce. In return, Helena confided that she had married Stephen in defiance of her parents, who had wanted her to continue along the path of debutante balls and corporate connections they had so purposefully set her on. "But Stephen has proven himself to the family. I suppose we'll never be in Daddy's tax bracket, but even Daddy admits I could never find anyone else so devoted."

When Stephen and Paul stepped through the door, the air in the room was thick with intimacy.

"I've decided," Helena announced with an imperious toss of her glossy, chocolate-brown curls, "that in a few days I'll be able to walk. Probably a grotesque parody of a walk, but I want you all to know I'm improving."

"Good news," Stephen said, toasting his wife with a triangle of watermelon.

"We'll be able to leave Florence," Paul said.

"Where is it you want to go?" Betsy asked, trying to draw him out, trying to draw him in.

"I don't know. Zurich maybe. Lausanne. Someplace cool. Someplace else."

The next day Betsy and Stephen inched their way through the Duomo at Stephen's suggestion. The day after, he asked her to choose their course. A pattern had established itself. Each morning Stephen would tap on Betsy's door and together they'd breakfast in the comfortably crowded dining room, sitting at one of the tables close to the balcony with its tumult of red and pink flowers. Stephen would butler a tray back to the sleeping Helena, and Paul would arrive from his solitary breakfast—he had managed to secure one of the city's single rooms on the other side of the river. While Betsy and Stephen followed the crowds of tourists through Florence, Paul remained with Helena. In the late afternoons Stephen relieved Paul at Helena's bedside and then Betsy and Paul found themselves thrown together. Betsy suspected they would both prefer some solitude, but Paul's hotel was too far away and, besides, neither wished to disappoint Helena. They developed the habit of reading or writing letters in each other's company.

During these siestas, she sometimes imagined Stephen and Helena behind their closed door. They were a handsome pair, pleasant to look at, another of the works of art that belonged to this city. She pictured him cradling Helena's heavy curls in his lap while soothing her temples with long, tapering fingers. She thought if that was marriage, then perhaps she had never really tried her hand at it.

"How long have you known them?" she asked Paul.

"What? Oh, Steve and I were in school together—engineering. I took a job in Venezuela for a year. The money was good but that was as long as I could stick it out. Anyway, that's when he met Helena. I flew back for the wedding." He tilted his head modestly and shrugged, "Best man."

"How long ago was that?"

"I don't know. They've been married pretty long now. About four years, I guess."

Betsy was conscious of being older than the others only when she was alone with Paul.

Every evening the four would come together. After the first night these gatherings were transferred to Betsy's considerably larger room. (A room for one person became available at the Pensione Désirée, but Betsy, in a burst of extravagance, rejected it as too small. It was not so much that she was choosing the more expensive room, she rationalized, but that this room had been allotted to her by the Fates for this purpose.) They'd position the little writing table between the single and double bed and lay out the various foodstuffs on it. Stephen had discovered a bar that sold good, extremely cheap, chilled wine by the bottle. Paul would drink only chilled wine and the others wordlessly agreed he was most in need of lubrication. The parties went on until all hours, the same participants each night. The arrangement appeared to suit even Paul.

Each evening ended in the same way: Betsy passing whispered good nights through the door as Helena left supported on either side by the two men. It was an unfailingly comic departure, none of them as steady as they should be, white-swathed foot extended before them, all three staggering the length of the marbled hall with the heightened caution of inebriates in a sleeping house.

Each night Betsy wondered if she would hear Paul's muffled tap upon her door as he made the return trip down the corridor. Once, his steps stopped just outside her room. She wondered how she would respond to Paul. She wondered if she would let him make love to her. A new love to—as Stephen said—erase the old. Could she and Paul—poles apart—come together for anything more lasting than an interlude in Florence? The strongest force between them, after all, was Helena. She waited, her fingers now unmoving at the buttons of her shirt, until his steps retreated.

Her sixth morning in Florence, Betsy proposed that she and Stephen visit the Palazzo Vecchio. She was conscious of Helena's too bright smile following them through the open door. And conscious of a complete absence of expression on Paul's face.

"Aren't we neglecting Helena?" she asked dutifully after Stephen led her down the flights of stairs and into the open air. She was afraid he would agree.

"Not at all. She wants us to go." He settled a reassuring arm around Betsy's shoulders.

"Well, Paul then. Maybe he's ready for adventure again. You two could have a day out on your own. I'd be happy to spell him."

"Trust me. We'll all be happier if you don't."

Touring the Palazzo Vecchio, Betsy felt sick with a kind of vertigo. There were paintings and altarpieces, statues, goblets—the art and artifacts of too many ages, all against a backdrop of ceilings, walls, and floors that were painted, carved, molded, and inlaid. The objects so filled her senses that they became obstacles to seeing. Outside, she took deep breaths of hot air, steadying herself against the cool stone at the entrance to the Loggia. The sculpture garden offered sanctuary, but Stephen pulled her on to the Uffizi.

She hardly looked, holding something of herself in reserve, until they arrived at the *Primavera*. She had seen so many reproductions of the vast canvas, so many fragments isolated into postage stamps or book jackets, yet the Botticelli was as fresh as the season it celebrated.

Like two children, they stood motionless for some time and then bolted from the room. Without words they left the building and its endless rooms of exhibits.

"Let's walk," he said.

"But I'm so tired."

"Your eyes are tired. Your mind is tired. Walking will help spread the tiredness around."

"All right."

Crossing the Ponte Vecchio, they lingered occasionally to look at a sketch by a sidewalk portrait artist. At the left bank of the thick, green Arno, they did not stop but immediately returned through the tunnel of shops and street vendors. Blindly, Betsy followed him along the streets that intersected without plan or reason.

When they arrived at the *pensione*, the door to Helena's room was closed.

Stephen turned to Betsy. "Let's go out for a drink."

"But —"

"Don't say that you're tired and that we only just got here—say yes."

"Yes."

A few blocks from the *pensione*, he took her hand lightly in his. Betsy felt something flutter, birdlike and distantly familiar, in her chest. Farther on, he drew her off the pavement into one of the openings that held immense wooden double doors with colossal brass globes as knobs. He leaned in against the door with his left hand and slowly traced the line of her throat with his right. Involuntarily, she closed her eyes.

He moved as if to kiss her and she pulled away, feeling the cold press of brass upon her spine. "We ought to go back. Helena might be awake now."

"Sorry," he said. "I didn't mean to frighten you." He smoothed the worried crease in her forehead with his thumb. "Don't be upset. I'll behave."

There was something about his mouth, not quite a smile, that reminded her of the *David*. She frowned, straining to see what was still unclear. Suddenly her face froze, blank and cold as virgin marble. "Helena wasn't sleeping," she said dully. "Paul was with her." A child's half-sob escaped her. "But I thought Helena had picked *me* for Paul."

Had she instead been chosen for Stephen? Or was it enough that she merely seem to Paul to belong to Stephen?

Stephen ran the fingers of one hand through the front of his crisp, wavy hair. "I don't suppose you'll go on with us to Venice now."

She knew then she would never see Venice.

"We'll all be disappointed."

She blinked back tears. Helena's Daddy was right: there could be no husband more devoted than Stephen.

Fumbling for her key in the hallway, she saw through the now open door of Helena and Stephen's room to Paul sitting rigidly on the straightback chair.

Betsy settled her bill with the concierge that night. It was necessary to leave before breakfast if she wanted to be certain of not seeing any of the threesome again. Before she hunted out another *pensione*, she would look for a schedule of trains that could take her to the Italian Lake District where, the guidebooks promised, the air was cool and Americans seldom went.

Monkey Business

8.

Paul had a problem, a mathematics problem. He was headed toward the room shared by his best friend, his best friend's wife, and Paul's lover and there were only two people in that room.

He stopped on the second floor of the Pensione Désirée and caught himself before he knocked on the door of the room to the immediate right of the stairs. Fist in midair, he glanced up. Another numerical befuddlement. He shook his head at the 1A painted in gilt on the transom. Paul recalled with annoyance that Italians called the second floor the *primo piano* and the first floor the *piano terra* or something like that, something meaning the ground floor. He was looking for 2A which was up on the third floor, which they persisted in calling the *secondo piano*. And if that's what they called the levels in buildings, what did they call pianos anyway?

It wasn't that he was unfamiliar with the layout of the Désirée or that he hadn't mounted the steps to Steve and Helena's room at least twenty times by now, but he was addled. This morning his complex mathematics problem had suddenly become exponentially more complicated.

He had stopped at the front desk on his way into the *pensione* to learn the Désirée's checkout time and to deposit his suitcase behind the desk before climbing the stairs to collect Steve and Helena and their belongings. The proprietress accepted his case and gave him a deadline of eleven o'clock. In the interest of clarity, she held up both hands and then added an index finger. As he started to turn away from the desk, she offered some additional information.

"*La signora è partita stamattina presto.*"

He looked at her blankly.

She sighed heavily. "*La signora*," she tried again, this time going with a minimalist approach.

He nodded.

"*Partita*." She pointed toward the massive wooden exterior doors.

"The *signora* left?" He could feel panic erupt lava-like in his stomach and then rise quickly to his chest. He had heard of situational depression. He supposed this could be the onset of a situational heart attack. Unaccustomed to locating himself in his body, he concluded that his physical relationship with Helena had set into motion a whole series of physical and chemical reactions and interactions. Something more over which he had no control. "Which *signora*?"

"*L'americana*."

"But which Americana? Helena or Betsy?" The thud he thought he heard could have been him stomping his foot in frustration or it could have been his heart. Either way, the body asserting itself.

Could Helena have left Steve because they had been found out? Did her going mean Steve knew about the two of them? Had she confessed? Was she right now headed toward the pensione where he'd been staying, trying to find him, trying to negotiate the streets with her enormous suitcase and a messed-up foot? Did it mean that from this day forward they would be together? And what about Steve? Had he lost his closest friend? His only close friend? Was it too late to start worrying about that now?

It seemed an intentional torment before the woman finally answered, "*Elisabetta*."

Betsy. Then Helena was still upstairs.

Was he disappointed?

A reprieve. Of sorts. He could continue to assume his best friend did not know that Paul had slept with his wife.

But Betsy's leaving was bad enough. It had changed the equation. Instead of Betsy and Steve pairing off to go sightseeing while he "kept Helena company" until her foot healed, they would be reduced to a threesome. A threesome was not divisible by two. Not anymore anyway.

When he reached the *secondo piano*, he tapped lightly on the appropriate door and it flew open as if he'd released a spring.

"Good morning," Steve said.

"She's gone," he blurted, never adept at small talk.

"Betsy?" Steve returned after a moment's hesitation. "Where?"

"I don't know."

"What do you mean—'gone'?" Helena said. She was lying on the bed fully dressed, a cool confection in the sultry air, iced in filmy white cotton scattered with yellow rosebuds. Paul imagined a convent of small Italian nuns bent over the cloth, embroidering the tiny flowers.

"I don't know," Paul repeated.

"Did you see her?" she frowned.

"No. The lady at the desk. The one with the frozen eye —"

"The owner," she encouraged him.

"She told me. But I'm not sure I got it right."

Helena picked up the receiver next to the bed and immediately launched into Italian. At the close of the conversation, she said, "*Sì, sì. Grazie, signora.*" They awaited her report. Helena left them dangling a minute, as though she had forgotten they were there. "Oh," she said. "She's gone all right. She paid the concierge last night and took off before breakfast this morning. The owner saw her leave with her backpack." She tapped her chin. "Before breakfast. That shows determination. Or extreme cowardice. I wonder what you could have done to scare her off like that?" She was looking at Stephen.

"I don't think it was anything in particular I did," he said slowly, choosing his words with as much care as he'd chosen the souvenir he'd purchased for Helena's father. "I got the idea she didn't want to be part of our quartet anymore."

"Really. I would have said she liked us all very much. Was

devoted to our merry little band of wanderers, in fact. I can't believe she left without coming to say goodbye."

"Devotion lends itself to disillusionment and sudden departures, don't you think?" Stephen said.

Paul said, "But she knew we were expecting her to go to Venice with us today."

He was bewildered. Not by Betsy's departure—though he was certainly surprised that she had left so abruptly—he was bewildered by himself.

He had lain awake most of the night trying to reconstruct the afternoon, the minutes immediately after Helena had asked him to close the door so they could talk without being disturbed by other guests of the Désirée. There was talk and then somehow there was kissing and then . . . He shook himself. He wanted both to relive each touch and to erase the entire episode from his memory, like wiping discarded design specifications from a blackboard. A clean slate, that's what he wanted.

He never planned to make love to Helena. He didn't know what had come over him. When she confessed that she was afraid that Steve and Betsy were falling in love, he had wanted to comfort her, reassure her.

Everything was a blur—not just the . . . the event itself, but the future.

It seemed to him that he went from being Steve's best friend—his best man—to Steve's worst enemy without anything—any thought—in between.

He wanted everything to be just as it had been before yesterday.

Or did he?

*　　*　　*

Helena glanced at Paul dismissively and then erased the expression before he caught her.

Paul would've been flattened by the knowledge that she occasionally referred to him as "Stephen's dogsbody." Not that he would have understood a dogsbody as the British equivalent of a drudge, but he would've recognized the intent to demean, to discount him. She was more widely read than either Paul or Stephen and that was not surprising. It would have been surprising had she not been, for she exuded leisure where they projected industry. Like practitioners in the medical field or the sciences, the bulk of their reading came from trade publications. Between them, at any given time, they had subscriptions to five different engineering-related journals. Helena enjoyed sprinkling her conversation with vintage words and arcane phrases, much as she liked wearing vintage or otherwise unexpected clothing: she took pleasure in being noticed.

Baiting Stephen, Helena had also conferred upon Paul the title "Your Man Monday Through Sunday." (Had he overheard, Paul could have convinced himself that she was praising his loyalty, his steadfastness as Steve's closest friend. Of course, now he had proven himself profoundly lacking in that quality.)

Until their trip to Europe, Helena had been equal parts amused and annoyed by Paul's attachment to her husband. She probably would've continued on just so, ricocheting between warm benevolence, tepid tolerance, and icy irritation, had it not been for having to take to her bed. This absurd injury to her foot meant she couldn't do any of the things she had planned to do in Florence. Helena cast about for a new plan. She could have settled on improving her Italian or learning to knit. Instead, she decided upon seducing Paul.

Helena liked a challenge and Paul offered that in spades. He was too straight an arrow and too devoted to Stephen for an unambiguous seduction. The real conquest lay in making Paul believe that he had seduced her.

It wasn't that Helena was promiscuous; it was that she was bored. She hadn't strayed from her marriage vows before now, largely because she was in love with her husband. And in some small part, she'd been determined to parade her fidelity before her father, who thought she had married beneath her.

*   *   *

Stephen squinted at the Florentine sunlight glinting off the diamond he had purchased on a monthly payment plan. Staring at Helena's ring took him back to the gathering at the Thorne house to acknowledge their betrothal. Mr. Thorne had given Stephen a first edition of Oscar Wilde's fairy-tale collection, *A House of Pomegranates,* as an engagement present. "I think this story will interest you particularly." He had placed a leather bookmark at "The Birthday of the Infanta," the fable of a princess who is given a hunchbacked dwarf to dance for her on her birthday. When she asks for him to be brought back to perform for her again later, the Dwarf believes that this must mean the Infanta cares for him. But seeing himself in a mirror for the first time, he realizes that the Infanta only cared to ridicule his freakishness and he drops to the floor, kicking and flailing. When she comes upon this new performance, the Infanta demands an encore. Her servant tries to prod the Dwarf into action and then announces that he has died of a broken heart, to which the Infanta replies, "In the future, let those who come to play with me have no hearts."

Stephen had been furious with his prospective father-in-law, but he'd also felt a shiver of fear. Both he and Mr. Thorne understood that a bored Helena was a dangerous Helena.

*   *   *

Paul supposed he understood nothing about relationships except that he felt closer to Steve than to anyone ever since they had first met back in the civil engineering program at Cornell. Steve had even accompanied him to Akron for his father's funeral. Paul barely remembered his mother, who had died from some kind of cancer when he was eight. An only child, he had no reason to go back to Akron anymore. Steve helped him with the paperwork in putting the family split-level up for sale. The following Christmas, the new-minted orphan was invited for the holidays to Eden, outside of Buffalo, where he was welcomed by Steve's parents and tolerated by his siblings. And the Christmases after that. But all that changed, naturally, when Steve acquired a fiancée.

From their introduction, Paul had admired Helena's appearance and her poise and stood more than a bit in awe of her self-assurance. He confessed to Steve that he kept having to shake off the feeling that Helena had just been dethroned somewhere. "In some kingdom that has recently shifted to a parliamentary form of government or been taken over in a military coup." Steve had laughed uneasily, the story of the unfeeling princess too recently read, and clapped an arm around Paul's shoulders, saying, "Sometimes she *can* be a royal pain in the ass, but mostly she's wonderful." Then he asked Paul to be his best man.

Steve had fallen for Helena during the year Paul spent in Venezuela where the main project he had worked on involved designing and building a telephone station for CANTV, Venezuela's phone company. The actual construction part of the job ranged from overseeing the laying of concrete to installing an electrical network and a grounding system to building perimeter fences. It also ranged from all-consuming concentration and busyness to unpredictable delays and abject loneliness. He didn't attempt to learn Spanish. What was the point? He couldn't get Steve to join him down there so he knew he wasn't staying.

*   *   *

Three years into the marriage, Steve and Paul finally managed to get hired on a project together. An architect Steve referred to as Frank Lloyd Wrong hired them as a team to engineer his design for a residence built into a diabase mountainside. Paul, having building experience on a range of projects in South America and, later, in Montana's high country, and Steve, with his master's emphasis in geotechnical engineering, were employed to oversee the excavations and make the outcroppings of wood-and-stone rooms secure. In keeping with Steve's not-Wright theme, and because the building with its extensions protruding at right angles was located in Pennsylvania (though at the eastern, opposite end of the state), Paul christened it *Fallingrock*.

They both admired the lines and the sheer cussedness of the finished product, but neither could imagine anyone actually living there. If the landscape's starkness and isolation didn't get to you, then the indigenous toxic creatures surely would. Like a pair of closely related monkeys, Steve and Paul picked numerous ticks off each other at the close of each workday, fraternal primates unselfconsciously engaged in a practice that affirmed their bond and preserved their well-being. And then there was their shared instinctive response to the snakes.

Steve announced to Helena that the architect was an amateur herpetologist.

"Actually"—anytime Paul began a sentence with "actually," Helena was instantly irritated—"he's an amateur ophiologist. A herpetologist has made a study of all reptiles. Ophiologists confine themselves to snakes."

F. L. Wrong told the two engineers that, being of a scientific bent themselves, they would be interested to know that of the twenty-one species of snakes native to Pennsylvania only three were venomous and, of those, only the timber rattlesnake and the copperhead could be found locally. And, he assured them, they could readily tell those apart from the harmless species.

"Wrong said we could tell the difference by looking the snake in the eye. 'Poisonous snakes have slit-like pupils, like cats' eyes, and the nonpoisonous ones have round pupils, like humans,'" her husband quoted to Helena.

"Actually," Paul corrected, "he said 'venomous.' A 'poisonous' snake would be one that sickens you upon ingestion."

"Right," said Steve. "He also said that venomous snakes store their venom in sacs on both sides of their heads, giving them a flat sort of triangular shape that's distinctive from the nonpoisonous—I mean nonvenomous ones."

Helena shuddered. "Here's hoping you guys never make acquaintance with any, poisonous, venomous, or non. I'd rather you didn't get into a staring contest with a snake."

"No worries there. We're both the act-now-ask-head-shape-questions-later type," her husband reassured her.

Paul shrugged. "Between us, we've killed five so far. All round-eyes as it turns out."

"We don't dare tell Wrong. He's trying to get them all on the Endangered Species list."

Paul nodded, "But we're not taking any chances. I looked up the timber rattler. Its Latin name is *Crotalus horridus*. That's enough of a warning for me."

*   *   *

After *Fallingrock* was completed, the trio decided upon a trip to sinuous Italy to counter the months of sheer escarpments and stark perpendiculars in Pennsylvania. Helena maintained that Stephen first needed the antidote of the City of the Seven Hills so the two of them went to Rome for a few days while Paul flew directly to Florence. Steve and Paul had never been anywhere in Italy but Helena had spent two semesters in Florence during college and was looking forward to feeling the same kind of exhilaration she had then.

If only she hadn't broken her toe. Or, *actually*, if only Stephen hadn't broken it by sending that damned travel iron crashing down on her foot. Her middle toe had swollen like a leech glutted with blood. And the whole foot had throbbed horribly. Even now, the top of her foot was bruised and sore to the touch. When she wasn't concentrating on pouting prettily, she'd wonder if she hadn't decided on diverting herself with Paul in part to punish Stephen.

"What to do? What to do?" Helena tapped her chin again, as though entering impersonal integers into an adding machine and waiting for the calculation to appear. She looked from one to the other of the men looming at the foot of the bed. "No matter what, we are leaving the Désirée this morning as planned. It's time to move on. I guess you two should take our bags downstairs for a start. Then we'll all go down for *la colazione* and decide what's next."

They went down to breakfast with Paul wondering exactly who was supposed to be making precisely what decision. Ever since he had found himself in bed with Helena, Paul had been wildly confused, but never too rattled to recognize that he had turned out to be the worst kind of snake in the grass, the vile *amigo horridus*. Turning away from the mirror this morning, he could see cat's eyes in his reflection. He knew what he had done was as venomous as could be. Remorse and pride struggled within him. Just a few days ago, he would have reckoned that Betsy was out of his league. But the amazing Helena? Out of his universe. And yet.

Paul and Stephen each downed a *caffè doppio* and Stephen made quick work of a sour-cherry *crostata* while Helena sipped her *caffè latte* and picked at her croissant-like *cornetto*. Paul, having eaten earlier at his own pensione, vibrated with impatience and yet wished he could stop the clock. Make time stand still. He couldn't go back and undo, but he dreaded going forward. He sat stupefied by the thought: *everything changes now*.

When Helena had finally finished, Paul scraped back his chair against the marble tiles and stood. Still seated, Helena looked up at him. "Stephen and I have decided to take a pass on Venice, but we don't want to interfere with your plans."

His plans? He gaped at Stephen, who shrugged in his direction.

Helena continued, "We're going on to Madrid. We'll be just in time to catch the Spanish Grand Prix tomorrow. We know you're not interested in racing. Or in ever hearing Spanish again for that matter"—she flashed her smile full at him, inviting him to pretend he was in on the joke—"but that doesn't mean we can't all share a taxi to the train station."

Paul stumbled backward, jostling the chair of another diner. As he retrieved the elderly gentleman's fallen napkin, he had time to wonder when this itinerary had been hatched. Steve and Helena hadn't had a moment alone together since his arrival at their door.

He felt betrayed. By both of them. And then he had to strangle a laugh. What right did he have to feel outrage? Forget outrage. His body told him that this intense feeling was, actually, relief: he was going home.

* * *

Steve, too, felt a relief as cool as Pennsylvania mountain air wash over him: he was not the Dwarf.

* * *

No one could guess what Helena felt. Helena least of all.

An Innocent/A Broad

9.

Betsy removed herself from the Desirée and the clutch of Americans staying there to another *pensione* but she knew she had not gone far enough. She had to get out of Florence.

There was the heat, of course, which filled not only the air but everyone's conversation. She showered twice each day—mornings before the breakfast of hard rolls, apricot preserves, and *caffé latte*, and evenings before she foraged for a trattoria with a menu turistico. In this way she was able to dine with some dignity, some poise—what was the Italian for *sangfroid*?—but by the time the bowl of floating fruit arrived at her table she was reduced, like those around her, to fanning herself with one hand, trying to move the hot, heavy air that breathed down her neck like an ardent dragon.

She blamed the heat, but it was heat of a different sort that troubled her. In all her vague plans, the itineraries of daydreams, she had seen herself regretfully leaving Florence—how much better the Italian name, Firenze, captured the climate and the overwhelming closeness of the city—for Rome and Naples. Now the prospect of going south, where it was yet warmer and the men were purported to be warmer still, made her feel faint.

She had not expected, at the age of thirty-two, to have her footsteps dogged by strangers, to be barked and worried at like unprotected game. Chestnut hair, dark wide-set eyes, trim figure, Betsy knew she was reasonably attractive, not unreasonably so. The face she saw in the mirror had never stopped traffic before. She was certain the attention she was receiving was a by-product of culture and climate and something indigenous in this species of male rather than inspired by anything in her. She found this exaggerated interest peculiarly impersonal.

In Florence she had introduced herself as Elisabetta, hoping the sheer formality of her name would serve as a mantle of protection, her way of taking the veil, but nothing could shield her from total strangers. After she was spun round on the street by a passerby who planted a kiss upon her protesting mouth, she decided to about-face for Ireland, where the weather would require wearing a cumbersome sweater and where the men would be properly repressed. On her way north she would visit the Italian lake country.

Even the words sounded cool and crisp and clean. She fled by rail to Milan, where she connected with the unabashedly third-rate second-class train to the city of Como. The Lago di Como was the only one of the lakes she recognized by name. From Como she rode a steamer (slightly cheaper and significantly more romantic than the bus) to one of the little towns on the water's edge, where she took a room in a well-kept, gracious middle-class hotel, the Albergo Giannino.

Nestled into the waterfront of the small town of Cernobbio, the Giannino offered the best accommodations of her trip thus far: a small but not cramped bedroom with an intoxicatingly modern private bath: sink, shower, bidet, toilet, shimmering stainless steel and salmon-colored tile everywhere. She had not minded walking down the hall or paying an additional fee for the use of a shower, but she had come to dread the water closets as she had dreaded having to use the outhouse when visiting her grandmother as a young child. The WCs were exactly that—indoor outhouses: windowless, airless, without even the aperture of a crescent moon hewn into the door; barren except for a commode which invariably did not flush properly. So the Giannino offered both charm and luxury for surprisingly less than she was accustomed to pay for neither.

She took full-pension accommodations, knowing after her first meal that nowhere else could she eat so cheaply and so well. She had learned variety and motion were not, for her, the essential ingredients of travel. Instead, they were distractions. Betsy was soothed by her increasing store of familiarities: set hours for dining, the same young waitress to serve her, the small carefully laid table with her room number discreetly displayed, her own napkin folded and tucked after each meal into an oversized paper envelope bearing both her name and that of the Albergo Giannino. For the first time since she had landed at the airport in Paris, Betsy relaxed.

Her host and hostess at the Giannino were a pair of perfectly matched opposites—he at once both officious and friendly, anxious to impress, and she sullen, with eyes half closed so she might be excused from returning a smile. *Signor* Alfieri spoke hotelkeepers' English, as well as a smattering of French and German. He was proud of his hotel and his accomplishments. The *signora*, also receptionist and chief cook, chose not to understand a word spoken by her few alien guests. Quickly Betsy learned to avoid complications and confusions by dealing only with the *signore*.

Her first morning at the Giannino, Betsy awoke in time to indulge in a shower before breakfast, which was served hours earlier than in the cities. Halfway through her ablutions, the lights in the bathroom went out. After pressing the various switches in the bedroom and discovering she was completely without electricity, Betsy resolved to withhold this announcement from the *signora*. With her impoverished Italian, she worked up a formula for explaining to *Signor* Alfieri both the electrical failure and her own lack of responsibility for it.

Signora Alfieri was ensconced behind the desk, wearing the same shapeless dress and well-formed frown of the evening before. Betsy offered a *buon giorno* in which she felt every one of her teeth was displayed. When the *signora* realized she could not pretend ignorance of her native tongue, she grudgingly reciprocated the greeting. Betsy decided henceforth to ladle pleasantries onto the *signora* like sauce. Her own smile and salutations would be frequent and unavoidable, the tariff her hostess must pay to keep Betsy's room occupied. She said nothing about electricity.

During breakfast, the same fare as in Florence with the addition of individually foil-packaged slices of cold, dry toast, *Signor* Alfieri stopped by the table three or four times to make sure she was satisfied with his hotel. "And did you sleep well in this night?" he asked with a degree of seriousness that made Betsy lend greater than usual enthusiasm to her reply. "Very well, *grazie*. I can't remember when I've slept better."

Signor Alfieri shook his head dismally so she could only suppose some error in his translation. He was gone before she thought to tell him about the electrical failure in her room.

Later, as she mounted the stairs, *Signor* Alfieri called her to the desk. He had replaced the *signora*, who was presumably off somewhere rechiseling the hard edges of her expression. "*Signora*, the lights in your room, they do not work?"

"Pardon? Oh"—Betsy felt herself flush as though discovered in a compromising position—"that's quite correct," she said stiffly. "I'm sorry—I forgot to tell you. I can't imagine why they went off. I'm sure it was nothing I did," she heard herself apologizing.

"You will go now to your room, please, and call to me if the lights do not work more?"

"Yes. Of course."

"Dial four, please." His voice was stern and his manner distant, showing no trace of the congeniality of the dining room.

"Sorry?"

"Two is for the outside line. Nine is the number for night service. You dial four, please. It is here, then I come."

"I see. I'll go right up and try the lights now."

"Yes. Then you call me."

Betsy hurried to do as instructed. When she phoned, *Signor* Alfieri didn't give her a chance to speak. "*Si*. I come now, *signora*."

She left the door to her room open and stood folding

her washing of the night before. She expected *Signor* Alfieri to enter armed with tools and expostulations. While mentally preparing for the onslaught, she found herself unceremoniously spun round. *Signor* Alfieri pressed his hips to hers and more gently placed his mouth on her lips. Betsy pushed off from him with the heels of both palms. *Signor* Alfieri's eyes darted back to the passage visible through the open door. His face was illuminated by the light pouring out from the sleek silver fixture in the renovated bathroom.

"*Signore!* You work very quickly," she said.

He moved toward her again with another furtive glance over his shoulder, but she kept both arms rigidly extended. "How long you rest here?" he panted.

"I don't know." She was torn between laughter and dismay. "It is a very nice hotel."

"It is my hotel," he wooed. "I own this hotel."

"I would be sorry to have to go," she warned.

"We talk later," he said, eyes fixed on the corridor behind him.

After she had shut and locked the door, Betsy snorted. She had just been congratulating herself on having discovered such a cozy refuge. She resisted the urge to run after the *signore* and tell him she had already met his younger, more handsome cousin on a street corner in Florence.

Standing at her window looking out upon the lake, instead of giving in to outrage, Betsy decided to be amused. *Signor* Alfieri had so overacted his part in this tired, clichéd drama. She chose to think of him as a stock character.

Later that day, with a great rush of agitation, Betsy saw it was she who hadn't been following the cues properly. She suddenly understood that *Signor* Alfieri had shut off the electricity to her room himself. That was how he knew to ask her about the failure even before she had reported it, and also how it came to be instantly repaired. She wondered if his maneuver was intended to be as obvious as it now appeared, and if her phoning down to the desk was taken for complicity, an invitation.

Betsy became angry at last. She had forgiven him when he was merely an opportunist, seizing the advantage against Ladies Luck and Elisabetta. Now that she saw him as master of his fate, she railed inwardly against him.

The following morning *Signor* Alfieri again stopped at Betsy's table to inquire how she had passed the night. Frostily she assured him she had again rested well. When she was passing through the lobby, he summoned her to the reception desk.

"*Si, signore?*"

He brought a printed card from behind the desk. On it were listed three single digits and a brief explanation for each in four languages.

"You see, to dial two for the outside line. Four is in the day. You remember you dial four for the lights?"

"I remember," she hastily summoned some hauteur.

"Good. Nine is the number of the night service. This night you dial nine."

"I don't understand. You mean to order something? Room service?"

"*Si*, room service."

Betsy had seen the small tables at intervals in the corridors where trays laden with crockery were deposited. "*Grazie, signore*, but you feed your guests too well."

"Tonight you cannot sleep. You dial nine. I come and you sleep."

Betsy had discovered in these weeks of traveling alone that the quickest way to avoid unpleasantness was by feigning tight-lipped, wide-eyed innocence. She often pretended not to understand an unsavory suggestion. Certainly she was blind to looks and deaf to innuendo. When pressed, she pleaded ignorance of language, as though a Berlitz course were needed to comprehend the meaning of street-corner lotharios. She wasn't young enough to have expected such unwanted attentions, or cool enough to dismiss them.

She wondered now if her practiced innocence had indeed become second nature.

"I am quite sure I will not need any night service."

Signor Alfieri, too, was practiced in the art of convenient deafness. He nodded his head, "You dial nine."

Betsy at last appreciated the *signora's* discriminating hostility, but this recognition did not eradicate the injustice to herself—the *signora* should place all the blame where it belonged—so Betsy continued her campaign of cloying sweetness as retribution for the personal offense. Unfailingly she spoke to the *signora* whenever possible and the *signora* was forced to reply. Her coldness, Betsy decided, was perhaps some explanation, though no excuse, for the *signore's* behavior.

In the meantime, *Signor* Alfieri did not give up. Betsy was impressed, almost touched, by his dogged persistence. When she sat out on the pier, with its cultivated appearance of a formal garden, reading a novel or the collection of poems she had brought from Florence, *Signor* Alfieri was apt to appear at her left shoulder talking out of the right side of his mouth. "You rest here the day. Maybe later I can come to you. The afternoon we are together." Betsy would only shake her head and laugh, careful neither to encourage nor discourage him, for either of these would mean she took him seriously. Still, to be safe, on those afternoons she reluctantly took herself away from the pier to wander the streets of the village or steam into the throbbing city of Como.

The lake itself surpassed Betsy's airy anticipations. According to a local brochure, Shelley had written to a contemporary declaring his intent to find a house on Como: "This lake exceeds anything I ever beheld in beauty, with the exception of the arbutus island of Killarney." Betsy would soon have the chance to make that comparison for herself. Such a funny guide, Chance, to bring her here where she had never meant to come.

In the daylight, after a night's rain—and it seemed to rain every night yet never before sundown—the green of the hills shimmered. The color was so lush that merely taking in the view seemed an exercise in hedonism. Scattered amid the thickly verdant growth were collections of dwellings, pale buildings hooded by faded orange tiles, crisp geometric shapes among all the undulating green. In the morning Betsy could sit contentedly, just looking, for hours. But at dusk, when the lake was more beautiful than she could bear, she would walk restlessly up and down the meticulously raked pebble-banked promenade, beneath the manicured trees, her eyes and her feet never still.

At dusk the light over the water softened and lied. Hill beyond hill beyond hill was shrouded in deepening veils of mist, making each seem a false shadow of the one before. In the haze the house lights shone yellow and warm, like fireflies or lanterns or candles in the windows. When dark came, it transformed all parts of the picture, smoothing the ripples on the water, absorbing the repeating hills, and draining the house lights until they were a thin, starry white. After only the second night, Betsy lost all sight of leaving.

*   *   *

On the third day, immediately after breakfast, she slipped out on the boat for the two-hour journey to Tremezzo. She visited the Villa Carlotta with its fecund botanical gardens, its statuary and paintings and period furniture, and returned to the hotel only moments before *Signora* Alfieri closed the immense wooden doors of the dining room.

Betsy loved the nightly collection of people, all guests of the hotel and almost all Italian—in Florence every third person had been an American. The Giannino was a family haven. In one corner of the dining room were grouped three tables representing three adjoining suites. A handsome couple in their mid-thirties and their two very prettily spoiled daughters occupied the first table. At the next sat the parents of the wife, and at a third sat her mother's parents. Four generations of women. Betsy feasted upon the flurry of kisses that hailed the beginning of each meal.

That evening she missed all the greetings. Most of the guests were well into their main course before she sat down. *Signor* Alfieri bent at her table to translate that night's menu and then lowered his voice to say, "Where were you?"

Betsy was taken aback. "I'm sorry if I held things up in the kitchen. Please apologize for me to the *signora*."

"Where were you all this day? You were not in your room or to the lake."

She found herself meekly reporting her trip to Tremezzo. "Today was not good for me," he said more audibly. "My liver was sick. I spend all this day in bed."

Betsy offered polite sorrow for his troubles though she supposed his incapacitation had been feigned to give him a day free for pursuit. When he left her table, she saw the *signora* staring at her from the kitchen doorway. Betsy beamed at her but the woman went temporarily blind.

As she was eating her dessert, the familiar, sweet smell of *Signor* Alfieri's cologne sidled up to the table a moment before him. Betsy laid her spoon down and waited. "Tonight you dial nine, yes?" and then he was gone.

That night Betsy pushed the writing desk against her door before settling into bed.

*   *   *

Restively she observed the stage business of *Signor* Alfieri's suit coat. The plague of heat had stretched as far north as Lake Como, and there what wasn't felt as heat was doubly suffered as humidity. None of the men staying at the Albergo Giannino wore jackets. The most proper among them carried theirs, limply, over one arm. On the evening of Betsy's arrival, *Signor* Alfieri had directed traffic in the dining room in his shirtsleeves. Now a pattern established itself. The *signore* attended to his duties in a comfortable short-sleeved shirt, but he would repair to a small room behind the reception desk when Betsy appeared. He would emerge with his suit coat buttoned over an incipient paunch, silk tie and matching breast-pocket handkerchief in place. Betsy was aware of the timing of *Signor* Alfieri's toilette though no one else seemed to notice, with the exception of the hollow-eyed *signora*.

He strutted and preened like a male bird, flashing his colors, while the signora remained on the nest, silent and glowering. *Signora* Alfieri wore the drab, dull coloring that camouflages the female; one could barely discern her shape behind the lusterless wood of the reception desk. She did not appear womanly and rounded but thick and congealed, like some perishable clotted from neglect.

Betsy began to sense *Signor* Alfieri's hovering even when she did not see him.

Sitting on the hotel terrace with its white wrought-iron tables and chairs, Betsy discovered that everyone seemed to have more English than her poor sampler of Italian. When, after a day or two, she was seen to neither behave badly nor be swept along by the Grand Tour, some of the guests made room for her in their circle of family and friends formed during annual visits to the hotel. For her part, she was more than content to spend the evenings mangling the language with new friends.

On these evenings, convened around a bottle of wine on the narrow border between the Albergo Giannino and the rain which connected Lake Como to the sky, the mother of a high school philosophy teacher would retire early, leaving her son free to wait on Betsy, but while he paid her respectful compliments, she paid attention to the shifting shadows. Then somewhere at the corner of her eye, Betsy's glance would snag on *Signor* Alfieri. She would be laughing and the laugh would die, asphyxiate in her throat. The *signore* would stand at a distance, too proud to presume to mix with his guests. If he saw that Betsy had spotted him, he put on his bustling, officious manner befitting the proprietor of a prosperous hotel. Betsy could not avoid feeling flattered.

*   *   *

She had trouble sleeping. She found herself listening for something. When footsteps came down the corridor, she held her breath until the sounds were long past her door.

It was preposterous, she told herself. She did not find *Signor* Alfieri physically attractive. If he had ever possessed it, he had outgrown the gracefulness necessary to this role. And then there was the way he treated his wife.

Betsy was sure women fell into one of two categories for the easily categorized *Signor* Alfieri: either unwieldy obligations or inconsequential pleasures. She couldn't think of a single thing she liked about him.

The next morning *Signor* Alfieri stopped at her table. She waited for him to ask how she had slept.

"How many more days you rest with us?"

"I don't know." Her fingers fluttered beneath the heavy damask napkin on her lap, as if they were curious, quite apart from her, to touch his shaven cheek.

"You call for night service this night?"

"What am I to ask for?" She tried to make her voice sound arch.

"Ask nothing. It is only necessary that you call."

"And if the *signora* answers?" Betsy had meant to make her inflection deep with disdain but she was listening so intently for his words that she forgot.

"She does not answer." He looked around the dining room to find their exchange had pass unremarked. "*Si,*" he sighed. "This night," he said as he moved off.

Despite her resolve, Betsy spent the whole of that day vibrating between predictable repugnance and unforeseen anticipation. It was his willfulness perhaps, his determination to have her. She was no longer either annoyed or flattered by his attentions: she was impressed by his decisiveness.

During dinner, she kept her eyes fastened to her plate, allowing them to stray only as far as the small pink blot on the tablecloth in the shape of Illinois where she had spilled some wine the evening before. Betsy took particular care not to smile at the *signora* when she came out of the kitchen to survey the dining room.

Following dinner, she walked up and down the pier, not altering her schedule in any way. Afterwards she joined a young Venetian couple on the hotel terrace for a tumbler of bright blue anisette mixed with water. At eleven o'clock she slid her key from the rack beside the desk behind which *Signor* Alfieri sat stiffly in his coat and tie. Her fingers nearly grazed his shoulder while his eyes fixed on her breasts.

In her room she executed her nightly routine, all her cleansing rituals. This time she didn't push the desk against the door.

Pulsing to the steady lap of lake against shore, Betsy lay there, alternating between replaying the speeches of *Signor* Alfieri and those of her ex-husband until three o'clock, wondering just how many women Greg had pursued while they were married, and how many of those had at last given in to him. Was he as dogged in his chase as the *signore*? Did he have to go after five to get one? Or had he been successful with them all? Did they pretty much fall into his arms, one after another? A domino effect? And what was the hotelkeeper's success rate? Surely *Signor* Alfieri enacted the same dance with other female guests traveling alone.

*   *   *

As she passed through the lobby on her way to breakfast, *Signor* Alfieri called her over to the desk. He was not wearing his suit coat. The *signora* was beside him, the two of them filling the space behind the desk like wooden pegs.

Signor Alfieri officiated. "You leave the hotel this morning, *si?*"

"*Scusi?*" Betsy was bewildered.

"You say you leave this day, so I give your room to another one person."

"But I never said—" Tears pricking her eyes, Betsy started to protest but found she could not claim innocence of any kind.

The *signora* spoke in English. "It is mistake," she said and patted Betsy's arm. She turned to her husband and began to argue. Betsy understood that *Signora* Alfieri was suggesting they give her the vacant double room for the price of a single. But the *signore* was adamant: that was no way to run a hotel.

The *signora* herself—the task was too menial for *Signor* Alfieri—insisted on helping Betsy shift her belongings to the end of the pier, where the boat would remove her from the Albergo Giannino. Slumping at the water's edge, Betsy waited to be carried away.

La Donata É Mobile

10.

By the time she had turned fifteen, Donata was already taking orders and turning down offers.

She had been waiting tables at the restaurant of her family's hotel, the Albergo Giannino, every summer since she'd entered upper secondary school. During the off-season, her married cousin Allegra could manage the dining room on her own with occasional assistance from Donata's father, but during the tourist season two young, energetic servers were indispensable during both the breakfast and the dinner shifts. Guests were left to fend for themselves at lunchtime.

Donata's mother oversaw the workings of the kitchen and supervised the culinary efforts of Donata's older sister, Glorianna, who would be replacing their mother as head chef when the swelling in the *signora's* legs finally made standing over the stove too difficult. Like their mother, Glori was an excellent cook. Unlike their mother, she worked just as hard at having a good time. She called it "letting off steam," a phrase she'd picked up from one of their guests. "When you cook pasta, you are always creating steam," she grinned. "I need to let it off before I wilt. Or explode." Donata worried about her big sister, that Glorianna would come to No Good, which she pictured as a small desolate island where Glori would mistakenly disembark and be forever marooned.

Donata also worried about their mother. Mamma, with her arthritis and swollen feet replete with bunions and hammertoes and fallen arches, struggled through her days. And with a husband like *Signor* Alfieri, nights were an ordeal as well. Once Donata asked her mother if her father had always chased other women and the *signora* had only shrugged wearily in reply. If he hadn't, she couldn't remember that far back.

One of Donata's worries was that Glori took after their libertine father. Another of her worries was that she herself took after their mother.

Now in the steamy summer of 1981, at age twenty-two and with her degree completed and with Allegra expecting her first child, Donata's parents let her know they were expecting her to take her cousin's place serving in the hotel's restaurant year-round. She had other ideas. Travel being the chief one. She wanted to check out the places the tourists were escaping from.

But because her parents were counting on securing her service for the foreseeable future—ideally at least until after she wed and was expecting her first child (fortunately for them, there were no likely prospects in sight)—she had some newfound leverage in her dealings with them. Otherwise, she would never have been able to persuade her father to put out the American woman he had been prowling after all week. Well, perhaps *persuade* was not precisely the correct word. Donata had threatened to quit the dining room, not at the end of the tourist season as he'd feared, but that very day, before the dinner seating.

Donata had studied her father in his pursuit of the American woman. He was relentless. A pomaded, scented wave of water wearing away the edges of an iceberg, eroding the American's considerable disdain until a chunk of her rectitude was ready to split off. Donata had witnessed it many times before. His clumsy, clownish wooing. He wasn't afraid to make a fool of himself. She thought it was this—as much as his persistence—that sometimes made him successful.

He was a sportsman, ever on his game, focused on the goal. Unfortunately for his wife and daughters, the unwilling spectators of his sport, his goal was always that small delta between some woman's legs. Despite his past conquests, Donata was each time surprised when he scored. It made her think less of her own sex. Women were so easily won. They craved attention and admiration, even from her buffoon of a father. She recalled with disgust what her sister had discerned about Cernobbio's middle-aged postmistress: "She is a whore for compliments."

Donata had delivered an ultimatum to her father that morning as the thermometer rose toward a record-breaking high. "Send the American away on the ferry or I will be the one leaving on it."

So he had sent the American female packing, quite literally. He wasn't sure he had been getting anywhere with her anyway. Another battle of the sexes lost. But that was a minor skirmish compared to the open warfare his daughter had declared. *Signor* Alfieri felt very much wronged, but he also felt he was not in any position to dictate terms, grooming Donata as he was. The job of managing the hotel was meant for her, *era fatto per lei*. Glorianna knew her way around the kitchen but was otherwise impractical. Her hands were deft but her head empty. She would have been more at home in a family of obsessive Scopa players or television addicts. Bookkeeping, managing the cash flow, keeping track of reservations, controlling the purchasing processes—these were beyond her. The only part of running the hotel that he worried Donata couldn't handle was customer service.

Donata knew too well that her parents did not want to bring strangers into the hotel and restaurant business. They trusted only family, and with that as their guiding principle, business had prospered. Except for the positions of limited scope—those of the housekeeping staff and the gardener—hiring from outside the family was not even considered. To do so meant that cash would be pocketed, wine would be pilfered, silverware would go missing, and secrets would be stolen. Not just the *signora's* recipes for *capriolo alla valdostana* and her celebrated linguini with fried lemon sauce but also the *signore's* practiced methods of seduction. On so many levels her father did not want outsiders knowing the family business.

Perhaps in this one instance Donata had felt sorry for

the American (she always felt infuriated on behalf of her mother). At any rate, she knew she couldn't keep demanding that her father oust every woman who aroused him. Hotel owners could not be in the business of turning away half their female guests. Luckily, not too many lone female travelers found their way to Cernobbio, let alone to the Giannino.

Despite dreaming of becoming a tourist herself, Donata found people in transit tiresome. They took so much for granted, expected so much to be granted to them. Away from home, among strangers—without baggage, so to speak—they could transform themselves into anything they wanted, anyone they wished to be for their two-week Lake Como vacation. Apparently, they spent the other fifty weeks of the year aspiring to be privileged assholes. "Assssa-hole," the waitress would hiss in sibilant English under her breath no matter the native tongue, age, or gender of the offending party. She had studied English in school but her working vocabulary came chiefly from listening to tourists and watching the occasional film.

Her disenchantment with the hotel guests, who made up most of the population of the restaurant, was becoming increasingly manifest. A few days before, during the dinner service, she had put the entire dining room on edge. No one heard what the Londoner had said to her, but several caught her reply in English. "You know how they say we Italians always talka with our handsa? Well, they are correcta," she delivered with an exaggerated accent before slapping him smartly across the face.

No one in the dining room needed to be bilingual to get the message.

Her victim smiled thinly for the benefit of their rapt audience, "And now you have illustrated the origin of the expression about the Englishman's stiff upper lip."

Signor Alfieri bustled over to the red-cheeked guest with an unopened bottle of Montalcino red. "All Sangiovese grape," he confided, as though hastening to fulfill the Londoner's straightforward request that had discombobulated his

capricious daughter. "*Per favore,* our gift to you," he spoke
softly as he sliced the foil from the lip of the bottle and
withdrew the cork in two deft motions. He mentioned the
oppressive heat and how it seemed to agitate everyone, even
the bees on the promenade, but his goal wasn't to defend or
excuse his daughter, only to return the room to its accustomed
hum, the clatter of silver and china, the fizzy intersection of
voices, the sighs of satisfaction.

That night, after the dining room had emptied, Donata
took a seat at one of the tables on the *terrazza* looking out
on the lake. This was an act of defiance, the first in the civil
war she'd declared against her father. It was forbidden to the
family to sit at the tables, indoors or out, at their hotel. "It
is not professional," *Signor* Alfieri decreed periodically when
he thought his family/staff's standards might be weakening.
"Not the custom at fine establishments."

"Because we are their inferiors?" Donata had inquired
at the peak of her mutinous secondary-school years with a
sneer that would yet ripen over time. "Because we are here to
serve them?"

"*Per niente.*" He tried to illustrate. "Sometimes a guest
insists I join him for a drink. I accept and raise my glass in
acknowledgment, but I never lower myself to his table."

"Because we are superior to them?" This notion more
closely conformed to Donata's sense of the world.

Her father shook his head. "Because it is not done.
It is like . . . like finding one of the Sisters of the Order of
the Visitation smoking a cigarette. Not just improper—
impossible."

*   *   *

On the night she slapped the Englishman, when the dining
room was finally closed and she had changed from her
starched white shirt to a shimmery lime-green one, she took
the only open table on the *terrazza*, brazenly, in the manner
of a woman who was above convention. When her father
headed in her direction—his agitation evident only to his

daughter, the familiar sight of his arms straight down at his sides while he vexed both thumbs against his index fingers as though he were appraising invisible fabric—she was saved by two of her vacationing countrymen who asked if they might join her. "We wish to thank you for protecting our national honor," grinned the younger and more handsome of the two.

Signor Alfieri's mouth pursed and his forehead collapsed onto his eyebrows in furrows, but he started to back away from the table.

"*Signore*," the younger said, "we would like to buy the young lady a drink."

"I'll have a glass of the Valtellina," she said dismissively to her father, as if she didn't recognize him from her seated position.

"*Signorina*, may we tempt you to try a wine of the Piedmont also from the Nebbiolo grape?" the storybook-handsome prince earnestly proposed. "Unless you would prefer something iced in this heat."

She shrugged.

"A bottle of the Barbaresco, *prego*." The young man turned his attention back to the daughter. "Have you been to the Piedmont, *signorina*? After all, it is quite close. My brother and I were fortunate enough to be born in Turin and live there still. Not that Cernobbio isn't beautiful, with much to attract the visitor."

"Easy traveling distance, but a world away," the older of the two said, mostly to himself.

"I think *you* are a world away," Donata said, eyeing him.

"You are the type of woman who notices things." He nodded. "Yes, I was drifting back to Turin."

"I've never been to Turin," she said bitterly. "I've never gone anywhere. Unless you count commuting to university in Milan twice a week. When I was thirteen I went to Rome with my school class. When your parents own a hotel with a restaurant, you are either in school or you are working. When there is a school vacation, that's when you're at your busiest because that's when all the families come for their vacations."

"This is your hotel?" the older asked with mild surprise.

"His hotel." She inclined her head toward her father, who was approaching with the wine and three glasses. "His and my mother's. I am Donata Alfieri. If I were someone else, after tonight, I would be out of a job."

As if reminded both of his manners and of Donata's earlier response to the ill-mannered, the younger said hastily, "*Mi scusi!* I am Gian Marco Ingria. And this is my older brother, in fact, my only brother, Neri."

Neri Ingria bowed his head in her direction as *Signor* Alfieri opened the bottle, poured, and then seemed to disappear. Gian Marco took Donata's lead and said nothing to the proprietor's shadow but a curt *grazie*.

Only Donata realized her father was still hovering somewhere in the dusk. And the *signore* did not like the view from behind the trellis curtained with clematis blooms. Ever since the Ingrias had arrived three days before, he had been aware of the younger one mooning after his daughter, gazing at her with eyes the size of chinotti, sighing like a soccer ball leaking air. Donata had been oblivious, but he recognized the signs instantly and assigned the brothers the farthest table at Allegra's station in the hope of keeping them apart. Now Donata could not help but see the love sickness too. What if it were catching? What if they married? What if she and this man, her new husband, moved out of the hotel? Away from Cernobbio? To Turin? Such things happened every day. The boy was good looking, wealthy enough to afford a vacation at the height of the season and to drink the best of the Giannino's wines. Why couldn't he be attracted to Glori? She would play with him and then send him home. *Signor* Alfieri shook his head. He slid out from behind the screen of purple clematis and inquired at another table whether there was anything else he might provide.

Gian Marco peppered Donata with questions about her life at the Giannino, calling for one disclosure after another until she felt all her limited mystery on display, like the ho-hum revelations of nudity at Gavano Beach that Allegra's husband had reported. "Better to see less and wonder more," he'd said.

"Where are your parents, wives, sweethearts, children?" she said to the Ingrias, pretending indifference to the answers. "The Giannino plays host to many families, but this is the first time I remember two brothers staying here on their own."

"It was my wife's idea," Neri said. "She is a saint and this trip was her benefaction."

Gian Marco looked at Neri, waiting for his slight, almost imperceptible nod of consent. "Neri's son is afflicted," Gian Marco said. "He has an uncommon condition called autism. His speech is difficult to understand—"

"What there is of it," said Neri.

"And some of his behaviors are . . . problematic."

"Ugo would be very sweet always if he could manage it," Neri shrugged, "unlike the rest of us."

"Annalisa, Neri's wife —"

"Ugo's mother," Neri said.

Donata nodded, "The saint."

"She wanted him to have some time away. And Cernobbio is only a couple hours by car. I came because he didn't want to be alone. And I am very glad that I did."

Donata turned her gaze questioningly back to Neri.

"On my own, I would not have managed to escape." He ran a hand through his already disheveled hair.

"And I was in need of an escape myself," Gian Marco said.

"From your wife and children?"

"I have yet to be so blessed."

"Gian Marco lives with our mother in the family villa that we will inherit when she dies."

"Today would not be too soon."

Donata jumped in her chair. Even when she hated her father for embarrassing her and humiliating her mother, she had never wished him dead or spoken of his misdeeds to strangers or anyone outside the immediate, suffering family. "I think perhaps you have had too much wine tonight," she said coolly.

"That is true. We have. Several glasses too much. It is also true that our mother is a monster," Neri confirmed.

"She tried to seduce Neri when he was seventeen. Of course, our father had recently died and she was feeling lonely."

"That's no excuse!" Donata gasped.

"Exactly," said Gian Marco.

Neri said, "For the several years after, she would swim naked in our pool whenever I or my friends were around, and for that there really is no excuse."

Donata tried—and failed—to imagine her mother or any woman she had ever known, even Glorianna, behaving so shamelessly. She shuddered and considered saying, "Maybe we should introduce your mother to my father." But she stopped short of speaking the thought. She wasn't prepared to betray her father, and anyway, she was confident this rapacious *Signora* Ingria would make a quick meal of her father, one bite, maybe two.

"But why do you stay with her?" She turned accusingly to Gian Marco.

"To protect our inheritance," he shrugged. "She still owns fifty-one percent of the family automotive parts business. And she says if I move out, she will sell everything and give all the proceeds to the Church."

"I think she has an idea that she might need to trade the properties in Turin for any hope of eventually acquiring some real estate there, " Neri said, pointing up to the twinkling heavens.

Donata wondered if she only imagined that he winked at her as he spoke.

"Besides, I like living in the villa," Gian Marco spoke defensively. "Neri and I like to remember the time before our father died. And when she's gone, Neri will return with

Annalisa and Ugo."

"And we will be able to sell off some of the estate," Neri added. "And still live well enough."

"The right school for Ugo will be very expensive," Gian Marco nodded.

"If we can find one," Neri shook his head.

Donata had little understanding of autism but it sounded to her like the boy's condition was severe. "He cannot go to the public school?" she asked.

"It did him little good and them less. This year we tried putting Ugo into one of the district's special schools. But he didn't learn anything. The school kept him from disrupting a regular school classroom and it kept him safe. But then ten days ago, he let us know he didn't like his cage. The bus that takes him home from the special school stopped at our apartment building and my wife met it as she does every day. But that day he got off the bus naked. The driver said Ugo had stood in the aisle and removed everything he was wearing and then put his shoes back on when his stop came. We kept him home all last week and this week my wife sent me on a vacation."

Donata looked from one brother to the other. "Well, I hope it has skipped a generation."

"What?" Neri frowned at her. "Autism?"

"This tendency in your family to take off one's clothes when not in private."

Both brothers laughed and Gian Marco slipped an arm around Donata's shoulders. "I think I am in love," he stage-whispered in the direction of Neri. "It seems I have at last found a woman, and a beautiful woman at that, who could stand up to our mother."

"Or knock her down," Neri smiled, inclining his head toward the dining room, alluding to Donata's blowup with the Londoner.

Signor Alfieri couldn't hear the words being spoken but he could see the younger man's arm snake across his daughter's shoulders. He cursed himself for having told the brothers they were unduly optimistic to believe there should be a room with separate beds still available at this point in the season. In the interest of a paltry increase in his revenue, he had installed them in his remaining two single rooms, keeping the last double with twin beds, which was more easily filled, still unoccupied. Had he assigned the brothers a shared room, Donata would be safe now. He had practically set up his own daughter to fall into the arms—into the bed—of this rogue from Turin. *Signor* Alfieri could only pray that he was a rogue, that his intentions were not honorable.

*   *   *

Since the night of The Slapping, *Il Schiaffo,* as Allegra referred to the incident when describing the scene to the women who had been busy in the kitchen, Donata had sat out on the *terrazza* with the Ingria brothers each evening. *Signora* Alfieri and Glorianna were curious about these young men, the silky younger one and his older, rumpled brother. As well as curious about this new Donata.

Glori longed to have seen her prissy, self-contained little sister striking the insolent Brit (with whom Glori had gone dancing in the city of Como the night before). *Signora* Alfieri wished she could have delivered the blow herself. Both now made a point of sticking their heads out of the kitchen from time to time to observe the brothers from Turin as they dined. As the mother and sister stole glances through the swinging door, they wondered what new transgression Donata might be contemplating.

On the morning of the departure of the American female (as a direct result of Donata's edict that would go unreported to either the *signora* or Glorianna), Donata, well pleased with herself, slipped into the kitchen and asked her mother and sister to prepare a picnic lunch for three.

"For the Germans?" Glori asked. "Lots of meat," she said to her mother. "Borzat sausages," she raised an index finger. "*Cotecotto,*" then her middle finger, followed quickly by her ring finger, "and sandwiches with the marinated Bresaola and arugula with lemon slices. Some *violino di capra*? Yes!" Her baby finger shot up. "You must remember to tell them this prosciutto gets its name from the tradition of using a violin string to slice the meat of the goat leg as thin as the skin on an onion. Foreigners like being told that sort of thing. And of course cheese. And plums. What do you think, Mamma?"

The *signora* drew her hand through the air like a priest giving a benediction. "That covers sheep, pork, beef, and goat. Enough even for the Germans. And put in some chocolate salame. They will be very happy."

"Will you tell them about the *violino di capra* or should I?" Glori offered. She had taken a fancy to one of the Germans.

"Not necessary. These are all Italians," Donata said as she passed back out through the swinging door. "But the menu sounds perfect," she called over her shoulder.

"*Qualcosa bolle in pentola*," Glori muttered the old adage as she reached for the wheel of Grana Padano: *Something is boiling in that pot.*

*   *   *

Donata led the Ingria brothers to one of the green benches facing the lake under the two rows of perfectly symmetrical lemon trees bordering the promenade. A few minutes into their picnic, *Signor* Alfieri appeared at the bench and inquired whether the young men were enjoying their stay.

"I, for one, did not think I could enjoy anything this week," Neri said, "and to my surprise I am enjoying everything."

"The *signore* is most generous," *Signor* Alfieri gave a little bow.

"You have a beautiful hotel." Gian Marco's gaze was fixed on the hotelkeeper's daughter.

Signor Alfieri's smile dissolved. His gleaming white teeth disappeared. He closed in on the bench.

"I was just telling our guests," Donata preempted, her eyes thorny, "that if we cannot find a peaceful place to picnic, we should pack up our lunch and get some more bottled water and head to *La Via del Monti Lariani*. It will be infinitely cooler up on the trail."

"Sounds great," Gian Marco chimed in. "How long a hike is it?"

"Five days," the father replied mournfully. "Five days of walking, even for the young, One hundred twenty-five kilometers."

Experience had taught the Ingrias to recognize a family feud. They fell silent.

"If you gentleman will permit," *Signor* Alfieri bowed again in their direction, "I will get back to the hotel. I'm afraid I can never stray for long at the height of the season."

When he was out of earshot, Neri said, "You do know we leave tomorrow morning?"

"Yes, I know," Donata returned.

"I gather you were just trying to annoy your father," Gian Marco said, "but I would like to hear more about this trail."

Donata shrugged. "It starts here in Cernobbio and goes all the way to the northernmost part of the lake. It's based mostly on old mule tracks. With some stretches of military roads that were built during the First World War. There are refuges for spending the night along the way and even some small inns in the villages the trail passes through. It is supposed to be littered with magnificent views."

"Supposed to be?" Gian Marco said. "You've never walked it then? Let's do it! Neri can go back without me. Can't you, Neri? The warehouse can do without me for one more week. I'll call Nardo and get him to open every day. He owes me." Gian Marco turned back to Donata and seized both her hands. "Tomorrow I can pick up whatever supplies we need for the hike and we could start out the day after." He had grown more enthusiastic by the second. "We'll have a great time, one fabulous picnic after another interrupted by magnificent views."

"I can't," Donata said. "I can't go anywhere, Gian Marco. You heard my father. It's the height of the season."

"Can't you get someone to take your place? It's just

for a few days. What if you were sick? They'd have to find somebody to substitute for you. You're always saying how you never get to go anywhere."

She shook her head. "Abandoning the hotel at the height of the season is like finding one of the Sisters of the Order of the Visitation smoking a cigarette. Not just improper—impossible."

*　　*　　*

That night in the dining room, Allegra inclined her head toward Gian Marco and whispered to her cousin, "See how he looks at you? Such big eyes."

"Yes, that one is always hungry," Donata agreed. "Unlike his brother. Neri settles for what life gives him."

"I can imagine waking up to that face," Allegra sighed, eyes still lingering on Gian Marco, startling Donata, who believed that a pregnant woman should confine her thoughts to the nursery, not the bedroom, and certainly not the bedroom of a man other than the father of her child.

After the dinner service had ended and the threesome sat at their accustomed table on the terrace, a young Sicilian couple tried to join them but were gently rebuffed by Neri. "Forgive me," he said, "but I think you would find our conversation very boring. We are are trying to make our travel plans." He shrugged his shoulders penitently. When the interlopers disappeared into the hotel, he said, "I had an idea you would prefer not to be disturbed on your last night. And with that in mind, I'll leave you. I have some phone calls to make and a book I've been neglecting." He stood and squeezed Donata's shoulder. "Thank you for a glorious week," he said. "I am going home much fatter and more relaxed than I have felt in years. Annalisa won't recognize me."

Donata raised her glass of wine, "You know how Jewish people are always toasting 'Next year in Jerusalem'? Well, let's drink to 'Next year in Cernobbio.'"

Neri took the glass from her hand before it reached her

lips. Looking at his brother, he said, "Better: 'Next month in Turin,'" and took a sip before returning the glass to Donata. "Good night, you two."

Signor Alfieri watched the older Ingria brother retreat into the hotel and, despite the slight breeze that had finally penetrated the heat, broke into a fresh sweat when Gian Marco took Donata's free hand in both of his.

"Don't say it," she pleaded.

"Don't say that I will take you to see the Shroud of Turin next month when you come to visit?" he smiled.

"I won't be coming to Turin next month. Or the month after. That's the month that I will graduate to most experienced server in the dining room. My cousin will be having her baby and my father will be having one of his dreams come true."

They sat awhile longer, settling back into aimless chat— about the tourists occupying the other tables, guessing at their occupations, their predilections and dispositions, entertaining each other with implausible genealogies and improbable biographies.

When Gian Marco finally stood, he bent to capture Donata's hand. Unfurling her fist, he pressed his lips against her palm. "You know, you can choose to please yourself. But first you have to believe you have a choice." After he left, she sat on alone, so still that no one dared interrupt her debate with herself.

*   *   *

Signor Alfieri had seen Donata take one of the duplicate keys from behind the front desk. He hadn't seen her take a foil-wrapped condom from her sister's drawer.

Donata went upstairs without looking back. She didn't want to feel her father's eyes following her. For once in her life, she was going to have what she wanted without thinking about what was best for anyone else. She turned the key in the lock and light fell through the open door into the darkened room. "Are you asleep?" she said quietly.

"No."

She stepped in and closed the door behind her and began unbuttoning her blouse.

"I love my wife," he said.

"I know. That's why you will never tell her about this night."

"And what about Gian Marco?"

"You love him, too. That's why you will not tell him either."

*　　*　　*

In the morning, when he saw the Ingria brothers slink out of the hotel before breakfast, *Signor* Alfieri was torn between the urge to bloody Gian Marco's too handsome face on behalf of his used and discarded daughter and heaving a sigh of relief.

Relief won.

Everything Changes Now

11.

When Betsy got off the train in Le Havre, she felt like a character in a Dickens novel, much buffeted about by fate and in imminent need of a deus ex machina. Arriving at the harbor after dark, she squeezed past the leering hulk blocking the doorway of the merchant marine hotel and prayed she had landed in Dickens rather than Mickey Spillane. It was too late to leave the wharf area to look for more hospitable lodgings. She hadn't seen a single taxi in the last half hour anyway.

Once in her room, with the dubious blanket removed to the dresser and the straight-back chair wedged under the handle of the door, she sniffed the pillow before taking pen to paper to try to convey to her sister the present assault on all her senses and sensibilities. The waft of oil thinned with brine. The moan of a foghorn and slurp of waves lapping against the docks. The featureless warehouses drained of all color, their skins peeled away by recurrent salt mists. The steel wool feel of the stained blanket. The man in the room opposing hers sitting astride a straight-back chair, bare-chested, suspenders hanging, staring out his open door into the hallway. It was the first time in her travels that she wished herself back in Milwaukee, but she would not tell her sister that.

She also wouldn't report that the middle-aged Italian hotelkeeper she had written about so condescendingly in her previous letter had cast her out. Even though she could tell both her sister and herself that nothing had happened between them, she felt soiled. And then disposed of. She let the paper and pen slip to the floor.

That night, as she had searched near the docks for a place

to sleep until the ferry's morning departure for Rosslare, she had seen only men—stevedores, sailors, wharf rats—slouching on and off the piers, smoking against buildings, and later, in varying stages of undress, passing between their grim cells in the merchant marine hotel and the fish-foul water closet at the end of the hall. And then there was the skeletal little man with the scar across his chin who had pocketed her francs and led her up the complaining, ill-lit stairs to a room that lacked both a number and a working lock. When she had held out her hand for the key, he shrugged and retreated down the steps. *"Le clef, s'il vous plaît?"* she called after him several times, her voice rising in mounting panic until she realized she was only alerting the rest of the floor to her vulnerability.

Her vulnerability.

What had happened to her in Cernobbio? And what had almost happened?

She had kept on the move since she boarded the steamer that took her away from the Albergo Giannino. Now she was not only stationary, she wasn't sure she'd ever get to leave this place, at least not upright. She would have said she was petrified, but that suggested that her insides had turned to stone instead of to liquid. She was sure she was intended to be the victim of some criminal, if not fatal, act before this night in Le Havre was over. Even as she wrapped her arms around the fear roiling in her midsection, she thought about how it was only men who had ever made her feel this way: *pathetic.* Greg, *Signor* Alfieri, the brute across the hall perched on his chair like a vulture.

She was getting used to thinking of herself as prey.

And what about the women Greg bedded? Were they his prey? Would that still be an appropriate term if they had been his coconspirators?

Had he preyed upon her? "Yes," she whispered into the night. Even though he hadn't needed to pursue her. He had preyed upon her gullibility. No, she wasn't being fair to her former self, to Greg's wife. He had preyed upon her trust in him.

Another hour trickled past.

Staring into the streaked mirror above the dresser, Betsy decided that it was not *Signor* Alfieri who was responsible for her humiliation, no matter what that louse had said or done. It was her willingness to consider him, no matter how briefly—in spite of finding his person unappealing, and his behavior grotesque—that made his dismissal humiliating.

What had caused her to lose her sense of herself? Had she been made vulnerable by her attachment to the twisted threesome in Florence? By the feeling that, once again, she had been easily duped, a too-willing believer?

A long-forgotten scene seemed to leap randomly into her consciousness. She could see herself and Greg and their closest friends Marilyn and Alan sitting around the mahogany dining table passing the teardrop-shaped jug of wine and patting their full bellies.

When the four of them would converge, at some point the men would commandeer the living room, to watch a sporting event or to talk national politics or philosophy department politics, while the women shifted into the kitchen to invent a meal together. "We should patent this one," Marilyn would say ritually when they had finished eating.

On the night that was revolving in Betsy's brain like a slow-moving zoetrope, Alan was keeping up a stream of patter and sweeping gestures, a mesmerizing stage magician sans cape. "Have you guys ever thought about wife swapping?" he said suddenly, pulling the rabbit out of the hat. He beamed as he emptied the last of the Almaden equally into the four glasses.

Betsy wrinkled her nose as if Alan had released a foul smell into her dining room. "What's there to think about?" she had asked with conversation-killing sincerity.

Alan shrugged. "I don't know. It seems like more and more people are doing it. Or at least talking about it." He affected an upper-crust English accent, "Thought it might be jolly for us to talk about it too."

"Really?" Betsy studied Alan to make sure he wasn't setting her up for one of his extended jokes. "What kind of people? Don't you assume that the people who are into wife swapping are just bored and boring? Not anyone you'd be interested in spending time with. But go ahead. Tell us. What are they like—these people who talk about wife swapping?"

"I don't know," Alan said, pushing away from the table and the conversation. "Not jolly after all, eh what?" Then, in his own voice, "Sorry I brought it up."

Marilyn turned the talk to the announcement of President Carter granting unconditional pardons to the Vietnam draft evaders, launching the foursome into an hour of speculation as to which of their friends who had escaped to Canada would remain there and which would be returning to the States.

Later, as the couple was leaving, Marilyn said to Betsy, "Alan didn't mean to upset you. You know he loves you. We both do."

Surprised that Marilyn could have thought she'd taken Alan seriously, Betsy assured her friend she hadn't been at all upset. And now here in this cramped, dingy room in Le Havre where she was expecting to be attacked, she wondered if she had been too dense to be upset. Now, as she replayed the scene she slowed the animation down and saw the looks, the nods, and shrugs that passed among the other three, saw the spark of possibility smothered by the wet blanket of their dismissal, saw their resignation.

As if she had been slapped awake, she was struck by this new comprehension of the depth of Greg's betrayal. That he had hatched this plot with Marilyn and Alan. That he had not first discussed the idea with her. That it fell to Alan to talk her into it. That her husband had never thought of her as his partner, not even in this.

Even in retrospect this episode didn't make her feel like a

woman who had kindled desire. It made her feel like a commodity. Something to be traded. *Swapped.*

She supposed that was why the memory had surfaced. It had been evoked by the feeling that her role in Florence was transactional. And by the certainty that the hotel owner in Cernobbio regarded her not as a person but as an object.

And yet she had to admit to herself that, on some level, she'd been seeking reassurance from Alfieri. Did she need him to convince her that she was desirable? To persuade her. To overcome her disbelief in herself. She supposed she wanted something—some*one*—to save her. Most probably a man. Someone who would obliterate her past—all those lost years with Greg, those squandered days in Florence.

Did everything come back to Greg's constant unfaithfulness? Ah, now there was an oxymoron.

Or had she been looking for a fling she could walk away from? Sex with someone she wouldn't care about. Someone it would be easy to forget.

All of the above, she supposed. Betsy shook herself. Men as saviors, men as predators—she was done with that. From this moment. *Everything changes now.* Suddenly it came to her with a flash, a cleansing fury: *They would never call it husband swapping.*

Prey no more, she resolved to stay up to meet any invaders, whatever their national origins (she had no doubt as to their gender), with both blade and corkscrew of her travel-sized Swiss Army Knife extended.

*　*　*

Surprised to be awakened at first light by bustling and cursing and heavy footsteps along the corridor and none of it pausing at her door, she sat up and stretched. Without shadows, what had appeared menacing by night became merely shabby in the early light. She hadn't undressed, lying on top of the sheet ready for her assailants, so she smoothed down her clothes, ran a comb through her hair, grabbed her backpack, and bounded down the rickety stairs two at a time.

She hadn't expected a dining area or a breakfast or other female hotel guests, but she found them all just the same.

Two rough-hewn plank tables, their tops worn smooth, stretched almost the length of the narrow room. Several men, including her neighbor from across the corridor, sat singly, scattered around the windowless room. She approached the table where three reassuringly prim, middle-aged women were clustered at one end. Theirs were the only voices to be heard, and hearteningly, they were speaking English.

"May I join you?" she asked.

"And wouldn't we be glad of your company?" said one with a short, tight perm of jet-black curls and a thick brogue.

"We would indeed," agreed the second, smiling, showing teeth like two rows of kernels of dried corn. Her hand shot up to shield her mouth from view and she nodded to one side, indicating that Betsy should sit.

"We're that glad of a new face!" contributed the third companion, whose protruding eyes put an exclamation point to everything she said.

"I was afraid this was supposed to be a hotel for men only," Betsy said gratefully as she dropped to the bench. "And I couldn't imagine why I was allowed to stay except that they were planning to . . . " Had she expected robbery, rape, or murder?

The woman next to her nodded and whispered from behind her hand, "I don't think any of us caught a wink all night, all those big hardchaws rambling about." She raised her voice, "You need to tell that chappy who's headed over would you want your sandwich with or without ham."

"Jam-bone," offered the one with the curls helpfully.

"*S'il vous plat, non jambon,*" Betsy instructed the same little man with the scar who had shown her to her room the night before. He slapped two long slabs of bread glued together with butter down onto the surface of the table in front of her. She reconsidered the sandwich. "*Pardon, monsieur. Avec jambon, s'il vous plaît.*" He whisked the bread away and returned with the same two slabs now plumped with ham as well as butter. Wordlessly he set a steaming bowl of coffee and milk down at her place before disappearing from the room. Betsy waited till he was gone to confide, "There was no lock on my door."

"Saints preserve us!" said the first woman, her suspiciously dark curls bobbing as she shuddered.

"Sure and wouldn't that frighten the bejaysus out of you!" said the one next to her from behind the hand.

"It would make you jump up and never come down!" exclaimed the one with the big eyes.

"I sat up armed with a corkscrew, but I must have fallen asleep. Nothing happened," she shrugged, "but I'd wedged a chair under the doorknob just in case."

"Aren't you the brave girl!" The eyes grew impossibly wider.

"But," said the one with the perm, looking around the room at the other diners and taking inventory, "you aren't here on your own surely?"

"I'm traveling alone." Betsy was surprised to hear the pride in her voice. She realized she was bragging.

"Well, I never!" said Big Eyes.

"No," came from the bouncing hair. "You never did and you never could." She turned her attention back to Betsy. "We're after havin' our first trip abroad, the three of us. To Dijon. Like that mustard. Our cousin Nola." Her voice dropped, "Nola married a Frenchie." She stopped and made the sign of the cross upon herself, much as Betsy supposed had been done through the ages at the mention of a witch or a wasting disease.

"A terrible tragedy," sniffed her benchmate and Betsy assumed she was referring to the unfortunate foreign marriage.

"That it was," said Big Eyes solemnly. "Taken in the bloom of life. Poor Nola."

"Oh!" Betsy realized they were on their way home from a funeral. "I'm so sorry."

"Too young," confirmed the black curls.

"That she was," clucked Big Eyes. "Not a day over eighty."

Betsy stifled a laugh, turning it into a genteel cough, and managed a few more words of condolence.

"We'll be getting into the queue out there," said the one next to her, head turned away. "We'll hold a place for you, but you'd best get your skates on. Boarding starts any minute."

"Mind you put on a jersey," cautioned the one with the improbable hair as all three stood in concert. "There's a wind up this morning."

"Imagine! And her door without a lock!" floated back to Betsy as the trio made their way out to the docks.

Betsy worked determinedly at her butter and ham sandwich, having no idea what food might be available on an overnight ferryboat. The only ferry she had ever taken anywhere was the five-hour car ferry from Manitowoc across Lake Michigan. She was eager to get outside and rejoin the women. She enjoyed the lilt of their voices and the sense of being young and adventurous they'd conferred upon her. After Italy, she hadn't expected to feel young ever again.

She cursed herself for relegating her sweater to the bottom of her backpack, necessitating that everything be removed and repacked, but she wanted to please them and they might be right about her needing it at least on deck. The whole process, eating and repacking, seemed to take forever. And perhaps it had for, by the time she got herself and her belongings outside, a sea of travelers covered the dock. It was hard to recognize this as the desolate warren of warehouses she had wandered through the night before. The sun had risen white bright and bodies were everywhere, a pulsing assemblage waiting to surge onto the ferry. She stood blinking, as much from the spectacle as from the light. She couldn't see her new friends or hear their voices. She would have tried calling their names but realized with a start that none of them had gotten around to introducing themselves. Disheartened, she fell in at the back of the throng.

"Is it a funeral yer headed for?" a male voice inquired in her ear.

"No," she snapped. Had he been in the dining room and overheard a snatch of the conversation about Cousin Nola?

"You've got a face on you like a Lurgan spade. Wouldn't you say, Colin?"

"What?" She whirled to confront her accuser. Though she had no idea what she was being accused of, she was determined not to project an air of vulnerability.

He had a full crop of springy red hair and a wide smile.

"Well, at least I'm not wearing a Ronald McDonald wig." Betsy couldn't believe her words. Apparently she couldn't find the middle ground between coming off as pathetically vulnerable and acting uncommonly offensive. She turned to face forward, wishing she could plead unfamiliarity with the language as her excuse.

"Fair play! Colin, we've got ourselves a Yank! And didn't she slag me off? Colin, come down off that cloud, will you." He turned back to Betsy. "He's mooning after that wan there."

When Betsy looked over her shoulder, she could see why. A few yards off stood a pair of raven-haired stunners, the girl with her abundant hair parted severely, the part like a weathervane pointing in the direction of the lovestruck boy. Hard to say which of the two was more striking, Colin with his chiseled chin and sea-green eyes or the nameless "wan" with the bale of hair.

"Those two met up in Paris, City of Love, City of Light, City of Pommes Frites. Her ladyship"—he nodded over his shoulder—"was traveling by herself alone after breaking up with her shite boyfriend and I might as well have been traveling by myself alone ever since. He's after wearing the face off her. She'll be needing the plastic surgeon. Do you believe in love at first sight? Despite the proof before my eyes every day since Paris, I was an agnostic. Until this minute, that is." He grinned at her. "Ah, it's grand to finally have another ear to bend—I've been talking to myself for the last two hundred kilometers. That self being Brian John David Samuel Beattie from the borough of Lisburn, which you might be knowing better as the 'Ringfort of Gamblers.' I'm an Ulsterman. And who might you be when you're at home?"

Betsy was eager to make amends for the idiotic Ronald McDonald remark but waited to make sure he would draw breath long enough for her to respond.

"Elizabeth Jane Baumgartner from Milwaukee, Wisconsin, which you might know better as Beer City, Brew City, or Cream City."

"Even more appealing than the City of Pommes Frites." He squinted at her in the sunlight. "It suits you."

"Being from Beer City?"

"Elizabeth. A name fit for a queen."

"Yes, well, mostly everyone calls me Betsy. A name fit for a social director on a cruise ship. Even if I introduce myself as Elizabeth, as soon as they hear someone hail me as Betsy, that's what they'll use. That's what I'm reduced to."

"The cheek."

"People think they're being more friendly or something."

"That's bollocks! You'll always be Elizabeth to me, no matter how friendly we get."

Betsy looked at him more closely. He gave the impression he was winking even with a straight face. He had what could fittingly be described as a *shock* of red hair. He was younger than she was, probably by a lot. He was desperate for company. And unflinchingly Irish.

"That's a fine lad of a backpack you've got there," he said admiringly. "It's class."

If she were going to be absolutely honest with herself, she had to admit that the Emerald Isle had never been on her itinerary chiefly because she was prejudiced against the Irish. Her bigotry was inherited. Her father, of solid German stock and descended from a prominent Pennsylvania abolitionist, harbored no ethnic or racial prejudices that she knew of, but her mother, whose parents came from the mountains of

Slovakia, could not keep herself from infecting her offspring with her antipathy toward the Irish, who became established in America before the immigrants from Slovakia made the crossing. According to Mrs. Baumgartner née Ciernik, Irish Americans made the Slovaks feel less welcome than dog excrement on white patent leather shoes.

When Betsy was quite small, she could have recited the lesson learned at her mother's knee: All Ireland is divided into two types, the lace-curtain Irish and the shanty Irish. When she grew older she figured out the underlying message: There was *really* only one type and all those pretended to lace curtains. Her mother warned, "They're often clever, the Irish, occasionally dull, but eventually they're all loud." And it was just common knowledge that the Irish often tippled until they toppled.

Betsy was comforted by her mother when Bridget Cullen pushed her down on the playground and when Patty O'Laughlin told the boys in their seventh-grade class at Our Lady of Lourdes that Betsy had arrived at school wearing her first bra. Never mind that all her mother's words of comfort came out sounding like "I told you so" and never mind that Betsy was also shoved on the playground by Angie Romano and that it was Margie Schmidt who took her Snoopy pencil case and Mary Jane O'Malley who returned it.

According to Doreen Ciernik Baumgartner—who had learned the proverb *Bad weed never dies out—Zlá zelina nevyhynie*—at her mother's knee, the oppressors had the nerve to grow up to be the ones bearing hard, flinty feelings with the aid of their elephantine memories. "Irish Alzheimer's," Doreen had taken to calling it. "That's where the only things they can remember are the grudges."

As Betsy didn't think she viewed Jews or blacks or Puerto Ricans through a noticeably warped lens, she let slide this prejudice. Betsy's bias was something of a family heirloom, tasteless and unsightly, granted, but still one of the first acquisitions her antecedents had made upon landing in the new country. Yet, looking at the wide-open face of Brian John David Samuel Beattie, she decided it was past time to let go of that tradition.

Betsy didn't stop to consider that all Ireland was indeed divided into two types—those who considered themselves part of Britain and those who considered Britain their oppressor. She didn't think about the differences between Northerners and those who lived in the Republic or militant unionists and members of the Irish Republican Army. She just imagined that this much-named young Irishman would be good company for the twenty-two-hour crossing. And he was, at least for most of it.

After they'd straggled aboard and learned that the cabins were all booked and the chairs all claimed, they dropped down in a less trafficked area of the deck, a safe distance from love-addled Colin and his young lady.

"Why did you ask me if I'd come from a funeral?"

"You had a puss that long on you. Like you had just buried your mother."

"No such luck."

He looked at her sharply. "That would be luck, would it?"

God, she thought. First the Ronald McDonald crack and now mother-bashing. He had to be desperate for company not to be making his way to the other side of the ferry. "Sorry," she said. "I didn't get much sleep last night."

Brian looked at the deck between his knees as though he saw something of interest there. "Ma could give out from the time I got up in the morning till the time I didn't get up the next. I admit I'm a bit of a dosser but she could make a holy show out of a sock left on the floor. It was three months yesterday she last had a go at me. She called me a bleeding chancer for sticking with our band. I'm drums and Colin there is lead guitar—he's got the face to play lead guitar and I'm hoping his fingering catches up. So Ma opens up on me and I slam off and she drops dead. Right there on the kitchen floor. Stroke. Trust me ma to make sure she got the last word."

"Good lord. I'm sorry. That's awful. Really terrible. But I hope you're not blaming yourself."

"Only on the odd days. On the even I blame her temper. 'Twas fierce, it was. Now, I take after me da. It took crockery to rile him."

"Crockery?"

"She could eat the head off him, even give him a clatter, and he'd maintain his composure. Until she'd go after the Delph. At the first plate into the wall, he'd be off and no knowing when he'd be back. Could be the next morning, could be the next week. Still and all, they had great craic together. Mad for each other."

"Mad, anyway."

He shot her a look. Well, she thought, that's it: three strikes. Not just bashing my own mother, but bashing his barely in her grave. But Brian shifted onto his back and squinted up at the sky.

"When Ma passed, the undertaker and his mute came to the house to wheel her away and he takes me da aside and asks in a loud whisper—I wonder, do they practice that at mortuary school? that piercing whisper?—about a proper dress and shoes to bury her in, how she can't go to her Maker in that costume. To be fair, she was wearing an old wraparound and slippers, but Da was feeling low enough without any help from this laudy daw.

"The old fella tells him we'll be having a closed casket so there's no need to tart her up. He says we were all remembering his mother in an open coffin, her hair curled, her face painted like a tinker's wagon, in a lacy dress and a necklace that had lived its whole life in a drawer. It wasn't just that none of us recognized her, but the old wan looked so much better dead. It wasn't proper.

"The wanker says that even so, they would still be dressing our ma before they put her in the box, open or closed. So Da nods and goes into their bedroom, his bedroom now, and comes out with the blue dress that set off her eyes, now permanently shut, and her open-toed heels.

"My sister Molly sees him handing over the things in the hallway. She screams, 'Not that!' before she can stop herself with both hands clapped over her mouth. 'Ah, that dress was her favorite,' she says. 'I just didn't want to think of it . . . in the ground.'"

"'You're bang on,' the old fella says. 'Your ma would be furious. She'd haunt me. You have it.' He takes the dress and shoes back from the body snatcher and gives them to Molly. 'Put these in your closet and pick out something that deserves to be buried. Maybe that green pantsuit your Aunt Eileen gave 'er.'"

"I think I'd like your father," Betsy smiled.

"You might at that. He's a grand old fella. You'd like my sister too. Not so sure about the brother. I got our ma's red hair, but Dennis got her feckin' temper."

Betsy grinned and tried on his brogue for size. "I'm after liking the whole family. Even your feckin' brother." She particularly appreciated that the representative of the Beattie clan that she had before her refrained from lecturing on how she needed to repair her relationship with her own mother while her old wan was still above ground.

"Kiss me if I'm wrong," he said, "but I'm guessing you're an only child."

"You're wrong. I have one sister."

"Well then," he leaned in for his punishment. She laughed and gave him a gentle shove with the heels of both palms.

For the next fourteen hours they talked. Rather, she worked a comment in here and there and he talked for twelve hours plus. She managed to insert a story now and then. She told him how her sister climbed onto the roof of their garage with a hose and turned it on the neighbor while Betsy was supposed to be babysitting her. "Ah, would you stop," he said. So she stopped. He shook his dramatically red head. "That means keep talking," he informed her.

He talked. About politics—"Your man in the White

House, the actor fella . . ." About questions of cultural import—"So, Elizabeth, you can tell us. Did you know who shot J.R.?" And international affairs—"I expect you flew over to attend the wedding of Charles and Diana." About his relatives—"Cousin Christey's a gas but she's the worst driver in County Antrim. Her idea of parking the car is to abandon it somewhere within view of a curb."

But there was one topic on which he could have lectured the whole of their crossing if Betsy had let him. "Can you believe New Zealand invited the Springboks to play the All Blacks this month?" He shook his head in disgust.

"I have no idea what you're talking about."

His eyebrows rose. "I know you come from a country where football is called soccer. And the Yanks play a peculiar game you call football and we call run-with-the-egg. But still, do you not recognize the sport?"

Betsy offered a shrug in reply.

"Rugby."

"I don't really follow any sports. Not even baseball, which is supposed to be our 'national pastime.' I didn't even know there's a players' strike in the Major Leagues until someone mentioned it in Florence the other day."

"The cheek of you."

"I gather Springboks are an all-white team playing against an all-black team?"

He whistled at the depth of her ignorance. "You got that half right. The Springboks are all white all right. They're the national team of South Africa. And the All Blacks are mostly white." He grinned at her confusion.

"Where are the All Blacks from?"

"New Zealand."

Betsy's frown deepened. "But if the team is named for the indigenous population, the Maori are Polynesian. They don't have African roots like the Aboriginals of Australia," the former anthropologist instructed. "So why are they called 'Blacks'?"

"The team gets its name from the color of its jerseys."

"Seriously?"

"That's the way they talk rugby in New Zealand. 'The whatevers versus the All Blacks.' All the other teams' jerseys have two colors, see. Anyway, the Kiwis are up in arms about the Springboks being invited to play. There've been massive protests."

"Because?"

It was Brian's turn to frown. "Apartheid."

"Oh! Of course. Like South Africa being banned from the Olympics."

"So you do follow sports a bit."

"The Olympic games are more spectacle than sporting events."

"So they are."

From time to time they napped companionably, snugged up to each other against the breeze. But eventually the wind changed direction and the waves swelled and tumbled all the way up to the ferry's gunwales as if the big boat were being slapped from side to side by an enormous unseen hand.

"Ah, that God fella, quite the practical joker," Brian managed between gritted teeth. No longer lying on deck, he sat cross-legged and bolt upright, as if his posture could save him. He finally stopped talking. After nearly an hour of stiff bravado, he announced, "I'm sick as the plane to Lourdes," before running to the rail and joining his friend Colin, Colin's girl, and the scores of others puking their guts over the starboard side.

Betsy discovered something consoling about herself that day: she was seaworthy.

She got into the long queue for the women's restroom and was still in line when the ferry docked. When she finally squeezed inside, she could barely wait to get out again. Tissue and toweling were strewn everywhere and the stalls reeked of vomit. By the time she returned to their spot on the deck, the area had emptied. She plunked down and waited awhile, hoping but not expecting that Brian would be coming back. She supposed he had been only too eager to plant his feet on dry land.

Betsy bought a train ticket to Dublin at the Rosslare Station. She presumed Brian and Colin were heading to their homes in the North. She had no desire to go where the Irish and the English Irish were lobbing bombs at each other. That much thought she had given to the political situation. She figured she'd spend a few days in the capital, seat of the parliament, pubs, and legendary *littérateurs*, before heading home. She might look for a walking tour—the places where the ghosts of James Joyce, Sean O'Casey, and Oscar Wilde could be found.

The train was crammed, as if the fifteen hundred passengers on the Saint Killian had been funneled directly on board. And perhaps they had. Betsy saw the three cousins from the merchant marine hotel seated opposite each other at the same moment the one with the bug eyes saw her and pointed to the fourth seat piled with their belongings. She looked around the car for Brian before nodding. Betsy struggled through the packed aisle. "How did you know to save a seat for me? How could you know I'd be on this train? In this very car? It must be some kind of magic! You can't be leprechauns—they're all male, right?" The ladies tittered as she plopped down on the seat they had emptied, her backpack swung round to her chest. "But then how do leprechauns reproduce, I wonder?"

"Sure listen, pet," the one with the bobbing curls leaned forward, "we weren't savin' the seat *for* you, though we're that glad to see you. We were savin' it *from* them." She nodded in the direction of a clump of leather-clad twenty-somethings of assorted genders with numerous piercings and gravity-defying Mohawks. "Imagine sittin' next to the loiks of that all the way to Dublin. Jaysus! It put the heart crossways in me," she shuddered. "Would you look at that filthy article?" She inclined her head at a fellow passenger within hearing distance who was wearing a T-shirt with several strategic rips, including one over his chest, showing the safety pin skewered through his nipple to its best advantage.

"It's a pure relief to see you, though," said the cousin with the dried corn for teeth, speaking into her raised palm. "We were that worried about you when we didn't see you out on the pier. We thought maybe you'd been captured by one of those pirates back at the hotel. And we worried that if you had escaped, you were all on your own on the Killian with every sort of ruffian on the prowl."

"Ruffians and a rough crossin' too," lamented the cousin next to Betsy. "I had a dose." She shook off the memory. "Did anythin' happen to you on board, pet?"

"No. Nothing. Nothing at all," she said, disappointing her audience, who settled back in their seats and began their inventory of Cousin Nola's furnishings. Throughout their chatter, her thoughts kept returning to young Brian John David Samuel Beattie, who was in the toilet in the next car— the only available seat—having a wank to her image painted on the inside of his closed eyelids.

The North

12.

The train from Dublin to Lisburn was not crowded, so Brian and Colin could sit together, which turned out to be a mixed blessing. The only thing Colin wanted to talk about was his sweet Aislin, her sweet face, her sweet voice, her sweet smile.

Brian stood it for the first hour. "Colin, I'm speaking as your best man now. Do yourself a favor and start rationing. Talk about her one sentence out of five. Then cut down to one out of ten. I'm not asking you to go cold turkey, but the sooner you get her out of your system, the better for us all."

"I'm off me nut about her."

"Sure it was all croissants and crepes suzettes while it lasted, but she's back in her world now and you'll soon be back in yours. It won't be long before your Aislin starts wondering how she came to get mixed up with a culchie. You're a gorgeous feen and all, but you're not in her class. You'd need a hape o' silver and years more schooling to climb that ladder. It's time you start to forget that hussy."

"Watch yourself, Brian. She's the one I'm going to marry someday."

"Would you ever cop on? Her father's a Dublin 4. Her mother pisses Chanel No. 5. Her and her brothers were nursed on Harvey's Bristol Cream. She's too posh for the likes of us. Not to mention she's a papist."

"I am, I tell you. Marrying her."

"It takes two to foxtrot, Colin."

"She feels the same."

"Did she say she would marry you?"

"As good as."

"I repeat: when the subject of marriage came up did she

say she would marry you or did she say, 'Grand weather we're having'?"

"She said she wished we could be together the rest of our lives."

"There's a great deal of room between a wish and a promise. About the length of a horse, I'd say. You get the promise from the horse's mouth. The wish comes outta the horse's ass."

"Aislin loves me."

"No doubt. No doubt. I love you too, but—prepare for it—I'm not going to marry you. And I'm a Prod. But I don't suppose her parents will even notice you're not Catholic with all that lovely love floatin' about."

"You're jealous," Colin said, as though a light bulb had just gone on over his head.

"She's a rare beauty and all, but not my type. I like a girl who talks as well as she snogs."

"Not jealous of Aislin. Of me. That I have someone and you don't."

"I was that," Brian nodded. "Paris was rough, I admit. It was supposed to be a trip for you and me but it changed into a trip for you and her. Which made me feel more alone than if I was on me own, if you follow my drift. Falling in with the American bird got me over that, though."

"The one on the ferry? She was only *ancient*."

"That she was, but she was only brilliant for all that. I could talk to her about anything."

"Jaysus, Brian, you talk to everyone about everything. At least that's what everyone says."

*   *   *

Brian could see that his sister was up to something. The table was laid when he walked in the door. "We're going to have a nice welcome home supper," Molly promised. "You and me and Da and Dennis."

"I'm knackered. Think I'll skip the meal and drop into me scratcher. Keep a plate warm for me."

"I will not! I've been cooking the whole day! We're going to sit down together, the four of us. And you'll tell us all about your adventures."

"I had none. There, that was easy."

"Bri, what's come over you? I was sure you'd be panting to tell us about France."

"Here it is then. Colin met a Dublin girl two days after we got to Paris. Quite the dote. The eejit thinks she's going to marry him. We were all sick on the boat coming over. That's it. Whole story. Now can I have a kip?"

"Wash up and have a wee lie down. We'll be eating at half six."

*   *   *

The meal was one of the quieter ones any of the Beatties could remember. Brian fended off more of Molly's questions; Dennis, Brian's younger brother, had found a way to both chew and act sullen at the same time; and patriarch Jack Beattie seemed to be absent from his body.

Uneasily, Molly ventured, "I've been thinking . . ."

"You're thinking? Mind you don't hurt your head," Dennis said because something of the sort was expected of him.

"Since Ma died," Molly persevered, "there's been a cloud over this family. A dark, broody cloud. And we're going to do something about it," she said firmly. "I've talked to a psychologist at the college. This Sunday afternoon at half three we're going to have a Balloon Release. I've already invited Aunt Eileen and she's bringing a bread-and-butter pudding— she's making that for you, Da—and Ma's favorite caraway loaf. And I've asked the Frawleys if we can use their garden chairs. So everything's settled. There." She sat back in her chair, eyes darting around the table as she waited for objections.

"What's a balloon release?" Dennis asked sensibly. "Are you after renting a hot air balloon with a big basket and all? That's a bleedin' fortune gone—gone up in the air—if you ask me."

"Not a hot air balloon," Molly said patiently. "Regular

ones, party balloons like. But they'll have hot air in them. The whole notion is that we each have a balloon that we let go up into the sky."

"A hot air balloon is overdoin' it," Dennis mused, "but a party balloon sendoff sounds a bit niggardly to me."

Molly reddened. "I don't like that word," she said too loudly.

"Ah," sighed Dennis, "you probably wouldn't like a chink in his armor either."

Molly said evenly, "The psychologist thinks we're all angry with Ma and that's why we're . . . like we are."

"It's called grief," Brian finally said. "She's only just gone."

"But it's not that, you see. Grief is sadness and loneliness, and fear maybe. But we're all angry. I felt it from you before you left, Bri. I feel it from Dennis and Da." She looked nervously at her father. "I feel it in me. And we're the kind of people who don't talk about these things."

"You seem to be making a profession of it," Dennis observed.

Molly ignored him. "So we have to find a way to talk about it, is all. That's what we're doing come Sunday. We each say at least one thing that we're angry with Ma for—it could be something recent or something that happened donkey's years ago—and then we let the anger go. And *then* we can grieve."

"Go way outta that," Brian shook his head.

"We're doing it," said Jack as he pushed away from the table. "And there's an end to it."

Brian's jaw hung open as he watched his father leave the room. Jack Beattie was the last man in County Lisburn he'd have thought would submit to such a show. Brian turned his attention—and newfound respect—to Molly. "You've got something on the old fella'. It's only blackmail could make him agree."

"He cares about his family is all," Molly sniffed as she started to clear the table.

Brian looked at his sister, then at his brother. "Did I

wander into the wrong house? Did the Beatties move away without giving me notice? Will someone tell me what is happening?"

"Ah, you know nothin' ever happens round here." Dennis slammed his chair into the table and blew out the back door.

"So tell me about nothin'," Brian said to his sister, his eyes like rods into her.

"Dennis was arrested last week. *And* the week before. The first time was a boozer fight. He went looking for it. The second time he went looking for it too. Ever since Ma died, I heard tales he was cozying up to the Ulster Defense. And then he and a bunch of gougers trashed the makeshift shrine to Bobby Sands at the Busy Bee shopping centre. That was the second arrest. Which saved his life. He came that close to being dismembered by a Catholic crowd that came outta nowhere. Da's been out of his mind with worry. Me too," she added in a small voice.

"What's this balloon thing supposed to do?"

"I don't know. Something. I hope something."

*　　*　　*

Came the knock at the door on Sunday afternoon.

"Ah, Colin, sorry. This sendoff is for the family. And you're that lucky you're not family on this day of days."

Colin was stunned. "But I am, Bri. I *am* family. Closer than blood. Who shared his last quid with you when you got fired from the grub store? Whose gaff do you take half your meals at? Who was there when you broke your tooth?"

"Who was the git responsible for the tooth breaking?"

"Who was there holding your head in the jacks when you got hammered and had a gawk after drinking your first poitín? You were only mouldy."

"And who was the lad that stole that piss from his father's press and dared me to drink it or lose me honor? I appreciate the sentiment, Colin, I do, but you should go home. You're like a brother to me, it's too true, but you weren't like a son to me mother."

"I got a letter from Aislin."

"Aw, sure look it."

Colin nodded. "A Dear Sean letter."

"This soon? Who woulda believed it?"

"You, you pox."

"Come on in then. You'll have to sit in here while we're all in the back garden for the exorcism."

"At least you have a good day for it."

*　　*　　*

Everyone was shifting uncomfortably on the folding chairs borrowed from the neighbor, not knowing what to do. They all felt foolish, even Molly, each grasping the string to a purple helium balloon, so they were looking down when the rain began, a fine mist.

"Ah, Ma," said Dennis, eyes lifted skyward, "you've kept your sense of humor, I see."

"We'd best press on if we're doing this," grumbled the senior Beattie. "I'll get mine done with." He cleared his throat. "Joan, you were me first love, me best and me worst love. If you didn't have a temper in you that could scorch the devil himself, you might be here with us still. It's murder thinking that every day, so I'm letting the thought and you go." Everyone gasped—his was a much longer speech than expected. They'd been anticipating something more along the lines of "Cheers." Jack Beattie released his balloon.

"I'll be taking my turn," Molly said, breathing deeply and raising her eyes. "When Brian was born I wanted a sprog of my own. I pleaded and wheedled and you finally had Da bring me home a cloth doll with yarn hair. But I knew that was just a doll and I wanted a baby. So Aunt Eileen bought me a doll that had shiny pink skin and real hair for me to brush and eyes that closed when I laid her down. And she cried. I loved that she cried. But you hated it. You said it made your milk come. One day I'm in the kitchen and there you were with a screwdriver. You were sticking it into my baby's back. You were taking out the batteries, I guess, but what I saw was you stabbing my sweet baby. And she never cried after that. Because she was dead. And you were fine with that. I forgive you for killing my baby, Ma." Molly let her balloon go.

Almost defiant, Eileen said, "You were the best big sister anyone could have wanted. It was you that got me ready for school every morning and saw to it I was neat and clean and brushed and braided. The teachers thought you were hard and that I was the sweet, well-behaved one because you made me look sweet and you taught me my manners. I'll never forget when I was in senior infants and somehow I forgot to put on my knickers one morning and the teacher said we were going to have PE that day and we would be tumbling on the mats and I knew it would be the worst thing that had happened in my life or ever would happen, that everyone would see me bum and all." She reddened at the memory as though she were five years old and it was only yesterday. "I told the teacher that I had to talk to my sister and I still can't believe she let me go over to the third form and your teacher let you come out to the hall. You took me into the bathroom and gave me your knickers. I knew you would fix it, but I didn't know how. I always knew that if anything went wrong I could go to you, Joan, and that's the hardest thing"—she choked back a sob—"knowing I can't go back to you now or ever." Eileen released her balloon. "You've caused the sadness and you're not here to console me."

Dennis said, "I'm up now, amn't I? Grand." He cleared his throat. "Ma, there isn't anyone here you didn't give a hard time, including your sister who you apparently taught to never speak ill of the dead. But we all loved you. And you loved all of us. And in the end, I guess that has to be enough." Dennis let go of his string and gave a flick to the balloon to urge it upward. "Well, Brian, we've never known you to sit quiet. Now's not the occasion to go mute. Get on with it before this mist turns into a lashing."

Brian said, "I'm sorry, Ma, that I was a disappointment to you. Says I to you, says you to me." He opened his hand and let his string go.

His relatives waited, knowing volumes more were to follow, but Brian lapsed back into silence. Suddenly Eileen shrieked, "Effing Christ!" before clapping a hand over her blasphemous mouth. She pointed heavenward. All eyes rose from Brian's face.

The helium balloons, all of them, even Jack's that had drifted up and away minutes ago, had been dragged down by the mist and were now massed together directly over Brian's head.

"Like bleedin' thought balloons in a comic strip," Dennis marveled. "Dark broody *purple* thoughts."

"Perfect," said Jack, shaking his head. "Now we know you were listening, Joan."

"Run for the house! It's bucketing now!" Molly instructed needlessly.

*   *   *

When they looked out the window after an hour or so, the balloons were still huddled over Brian's chair.

Come Here to Me

13.

Dublin did not take warmly to Betsy, literally or otherwise. It was like this: The weather was wretched, and the accommodations she found in the town originally called Dubh Linn, meaning Black Pool, were not all that accommodating. While she was relieved to find she had been right about Irish men keeping their distance, she was disappointed that the only conversations she'd had since her arrival were with the proprietress of her lodgings.

Beyond the front door of Mrs. Murtaugh's B & B, the days were gray and damp and chilly for mid-July. Searching out nooks to duck into when the damp devolved into downpour proved surprisingly tiresome and time-consuming. Betsy was spending too much energy staying dry (in a manner of speaking) in pubs. This proved dangerous. She didn't like beer, and while she didn't consider herself a connoisseur of fine wines, the wines she tried in those establishments weren't quite fine enough. She found the pub menus brief, all sandwiches, reminding her of breakfast at the merchant marine hotel, buttered bread with a slab of ham, or buttered bread with a slice of cheese and two slices of tomato, only this bread was not cut from a crusty baguette but fell out of a plastic sleeve, square and soft and flavorless except for the preservatives. She would start out determined to nurse her small glass of Irish whiskey until the rain stopped, but she was ending up either soaked or sauced.

Except for the mostly wordless barmen taking her orders, no one spoke to her. She had envisioned storybook taverns with flapping signboards proclaiming *The Three-legged Wolfhound* or *The Flying Sow* resounding with melodious voices raised in laughter or plaintive song. Maybe such places with such people existed somewhere, in charming rural villages where there were thatch roofs, and maybe there were dry, sunny days in those places too. She complained about the weather to Mrs. Murtaugh, she of the B & B, who quoted her husband, who was likely quoting someone else, "Summer is that week when the rain warms up a bit." She directed Betsy to a compressed bookcase in the breakfast room. "Weather makes for readers. I'm a great reader, I am. This shelf is Take One/Leave One," she instructed. "Some of the guests leave behind the books they've finished. Mind, I don't allow just any old thing a place on the shelf. I read each one myself and decide if it's worthy. Or just wordy." Mrs. Murtaugh smiled and lowered her eyelids, pleased with this sample of her affinity with words. She didn't look like someone who had spent her life indoors snuggled up to a book. Her skin was tight but coarse, like a top sheet tucked and taut over an unmade bed.

Betsy examined the top shelf: *Jonathan Livingston Seagull, Bury My Heart at Wounded Knee, The Thorn Birds, The Crystal Cave,* and several Stephen Kings and Agatha Christies, signaling the tastes of the travelers who lodged with Mrs. Murtaugh.

"Now take a gander at the lower shelf. These stay on the premises, mind, permanent like, though you're welcome to any while you're in residence."

Betsy's index finger stroked the spine of the first volume, *Ulysses*.

"I can't say I've finished that one myself," Mrs. Murtaugh confessed, "though I've had at it five or six times."

Betsy exclaimed, "Me too!"

"Those on that lower shelf would all have been written here. On our wee island."

As Betsy's finger grazed across *The Poems of W. B. Yeats: A New Edition*, Mrs. Murtaugh clasped her hands across her chest and intoned, "'Now that my ladder's gone/I must lie down where all the ladders start/in the foul rag and bone shop of the heart.'"

Betsy stopped herself from asking, "Wasn't Yeats an admirer of Mussolini?" and instead pointed to *Dracula*. "Bram Stoker was Irish?"

"In Irish *droch ola* means 'bad blood,'" Mrs. Murtaugh nodded.

The next were *An Béal Bocht* and *Dúil*. "My husband," Mrs. Murtaugh informed her, "himself could read Irish," she said with pride. "Gone these four years now." She made the sign of the cross upon herself. "And what about you? Traveling on your own and all and all. You're too young to be widowed and too pretty to be a spinster. Where might your husband be?"

Betsy bristled, but she told her, "I'm divorced."

"Is that so?" Mrs. Murtaugh's interest was aroused. "And did he keep the children?"

"I wasn't able to have children."

"Well, that's a blessing. Under the circumstances, I mean." She paused and then leaned in, dropping her voice though no one else was present, "And did he beat you?"

Betsy was startled into a laugh. "No. He slept around."

"Oh. That."

"That."

"Well, you can be disappointed, to be sure, but you can hardly be surprised, now can you? That's the way God made them."

Farther along on the lower shelf she came to *The Holy Bible* (Betsy didn't question its Irish pedigree) and *The Collected Plays of Oscar Wilde*. "I love Wilde," she said. "*The Picture of Dorian Gray*—that was his only novel, wasn't it?"

Mrs. Murtaugh sniffed, "Mr. Gray had an honored place on the shelf but a langer from Suffolk made off with him. You should visit Merrion Square."

"What's that?"

"Where Wilde lived. One Merrion Square. Yeats had his accommodations on the Square as well. He won the Nobel, don't you know," she sniffed confidingly. "Quite a bit of the old Georgian red brick still standing. They used to be private homes when I was young, but they're mostly offices now. And then it's a quick hop to Kildare Street."

"What's there?"

Mrs. Murtaugh raised her eyebrows in surprise. "Where the government sits. Ach, you know, like Westminster. And you might just catch a glimpse of the Taoiseach."

"Oh." Betsy was debating whether or not to ask what this might be. From the narrowed look that accompanied the strange word, she was afraid it might be connected to the unwelcome topics of divorce or childbearing or philandering.

"If seeing the government buildings and where the writers lived isn't your cuppa, then there's always the Natural History Museum and the National Gallery right by. They're all practically on top of each other."

"Sounds perfect for my last day." She shook her head. "Sounds like it should have been my destination each of these last three days." Betsy wondered if it had been the weather in Dublin that had dispirited her or, rather, the looming prospect of returning home. She had found herself more interesting on this side of the Atlantic. She was having trouble picturing a divorced librarian who lived with her sister's family as anyone she would want to get to know.

"Well, if you're going, you'd better get your skates on. The day's almost gone."

When she looked out through Mrs. Murtaugh's lace curtains, Betsy took heart from observing that not a single person in view was carrying an umbrella. When she stepped out, the skies were still sullen but the air was crisp.

On the bus to Merrion Square, she began composing a letter to her sister in her head. Gina shared her appreciation for the work of Oscar Wilde. Her timing as Gwendolen in *The Importance of Being Earnest* had been exquisite. After watching Gina in that and other college productions, Betsy thought her sister talented enough to head directly to Broadway, but was grateful that she hadn't.

The bus stopped and all the other passengers rose from

their seats. "Excuse me, where are we?" she asked the woman who had been seated next to her.

"That's Merrion Street right up there. At the crossing. Looks like we're in time."

"Oh. Thank you. I guess the Square must be nearby? I didn't realize that Merrion Street was the end of the line."

The woman raised her eyebrows but was already swept up in the queue to the door. Betsy glanced outside and gasped. The window framed a churning sea of humanity surging like the waves that had tossed the ferry on its crossing. Even the crowds in Florence were nothing compared to this. They couldn't all be Wilde or Yeats fans or interested in museums and government buildings. As she stepped off the bus, she was launched in the direction of a barricade. Segments of metal fencing and what looked like bicycle racks held together by chains bisected the street. A phalanx of police formed a second wall on the other side. "Is there a parade today?" she asked the man in front of her as she tried unsuccessfully to backpedal against the forward motion of the throng. He replied with a low laugh, dry appreciation of her dry humor. He was carrying what looked like an elongated axe handle. Glancing around, she realized that many of the men and some of the women, too, carried something in one hand or the other—pickaxe handles, shovel handles, bats, bricks, golf balls, bottles. She saw one crowbar and several men in a cluster holding what appeared to be fence pickets.

Betsy felt panic rising in her like an incoming tide. She tried to turn around, to move against the current, but the mob carried her along. There was no place to go but forward or down. "What's happening?" she asked of no one in particular. Then louder, "What is this?"

The crowd had been muted enough, grim enough, for a funeral march. Now shouting erupted as they neared the barricade and the sound traveled back like a wave. A roar. Betsy began to grasp how large the surging sea of bodies was. There were hundreds—thousands?—behind her still turning in from Northumberland Road. The bus had deposited her less than a block away from the makeshift barricade at the very front of the protest. "Let me through! Please!" she begged hopelessly as she felt shoulders and elbows jostling her forward. The crisp air was suddenly thick with insults and threats fired across the barricade at the uniformed men, followed shortly by the primitive, impromptu weapons. Bricks and bottles hurtled over her head. There were cries of "For the Blanketmen!" She saw the barricade collapse under the human deluge. A chant of "Burn it! Burn it!" rumbled up all around her. She watched for several minutes as the front row of uniforms and their handheld plastic shields crumpled unevenly to the pavement. Then she watched as the next line of police took their place and advanced toward the crowd—*toward her*—with batons swinging. The noise grew impossibly louder. She was amazed that she could separate sounds out from each other—the tattoo of heavy shoes on concrete, the thud of wood on flesh, the shrieks, the grunts. When a sudden sharp pain seared through her arm, Betsy involuntarily joined the chorus. "Oh!" and then "Ohhhh!" The men on either side of her dropped, one screaming, one silenced. As she stumbled and went down, legs tangled beneath her, she thought, *This is such a stupid way to die, not even knowing why.*

She was caught—miraculously—before she sank all the way to the pavement and then—astoundingly—lifted and carried, her injured arm dangling, her other arm around the neck of her savior, her face buried in the smooth cloth of his jacket, all of her shaking uncontrollably. Biblically, he managed to part the roiling sea of humanity that continued to swell and surge past them and over the fallen barricade as if irresistibly drawn to the swinging batons.

It seemed to her that they navigated through the mayhem for hours, but later he told her their voyage lasted only minutes.

They came to a sudden stop and a voice thick with worry inquired, "Can you manage the latch?" Eyes kept downcast to spare herself the sight of broken bodies, she had known him to be tall by how far away the ground was and strong by how easily he carried her. Betsy twisted her leg and lifted the handle with her foot and he shouldered them through the door. It was only then that she stole her first look. She gasped and was instantly embarrassed until he saved her with a murmured apology, assuming that the awkward passage through the door had caused her pain. It wasn't that he was so good looking—she thought his nose had been broken, maybe from the same adventure where he'd acquired the line etched into his forehead—but that his scars made him look fearless. She guessed this wasn't his first time marching on Merrion Street.

He deposited her gently onto a chair. "You all right? Should I be getting you to hospital?"

The realization that he felt an obligation to take care of her flowed through her like warm milk.

"I know you're injured, but I'm not sure where exactly." He looked away, reddening at being both indirect and still, perhaps, indelicate.

"My arm mostly," she reassured him of the decorousness of the location. "I don't know if I was hit by a policeman's baton or one of the bats in the crowd."

"You're a Yank!" he exclaimed. Then, focusing, "Is it broken?"

Betsy gingerly lifted her wounded wing. "Ow!" She slowly turned it this way and that. "No," she said, wincing. "Nothing's broken, I think."

"Ah, that's fine then." He turned on his heel and made his way over to the bar. That was when Betsy realized she was in yet another pub. This one was nearly empty, only the bartender and one other customer, and that patron had his head against the wall and was snoring with mouth gaping wide enough for Betsy to see he was missing several teeth.

"Is there someone waiting for you?" her rescuer called back over his shoulder. "Someone we should give a ring?"

"There's no one," she said, feeling the pathos of that

admission. "Speaking of no one, where *is* everybody?" she asked as he returned with chunks of ice wrapped in toweling. The pubs she had previously wandered into never seemed to lack for customers no matter the time of day.

Amused, he said, "Everybody is out there on Merrion Street." Then his face darkened. "I should be getting back meself."

"'Hooligans!" contributed the barman.

Her companion turned his attention back toward the bar. "You'd better get that rot out of your system before the lads come in or you're likely to see this place reduced to matchsticks. Or," he smiled sweetly and inclined his head toward the snorer propped up by the wall, "your man there will make up your entire clientele for a long time to come."

The barman mumbled something indecipherable and went back to polishing glasses.

"But weren't they hooligans?" Betsy asked as he wrapped the towel around her throbbing arm.

"No more than I."

"So you were with them?"

She had his full attention now. "You weren't? You were there in support of the gardaí?"

"What are gardaí? I came to see the building where Oscar Wilde lived."

"A tourist," he shook his head, marveling.

"I'm done with sightseeing. I've seen enough sights now, thank you. A memorable last day."

"Your last day in Dublin?"

"The last real day of my trip, period. I fly to Paris tomorrow to catch my return flight to Montreal and then home to Milwaukee. This was quite a grand finale." She grimaced in pain, perhaps more than necessary. "So what was it all about?" She wanted to keep him there talking to her—she did like looking at him—cleft chin, watchful eyes above the skewed nose, and dark blond waves that tumbled Prince-Charmingly across his marked forehead—and she liked listening to his voice, but also for his own sake. She felt sure if he thought she had recovered, he would abandon her and return to his comrades in arms. Where anything could happen to him. And none of it would be good. "You know, there's a Chinese proverb that says if you save a life, you are responsible for it."

"Ah, but I'm not Chinese and neither are you. And then there's this to be considered: no one ever died of a bruised arm, even a badly bruised one."

"Maybe not. But plenty of people have died from being trampled underfoot. Or from being beaten by batons." She shivered.

"You've had a fright," he said sympathetically.

Away from the chaos, she could still feel the bewildering rage that had flooded the street. Her eyes brimmed and her chin quivered as she nodded. She watched him waver between duties. Betsy sighed with relief when he went back to the bar and returned with two whiskeys.

"Medicine. For the shock," he said. "First you sip, then I'll talk." He waited until she obeyed. "You were caught up in a demonstration."

"That must mean something different here than it does in the States." He pointed to her glass. She took another sip and continued, "I've been to antiwar demonstrations and civil rights demonstrations—I marched with Father Groppi when I was in high school—and some workers' rights demonstrations. I even got to meet César Chávez when I organized the grape boycott at the A&P near campus." She saw that he didn't recognize the names she proudly dropped. "Anyway, nobody came to those demonstrations armed. Except the cops."

"Our lads are dying."

She was puzzled. "I'm not following. I mean, our lads— our boys—were dying too, in Vietnam and in our inner cities and across migrant worker camps. But we weren't carrying bricks in our hands."

"The best of us are dying in prison. As we sit here. In the

Haitch blocks. And it's killing the rest of us." He looked at her blank face with some irritation. "Do you know what's located on Merrion Street aside from the digs of your man the playwrighter fella?"

Betsy frowned. "The home of Yeats. The National Gallery," she ticked off. "Maybe not exactly on the Street? In the Square? Or nearby? I don't have a clear picture of the geography. Oh! The seat of your government."

He shook his head impatiently. "The British Embassy. The plan is to tear it down or burn it up."

The light dawned. "This is about your civil war."

"This is about centuries of oppression by an imperialist nation."

"And what are the Haitch blocks? I'm not familiar with that word."

"It's not a word, it's the letter Haitch."

"Oh! H blocks."

"The blocks are these Haitch-shaped units in a filthy prison called the Maze up near Lisburn. It's where Maggie Thatcher incarcerates political prisoners and has them stripped naked and tortured and beaten. Have you not heard of Bobby Sands?"

"The name sounds familiar," she lied.

"At Bobby Sands's funeral in May there were one hundred thousand mourners."

"A hundred thousand?" Her eyes widened. "I should know about him."

He jabbed at the base of his glass with one finger, pushing it away incrementally. She saw that he was again weighing the decision whether to stay with her or rejoin the fray. "I'm Elizabeth Baumgartner. But most people call me Betsy. I'd like to know the name of the man I have to thank for snatching me out of harm's way and who is about to become my tutor in matters Irish."

"Declan Jones," he said.

"But Jones sounds English."

"It is. I'm not. Leastways not the Republican half that carried you into the pub." He smiled for the first time. Betsy took note of the crinkles that puckered the skin around his startlingly intense eyes and was surprised to realize her champion was several years older than she was. *Late* thirties, she decided. She shifted on her chair to reposition the ice pack and the movement sent a blade of pain twisting through her.

Watching her wince, Declan seemed to come to a decision. "I can't leave you wandering about, not with that wing," he sighed. He set about fashioning a sling of toweling and ice, suspended it from the back of her chair, and gently lifted her arm to rest in it, then he reared back on his chair, arms folded, eyes closed. Betsy took advantage of the opportunity to stick the tip of her finger in the glass and apply several drops of whiskey as an antiseptic to her abraded knee. Declan began, "Bobby Sands lived in Belfast. He was just eighteen the first time he was arrested. Four handguns were found in the house where he was staying. After he was charged with possession, Bobby spent four years in the cages of Long Kesh. Back then, the Republicans had the status of political prisoners. They were deprived of their liberty, but they still had freedoms. They wore their own clothes; they could associate with each other; they had access to books and time for study. Bobby was a great one for the books. He even taught himself Irish.

"When he was released, he went back to his family. He was home less than six months before he was arrested again. There'd been a bomb attack on the Balmoral Furniture Company at Dunmurray. And after, there was a gun battle. Bobby was riding in a car near there with three other men when the RNC stopped them and found a revolver in the car. They were taken to Castlereagh and subjected to interrogations that were only brutal for six days. No matter what they did to him, Bobby would answer with his name, his age, and his address. Not a word more. He didn't put up a defense at the trial. He refused to recognize the authority of the British court. And there was no jury. Just the one judge who admitted there was nothing to connect Bobby or any of the other three to the bombing. So *his honor*"—Betsy watched a sneer transform Declan's open face—"sentenced all four of them to fourteen years apiece for possession of the one revolver.

"In the short span betwixt his first incarceration and his second, the bloody Brits stripped the Republican prisoners of their political prisoner status including their right to wear their own clothes. Most of the men refused to wear the prison uniforms seeing as they weren't thieves or rapists or killers but soldiers in the Irish Republican Army, so they went naked except for their blankets. So Bobby joined the blanketmen."

Betsy interrupted, "That's what they were shouting out there—'Blanketmen.'"

His eyes narrowed. Betsy couldn't decide if he was surprised that she wasn't familiar with the term or surprised to find himself sitting there relating this history to her while current events outside unfolded or combusted.

"The screws clubbed and kicked the blanketmen every time they left their cells, so the lads refused to wash or slop out and the shite was piling up in corners. The stench was ungodly but the lads wouldn't give in. Somebody had the bright idea to paint the walls of their cages with their own excrement to get rid of the stink. Conditions were pure brutal so, on the first of March, Bobby began refusing food."

"Oh! Of course! Bobby Sands was one of the hunger strikers."

"He was the first. At the end of March, he was nominated for a seat in Parliament for the Fermanagh and South Tyrone by-election. When Bobby won, the thinking was, 'Done and dusted, they'll have to grant the status now and the strike can end.'" He shook his head.

"After sixty-five days on the hunger strike, the right honorable Bobby Sands, duly elected Member of Parliament, died in the prison hospital at Long Kesh, just twenty-seven. He'd been a beautiful buck. You've seen the poster of him—

it's only everywhere—long hair, big smile, full of life—you probably thought he was a rocker or a film star. He was just a bag of bones when he died. Blind as well. Starvation is brutal."

Declan sat bolt upright, as if he had been prodded from behind. "Come here to me," he ordered.

Betsy was bewildered. They were sitting at a right angle to each other, their knees almost touching. "I'm right here."

He frowned, then saw her confusion. "Ach, it's only a local expression. It just means 'Listen to me now.'"

"I am listening, Declan. I'm all ears."

"It's that the hunger strike in the Haitch blocks is still going on." Declan's voice caught. "There've been five more died since Bobby. And still more languishing in the prison hospital as we speak. That is what it's about today. We're dead sick of it. Of being on a deathwatch. Waking up each morning and wondering who died in the night."

He cocked his head toward the voices that suddenly boomed outside and then the door burst open and the voices came crashing in, followed by dozens of bodies.

Declan laid his hand on the arm of a man headed toward the bar. "What's the story, Terry?"

Terry looked from Declan to Betsy. "It's all over but for the mendin' of the bones."

"We didn't make it to the embassy, but we gave better than we got," the man behind Terry nodded grimly. "There'll be lashings of gardai takin' up beds in the wards tonight."

"Declan," said Terry, "what happened to you? I thought you was down. One minute you was at me side, the next you was gone. I looked for yeh."

"I'm afraid I happened," Betsy hurried to explain. "I did go down and somehow he managed to rescue me. I don't even want to imagine what would have happened otherwise."

"A hero," Terry said flatly.

"To be sure," the second man seconded.

"You the damsel in this dress and him your knight hiding

in the armoire," said a third who suddenly appeared.

"Are you taking the piss here, Jimmy?" Declan said.

"I yam takin' the piss here, Declan. That I yam."

"I'm glad to see you lads are safe as well," Declan muttered. "We're off now." He telegraphed Betsy a look and she stood. "If the streets are clear, it's time we get you back to your kip."

Betsy made a show of cradling her arm and grimacing. She handed the towel to Jimmy. "Would you return this to the bartender, please? It's too crowded to risk doing it myself." Then she turned and started for the door, still cradling her arm. "Declan, could you walk on this side, as sort of a buffer?"

As the door swung closed behind them, he said. "Bloody buggers. They think I turned yellow. Can't blame them. I'd be thinking the same of any one of them."

"Well, I know better," Betsy said, watching the cloud that had descended over his face. "And they should too."

He perked up a bit. "Ah, to hell with that lot. Let's get you back to your kip now. You do look a sight."

Betsy was startled into taking inventory. Her dress was torn at the waist and the shoulder and there was dirt—a shoe print!—on the skirt.

*   *   *

When they pulled up to the B and B, the front door flew open as if on springs.

"Thanks be to Jaysus!" Mrs. Murtaugh cried from the doorway. "I was that sure you were lying in a pool of blood, the life draining out of you. And all my fault. It wasn't until I turned on the box that I remembered that today of all days was the march on the embassy. I thought I'd sent you to your death! I want to hear everything that happened. Don't you be leaving out a thing now."

"Oh, God," Betsy whispered as Declan helped her out of the car, "I need you to save me again. I'm going to tell her we have dinner plans. I don't expect you to stay with me. You can let me off at some restaurant. Just don't leave me here."

"You've been hurt!" Mrs. Murtaugh looked her up and

down, taking in the torn dress. "Did one of those brutes try to ravish you?" She shot Declan a look that suggested she suspected him despite his chauffeuring his victim to her door.

"I'm all right." Betsy wondered if it were the protesters or the gardai who were Mrs. M's brutes. "Well, mostly all right. Something hit my arm, but it's not broken. And I scraped a knee. It could have been so much worse. It would have been, but Declan here rescued me, got me completely away from Merrion Street. And really that's the whole story. I didn't see what happened. You probably know more about it— certainly more than I do—from the television."

"I guess I do at that. They said there were upwards of fifteen thousand protesters and only five hundred gardai. Two hundred injured were taken to hospital and most of those were gardai."

"Fifteen thousand," Betsy marveled. She thought about the marches she'd been on in Milwaukee, the ones she had thought of as large, and shook her head. And then she remembered the hundred thousand mourners at the funeral of Bobby Sands.

"Come in, lass. Come in. I'll put a kettle on."

"Thanks, but I'm just here to change my dress."

"Now, I'll not have you running off without a proper meal, not after all you've been through." Her eyes narrowed as she turned to Declan. "I can put another sausage in the pan."

"Thanks for the kind offer, Missus, but we'll be shoving off. We're due to meet up with some lads. Hurry on now," he said to Betsy. "We don't want to be late."

Betsy whisked past Mrs. Murtaugh and up the stairs. In her room, she surveyed her limited options. Gingerly, she slipped into the nearly clean, clingy yellow dress that revealed a slice of cleavage. Back when her sister Gina, then a nursing mother of twins, had admired Betsy's "perky breasts," Betsy had said, "My consolation prize for being childless?" She wrapped her perky cleavage under a cardigan buttoned firmly against Mrs. Murtaugh's appraising eyes.

"You'll be needing a good night's rest," Mrs. Murtaugh cautioned as Betsy descended the stairs, "after all the excitement. What with your leaving tomorrow morning and all and all."

"Oh, I can sleep on the plane," Betsy called back over her shoulder. "Don't wait up."

When Declan's car door closed, she said, "Thanks. You can drop me off wherever. I just couldn't face being the main dish at her table tonight." She hoped he wouldn't take her up on that option. She wanted nothing more than to spend the rest of the evening with him, but she wouldn't say that. She would barely admit it to herself.

"Sure I won't be dropping you off on your last night in Ireland. What would the Chinese say?"

Betsy grinned.

"You must be famished. Me belly thinks me throat's been cut. We'll be stopping at Dunnes to get what we need for a picnic supper. Then a quick stop to grab a blanket."

At the grocery store Declan filled their basket. "My plan is to stuff you with regrets so you'll leave Ireland planning your return. We'll start with a brick of smoked cheddar and a small wedge of this Kerry blue." They moved from aisle to aisle. "Some potato rolls to carry the Kerry. A nice loaf of spotted dog." They stopped in front of a glass cabinet. "Have you tasted our smoked salmon yet? Ah, it's only deadly. Some Guinness? No? Hard cider for the lady then. And a pint of tayberries. Grand that you're here in July. It's only in July that you get tayberries. And one banana."

"An Irish banana?"

"The banana is medicinal. You'll see."

"Let me pay for this, Declan. Dinner is the least I owe you."

"That's not how it works, see. I'm responsible for you, remember? That includes feeding you."

"All right then. I'm putting myself in your hands." She could feel the flush rising from her chest to her cheeks.

"I'll be taking me duties seriously. Including bestowing on you your rightful name. I don't see you as a Betsy."

"One of your countrymen said Elizabeth suits me." Betsy thought about telling Declan about Brian John David Samuel Beattie from the borough of Lisburn in the North, but she'd gleaned enough to know that it wasn't only geography that separated her Irishmen.

"Lizzie," he said. "From the first, I've thought of you as Lizzie."

He pulled up to the curb outside a two-story row house with a sunflower-yellow door.

"Is this where you live?"

"'Tis where my mother lives and 'tis where I grew up, but I'm only here for a wee while. Circumstances," he shrugged, leaving her to wonder what those circumstances might be. "I'm between flats."

"Should I meet your mother?"

He shook his head. "When I was a laddie, she used to say I was her 'child of grace made of butter.' Now . . ." he laughed.

He disappeared inside the yellow door. Betsy watched as the curtain on the downstairs front window was drawn to one side and a woman with a halo of white hair peered out, framed in the glass.

Betsy snuggled back in the seat and closed her eyes, reliving the improbable events of the afternoon.

"Would you be asleep now?" came a voice startlingly close to her ear.

Betsy's eyes snapped open to find the face of the white-haired woman bent down to hers. "Oh! No. No, I wasn't sleeping."

"You don't sound like you hail from these parts."

"I'm from the States," she said, sitting up.

"Well, look at you! The States now, is it? And how long have you known our Declan?"

"We only met today. He actually saved me from getting trampled on Merrion Street."

"Did he now?" The woman looked appraisingly at Betsy. "Are you one of them they call an 'outside agitator'?"

Betsy laughed. "Not me. More an innocent bystander."

"Are you planning a long stay here in Dublin?"

"I'm sorry to say that I am going home tomorrow." Betsy thought her interrogator relaxed noticeably, perhaps relieved at not having to perform any hostess duties.

"Ah, well. I wish you safe travels." She gave a little wave and disappeared into the house as noiselessly as she had come.

Betsy didn't quite believe in her. There was something of the fairies about their exchange. But then everything since she had left Mrs. Murtaugh's house in the early afternoon had been unreal or at least unimaginable. Why should this chimerical figure be otherwise? She shut her eyes again, resolving to stay within the dream.

The sound of the car door closing jolted her out of sleep. "Where are we going?" She blinked, sitting up. "Oh," she shook herself, trying to get her bearings. "For our picnic, I mean."

"Not too far from here. Your visit to Dublin wouldn't be complete now without going there."

"I'm not even going to try to guess."

They rode in amiable silence for several minutes, then Declan pulled over and parked. He grabbed the bag of groceries and the rolled-up blanket. "Follow me," he said, "walk this way," as he did a little jig down the sidewalk. Betsy laughed and he stopped on the corner and waited for her to catch up. "Have you tumbled yet?"

"Well, I would have if I tried to walk *that* way."

He turned to see her smirk dissolve.

"Oh! Thank you, Declan!" She stood gaping at the red brick corner building with its plaque stating the years of Oscar's Wilde's residence.

"These were called townhouses because they were the houses in town of the landed gentry. On their country estates they lived in sprawling residences; in town verticality was the thing. The rich did their living in their upper stories, far above the street noise and the street smells. Think cobblestones and horses' hooves and open windows and horses' shite."

"Merrion Square," Betsy sighed. "I'm sure Mrs. Murtaugh would approve."

"Not really square, you'll notice. A rectangle. They built them with a park in the middle so they'd have plenty of light pouring in. No buildings obstructing their view."

She surveyed the townhouses. "I'm finally seeing the celebrated doors of Dublin—they look enameled—and what do you call those arched windows above the doors?"

"Fanlights."

"Of course. Because they're shaped like fans."

"Clap your eyes on these," he tapped his shoe on a metal disk in the sidewalk the size of a large dinner plate. Then he walked to the next one.

Betsy's eyes swept down the pavement. "It looks like there's one in front of every unit."

"Coal holes. Where the deliveries would be dropped for each house."

They crossed the street and strolled along a wrought iron fence until they came to a gated entrance.

"What a gorgeous park," Betsy said once inside, turning her head to take in the perimeter of trees and the expanse of lawn studded with beds of flowers. "It's so lush."

"It is that."

"What's it called?"

"Archbishop Ryan Park."

"Seriously?"

"The park had always been private. That's why there's a fence all round. You could only get in with a key. The keys were rented out to the residents, the ones with nicker enough to live on the Square. This would be the park where your man Wilde would stroll." He unfurled the blanket on the grass. "Then the Catholic Church bought it—I dunno—maybe fifty years ago. The plan was to build a cathedral, but that never happened. So the Church went along renting out keys for the next several decades. Then about ten years ago, Sinn Féin started agitating to make it a public park. When the protests didn't change anything, Sinn Féin hit on a lethal plan. They distributed keys to all comers. The Archdiocese changed the locks and distributed new keys to the renters and the whole enterprise started all over again. And again. Costing the Church a continuous outlay of keys and time and money and aggravation. So Archbishop Ryan gave up and turned the park over to the city and got his name on a plaque."

"Well, I'm grateful to the archbishop." Her glance took in the few blankets that were scattered on the grass. "I'm surprised it isn't more crowded. This is by far the nicest evening since I've been here."

"A grand stretch," he agreed, "but most will be steering clear of these parts tonight, not wanting to be anywhere near the British Embassy, for fear the fighting will start again."

"Oh. Right."

He pulled the banana from the paper sack, peeled it, and offered her half. She shook her head. The fading light kindled sparks of gold and red in her hair.

"You need to be taking off your jersey."

Betsy was puzzled but did as directed, undoing the buttons with one hand and slipping the sweater off both shoulders with her good arm. Declan finished the banana and then raised his gaze. His eyes danced over her pale skin and yellow dress. "You're lovely," he said with an intake of breath. "All butter and cream." Then he blushed as though he just realized he'd given voice to his thoughts.

Not, noted Betsy, *That's a nice dress*. Or even *You look lovely*. But as if he were commenting on her essence as much as her appearance. Despite the chill air and her bare arms, a warmth suffused her.

Declan moved to her side and examined the injured arm. Then he placed the banana peel over the area where discoloration had begun to appear. "The only souvenir of my visit to Ireland," Betsy sighed.

He pulled a roll of surgical tape from one of his jacket pockets and began gently wrapping, creating a cast of peel and tape around her upper arm. "Am I hurting you?"

"No. You're baffling me. And I mean that in both senses of the word."

"Ah. Seldom do I meet such a well-spoken lass as yourself. Usually the ones I meet who speak well are speaking the lines of someone else."

"What is it you're doing?"

"This is me mum's remedy for bad bruises. Don't ask me how it works. Just trust that it will."

It struck Betsy that this cure was just the kind of medicine she might have expected that ghostly apparition to practice.

"There," he admired his handiwork, "that should hold till you get home." He helped her get the sweater on. "Toss me that yoke over there, will you? That," he pointed to a bottle opener. "When I picked up the blanket, I remembered to take that and the tape," he congratulated himself. He popped the cap on the cider bottle. "And these." With a flourish he pulled out two juice glasses and a knife from his magical jacket pocket.

"What did you mean before: 'They are speaking the lines of someone else'?"

"Actresses. I work at The Abbey."

"An abbey?"

"*The* Abbey. Not a monastery. The national theater."

"Oh! Are you an actor?"

"Not hardly. Lighting technician. I install, rig, operate, repair. Whatever's needed."

"Wait. Then how can you be here? Theaters are never dark on Saturdays. Is it because it's summer? Off-season?"

"Two shows today. One at three o'clock and"—he turned her wrist and glanced at her watch—"the other has already started. But I took the day off. Had other things to do," he said sardonically.

"Are you allowed to do that?"

"I told you I work in a theater, not a monastery. It's my job, not a religious vocation. Though my mother had hopes I'd go into the priesthood. *High* hopes, I guess you could say," he said, looking heavenward.

"My father wanted me to become a nun!"

"Did he now? And I thought you were a Prod."

"Me?" she squawked. "Me, a Protestant? I'll have you know I was one of the very few chosen to help clean the sacristy in our church every week when I was in eighth grade. And our family always said the rosary together after dinner during Lent. *On our knees.* Everyone I knew as a kid was Catholic. I mean *everyone.* I went to Catholic schools from kindergarten through university." She told him she had grown up in a city of neighborhoods referred to not by their geography but by the name of the parish in which they were located and how some of her classmates called the students who attended the city schools Publics, as though that were another religious denomination. "After all, we were Catholics and going to Catholic schools and as they were going to public schools. . ." She shrugged.

"Well, I can't claim your academic credentials, but I still serve on the altar at the occasional Mass, I don't eat meat of Fridays, and I never miss Mass on Sundays—I don't go in for the Saturday substitute."

Betsy was uncomfortably aware that he was speaking in the present tense, while she had talked only of the past. "Wow. That's pretty hardcore. I guess you didn't approve of the Vatican II changes."

"I guess you did."

"I did at the time. Now it all seems mostly irrelevant. I stopped going to church a few years ago."

"Did you now?"

"I think it came from studying anthropology. The whole 'One True Church' thing suddenly seemed so . . . antiquated. And"—she drew her shoulders up apologetically—"narrow-minded."

Declan looked at her noncommittally. He leaned over to cut hunks of cheese and bread and slivers of salmon and lay them out on paper napkins that came out of the pocket. "Didn't manage to bring any plates."

"Why, oh, why don't they serve this in the pubs?" Betsy said when she'd cleared her mouth.

Declan took off his jacket and folded it into a pillow and lay on his back, examining the darkening sky.

"You know, no one back home is going to believe any of this," she stretched out her arms to include him, their picnic, the park, the Merrion Street demonstration.

"Ah, sure, you'll be a celebrity. You'll dine out on your Dublin adventure." They both fell silent, perhaps both trying and failing to imagine her back home. As he sat up to fill her glass, Betsy reported that she would start her new job—"a children's librarian with a useless arm"—two days after her return to Milwaukee.

"What were you before?"

"A part-time textbook editor and teaching assistant, a full-time wife, and a sometime anthropology graduate student." She made a face. "I divorced my husband and my dissertation on the effect of clan identity on leadership roles among the Menominee Indians of Wisconsin and moved in with my sister and her husband and their two boys while I went back to school for a master's in library science. I couldn't afford to live on my own. The money I got from editing went for tuition. And therapy," she grimaced. "But living there has been about more than economics. It got me through a rough time. Like you, my sister is a rescuer. Oh, and by the way, Gina's an actress. Not professional, but really good."

"I can only say I'm grateful you didn't get bitten."

"I thought you theater people always stuck together."

"I'm not a 'theater person,' I'm an electrician." Declan moved near and, as punishment for improperly labeling him, began filling her mouth with tayberries, poking in one at a time, until speech was no longer possible. Betsy couldn't laugh for fear of choking. He took his thumb and wiped the juice from her lips. She closed her mouth over the tip of his thumb and nibbled until the tayberries were gone. Declan's eyes went wide. She looked up into them as she sucked his thumb clean. Then he leaned in and kissed her. It was a slow kiss, very like the kiss she had been imagining.

"Sorry," he pulled away. "Sorry." Not the words she had been imagining would follow.

"Well, I'm not." She couldn't keep the disappointment out of her voice.

Suddenly he barked, "Bollocks. What time is it?"

"I don't know." She glanced down. "It's gotten so dark I can barely see my hand."

He tilted his head back and shouted, "Anybody know the time?" His query was met with silence. "This is your last night gone arseways. Usually there's enough folk about that you notice a great migration around nine. Park closing is at half past. I'm guessing 'tis well onto ten now if not later."

"Well, it's not like they lock the park gates anymore."

"Ah, but they do. Every night. Promptly at half nine."

"Oh. God."

"Prayer might be your best option at that. Boosting you over the fence would be doubtful under the best of circumstances, but it's not on with that arm of yours."

"What will we do?"

"There's nothing we can do except wait till they open the gate in the morning."

"How early?"

"Parks in Dublin open at ten."

"You're kidding."

"I'm a right eejit. I wouldn't blame you if you was to eat the head off me. If you can't get the airline to honor your ticket for a later flight, I'll pay for another. The fault's mine alone."

"Maybe I can still make my flight. If you drive me to the airport."

"What time does it take off?"

"Noon. A few minutes after."

"We'll make it," he said. "I swear on me mum."

"Okay," she said, uncertain that it would be okay. She sighed deeply.

"You must be knackered."

"It's been a long day," she agreed.

"Feel around and see if you can come up with the bottle opener and what's left of the cheese. I think I've located everything else. I'll clear off the blanket and we can wrap up in it and get some sleep."

Betsy thought that might possibly be the least romantic speech ever made.

When things were put away, or at least off the blanket, Declan felt for her hand. He moved toward her, pulling the blanket around them, careful not to bump her swaddled arm.

"Sleep now," he said. "You've got two long days of travel ahead of you."

No, this was the least romantic speech ever, or at least a tie.

She settled into the crook of his arm and lay still but her thoughts were racing and her heart pounded to keep up. As when he'd carried her away from the protest, she lost all sense of the passage of time. Finally, she turned toward him and buried her lips in his neck. Declan didn't move. His passivity brought out the seductress in her. She raised her wounded arm and turned his face toward hers and her mouth sought his. Then she pushed his jacket open and drew her hand slowly down the front of his body until it rested below his belt. This was the reassurance she'd needed. Forget speeches. She didn't want words. With one hand she worked at his belt buckle and then his zipper until she could slide her hand into his pants.

She amazed herself. Not because she learned she was capable of acting the aggressor and not because this was the only man other than her former husband that she had touched in this way—and she had known Declan for less than a day—but because she was so sure. About *this*, the present, and so unconcerned about tomorrow. She wondered if that was how men felt. She raised herself cautiously and swung one leg over his prone body, straddling him.

"We can't, Lizzie," he said, breathing heavily. "I don't have any protection."

His resignation only emboldened her. "When I saw all the things that you produced from that jacket—a knife, glasses, napkins, bottle opener, even a roll of surgical tape—it did occur to me to wonder if you'd slipped a condom or two into one of those pockets."

Declan grunted. "You're thinking that would be simple, are you now? A quick stop at the chemist's? I guess you have no call to be knowing that contraception is illegal in our fair Republic."

"You can't be serious!" She could feel him shrug. "You *are* serious."

"A law was passed last year making it possible for married people to get contraception but by prescription only and they have to pledge to the doctor it will be used solely 'for family planning.'"

"Good lord. What a country."

"You've got that dead right. There is an outfit that gives out condoms for free, but you're expected to make a donation." He laughed. "The Family Guidance Company."

"What's so funny about that?"

"Other than their name? I just remembered where their office is located. Right on Merrion Square." He laughed again.

Betsy took a deep breath and whispered, as though the park were rife with listening ears, "It's all right, Declan. There's no chance of my getting pregnant. I'm not fertile."

Still he didn't move or say anything.

"I hope you're okay with my being on top," she said into the darkness. "With this arm, that's probably safer."

She felt his hands slide slowly up from her hips to

unbutton her cardigan. He slipped the sweater back from her
shoulders and carefully wriggled it off her arms. His hands
caressed her breasts through the thin cloth of her dress.
"Sweet Jesus," he said and she laughed and pressed his palms
against her.

"I think I can get my dress off okay but I'm not sure I can
manage my bra."

In one minute he had deftly lifted off her dress and
unhooked her brassiere. Given the fragility of her arm and
the utter dark, peeling off her underpants took a bit longer.
"I wish I could see you," he murmured.

"You will," she promised. "Since the gates don't open till
ten, we'll have a lot of daylight before anyone comes back in."

They made love twice that night, the first time was quick
and greedy, the second unhurried, as though they had the
rest of their lives.

Afterward, she lowered herself gingerly back into the
space he had made for her and dropped into dreamless sleep.

In the morning, Betsy prodded him awake, saying, "My
watch reads 7:20. We need to make the most of the time left."

He sat up and unfurled the blanket and dragged his eyes
down the length of her and then slowly back up. He nodded,
as if something had been confirmed for him, and then lay
back down.

A thin white line ran down from Declan's hairline
through his eyebrow like a snail's trail. Betsy traced the scar
with her finger. "Who were you demonstrating against that
time?"

Declan smiled and the skin around his eyes puckered.
"The most dangerous adversary a lad can have. That was put
there by my mother."

"What?" Betsy drew her hand back as though burned by
the raised skin. "That sweet white-haired woman did that to
you?"

It was Declan's turn to pull back. "You saw my mum
then?"

"She came outside and talked to me while you were getting things from the house."

"What did she say?"

"I don't know," she shrugged. "Nothing in particular. She asked about my trip. When I would be leaving. That sort of thing. I think she was just curious to see what her son had brought home from the demonstration. So how did that happen?" she said, pointing to his scar.

"I don't remember much—I was only five or six—but it was quite the story in the family. She had taken me down to the Grand Canal at Clondalkin to teach me to fish. Mum was demonstrating how to cast when the hook caught me right here." He touched below his eyebrow. "She didn't realize it was me she'd caught on the end of the line and gave a good tug. Seems the hook tore up my forehead and out my scalp. They tell me that she carried me into the dispensary and then fainted. There was so much blood from the scalp wound that my eye was covered and she thought she had blinded me, but it had missed my eye altogether. Later, my Uncle Colm went back to the canal to collect our fishing things and the picnic basket and whatever else was left behind and he delivered them to the house. Nana was after thanking him when my mother came to the door and grabbed both poles and broke them over her knee, each one. That was the end of fishing for the Joneses. As they tell it, my mother has always been a woman of firm decisions and strong convictions. And now," he said, lifting her and settling her on top of him, "if you don't mind, I think that's talk enough."

At twenty to ten, they were standing at the gate, as tidy as they could make themselves, gnawing on what was left of the cheese and spotted dog, the paper sack at Declan's feet and the blanket rolled and tucked under his arm.

The park attendant shook his head at the guilty parties. "Don't bother tellin' me the tale you've crafted, grand as it might be. Why add a fib to what you'll have to be confessin' to the priest?" He tsked. "And at your age."

They ran to the car. "No need to worry, Lizzie," Declan pledged, "I'll drive her like I stole her."

When they pulled up outside the B and B, the front door sprang open. Betsy wondered if Mrs. Murtaugh had stationed herself there through the night.

"You'll have to face her on your own," said Declan. "I'm waiting in the car."

Betsy ran up the path. "Were you worried about me? I'm sorry, but you shouldn't have. I'm really in a rush. My plane leaves at noon." She hurried past Mrs. Murtaugh and up the stairs.

"But where were you this whole night?" Mrs. Murtaugh called after her.

Betsy slammed into her room and quickly washed and changed into jeans and an embroidered peasant blouse and her sweater to cover her wrapped arm and stuffed the rest of her belongings into her backpack. She realized with a start that sometime after making love with Declan the first time, her arm had become considerably less painful. She considered throwing away the dress that had been torn in the demonstration, but decided her sister would appreciate a prop when the story of Merrion Street was told. When she opened the bedroom door, Mrs. Murtaugh was standing outside it.

"Where were you?" Mrs. Murtaugh repeated.

Betsy didn't want to give away a single word about Merrion Square. She said, "We had dinner with his friends and we all went to a pub and then Declan took me for a ride," moving Mrs. Murtaugh aside by proceeding with her backpack clasped in front of her.

Mrs. Murtaugh gasped, just a slight intake of breath. "You don't want to be saying that, pet. I'm sure it means one thing where you come from, but here it means quite another. 'He gave me a lift' is what you want to be saying to anyone who asks."

Betsy laughed. She said over her shoulder, "That's all

right then. No one else would ask."

Declan ran to the front door and took the backpack from her, ran to the car and threw the pack in the backseat, ran to the passenger side and opened her door, ran to the driver's side and had the car in motion by the time she got her door closed. Betsy half wished he wasn't in such a hurry. If she missed her plane, even if she missed the first few days of her new job, she was sure that all she had to do was present her injured arm and the story of a tourist blundering onto Merrion Street for allowances to be made.

Declan got her to the airport at twenty-eight minutes past eleven. He parked his car illegally, grabbed her backpack, and ushered her inside. He left her while she was collecting her boarding pass from the ticket agent and returned with a wheelchair and pushed her to the security checkpoint.

"I can't go further. Only passengers from here on since the Aer Lingus hijacking."

As she sat, she had been fumbling in her backpack and now pulled out the book she'd lifted from the Take One/Leave One shelf. She turned to the dedication page of *Bury My Heart at Wounded Knee*, printed her address in Milwaukee on it, and handed the book to him. "You'll write to me?"

"I'm not one for writing.'"

"Since about eleven o'clock last night, you haven't been one for talking either."

"Sorry."

"Don't be. I don't feel sorry, I feel lucky. I was damn lucky you came along yesterday afternoon. And lucky last night. And this morning."

The corners of his mouth turned up as he shoved the book into his jacket pocket. "And lucky to make your flight out."

"That's the one I'm not so sure about."

"You're a lovely lass, inside and out."

She blushed and then laughed to see him blush as well. "You will write?"

"I will that."

"Swear."

"On my mother's eyes."

She stood and set the backpack in the wheelchair. She put her good arm around his neck. "How do you say 'Until we meet again'?"

"See yeh after."

She reached up and tugged his hair. "I meant in Irish."

"Here's how." He leaned down and kissed her, the way he had the first time.

"I wish you could put that in a letter. Bollocks," she said with a grin. "I'd better hurry."

She went through the checkpoint and saw him waiting while she emptied her backpack and a gruff security officer poked through her things with a metal wand. She saw that Declan waited while she repacked. She didn't look back before turning a corner. She didn't want to see him gone.

The Opposite of Chance

14.

Declan turned the key and pushed open the sunflower-yellow door. He found his mother sitting just beyond it, hands folded in her lap, a rosary entwined in them, her eyes a stranger's appraising him.

"I hope you haven't been worrying all night," he said, trying to disguise his unease as concern.

"I sleep in a chair as well as not," she said.

"Since when?"

"Since me only son was replaced by a changeling. He looks like Declan. He has the voice of Declan. But he acts like he thinks he's Parnell."

He knew the Parnell reference wasn't so much about the politics of Irish Nationalism as the womanizing that brought him down.

"It's the stage you should've gone on, Mum. You've got a rare talent."

"I didn't have a voice for the stage. I lacked volume. And then there was me accent." Cliona Jones stood as though this were her exit line and walked stage left into the kitchen and put the kettle on to boil, thinking this was the one thing she shared with her deceased mother. The women of that generation had dealt with all difficulties by putting a kettle on to boil.

Declan was stubborn, but—Cliona thanked the God she had once renounced—not stubborn like his mother. He was not willful as a lad, her child of grace made of butter. He always listened—and then made up his own mind. She had been the headstrong one.

*   *   *

As a girl of seventeen, the first thing Cliona renounced was the wearing of girdles. The second was the Catholic Church, for much the same reasons. Neither seemed relevant to her. Both struck her as practices adhered to not out of conviction but out of custom. She was on the tall side and thin—willowy was the word often used to describe her—so she didn't see the need for a girdle. In her view, a girdle was something that was imposed by society on a lass to (a) keep her in her place (not just keep her buttocks in place), (b) promote restraint in all things (no wiggle room), and finally (c) add another layer of impediment to unmarried sex (a twentieth-century chastity belt). She thought religion functioned much the same way.

Once Cliona decided that the strictures of the Church did not apply to her, she stopped attending Sunday Mass altogether, to the horror of her devoted and devout extended family, who kept a tally of her accumulating mortal sins. No threats from her father moved her, so Monsignor McLafferty himself came to the Rooney house and gave Cliona a tongue-lashing followed by a penance beginning with a recitation of the Apostles' Creed and ending with ten Hail Marys, with five Our Fathers, the Act of Contrition, and a corporal work of mercy in between. Cliona declined to undertake the penance, and the monsignor, in a phlegmy fury, told her not to come near *his* church until she was ready to accept *His* authority, which suited Cliona just fine. But the priest's ostracism offended her father and petrified her mother, who fulfilled Cliona's penance on her daughter's behalf that very afternoon, reciting all the required prayers in her daughter's hearing and sending Cliona with a shepherd's pie to the McGintys, where Jack McGinty was out of work and Mairéad was swelled up with dropsy. Sheila Rooney hoped this errand would credit her daughter with a double corporal work of mercy as it entailed both feeding the poor and visiting the sick.

With her sisters and her aunts all making novenas on her behalf, Cliona had the sense to refrain from confiding her other recent conclusion: that she could discern no *earthly* reason to confine sexual intercourse within the bounds of marriage. Not that she had any plans, mind you.

Girdle or no, Cliona was accustomed to being appreciated by the other sex. With a cloud of flaxen curls, dewy skin, tipped nose, wide mouth, and clear blue-gray eyes, she drew attention. She had settled upon becoming an actress and all the ogling and flattery confirmed her choice.

She had no stage experience, excepting school pageants, but that didn't stop her from heading to London. Her parents tried to talk her into attending the local commercial college for girls that the Dominicans had opened. Then they just tried to talk her out of London. "Jaysus, Mary, and Joseph, lassy, they are evacuatin' people *out* o' London and that's where you're fixin' to go?" Her father took her by the shoulders and tried to stare some sense into her.

While several continents put the international havoc on the scale of an official World War, the Irish didn't even call it a war but referred to it by the diminutive "The Emergency," which naturally infuriated the English. Ireland was bent on maintaining her neutrality, and perhaps this contributed to Cliona's determination. "I have to be going to London," she shrugged. "That's where the Ealing Studios are."

*　　*　　*

Cliona was besotted with films. She liked viewing them and thinking about them and talking about them, so she was sure she would like being in them. The thing Cliona liked most about London was the number of cinemas she found there.

The thing she disliked most about London, the thing that made her homesick, was not so much the absence of family (she did miss them, but she was enjoying her independence) or the lack of familiar landmarks but the absence of lights. Cliona hated the blackout. As though *it* were the enemy. The blackout wasn't just visual but palpable. She could feel it coming on every afternoon, like the return of a headache.

To the surprise and dismay of the Rooney clan, who looked for her speedy return, Cliona was hired at Ealing, first as an assistant to the assistant to the script girl, and then as a stand-in for the likes of Gracie Fields and Anna Lee, and finally for bit parts.

She went out several times with one of the cameramen employed at Ealing. Invariably, they would end up at the cinema. "A busman's holiday," he called it. Cliona found that the only nighttimes she didn't feel stalked by the blackout were those she spent cocooned in a darkened cinema.

Rolly taught her about lighting and her face and the camera, the angles that were best for her, and she got more bit parts. Cliona was grateful to him. She liked him well enough but he didn't stir anything in her. She could tell he was quite smitten, though. Enough to ask her to marry him. With a ring and all. She said no.

He thought she was giving him the brush, but she was sincere when she said she didn't see why they couldn't go on as they were. So they did go on, but Rolly grew less satisfied and more morose. Cliona said it had become clear he no longer enjoyed her company and they "should call it a day." He told her that seeing her had become torture. Being so near but not close felt like she was punishing him. Or he was punishing himself.

She considered this. She didn't like the notion that she was making him suffer. "Is it doin' the bold thing that you're after?"

It was a few minutes before Rolly understood she was talking about intercourse. It wasn't just that he was unfamiliar with the Irish expression but that he was unused to sex as a topic of discussion. When he comprehended and then composed himself, he confessed it was all he thought about.

Cliona explained that, while she didn't know if she believed in the institution of marriage, she wasn't opposed in principle to the act of coitus. Finally, she said, "Well, you're a kind man, Rolly, leastwise you've been kind to me, and curious I am meself about the deed." She went on this way until Rolly realized she was offering to put him out of his misery. She suggested they set a date for it, but a glazed look had come over him, reminding her of her brother's middle son the time the boy had emptied the sweets box. Trembling, he took her hand and shook his head. "Now," he said.

Cliona decided she had no strong objection, so they went to his flat. It was the first time she'd seen where he lived, how he lived. Two rooms, minimally furnished, but the walls were papered with black-and-white photographs from films he'd shot—stills, he called them. Cliona wanted to stop to examine the images but he had clasped her hand and was drawing her into the second room with its neatly made metal-framed bed.

Pulling away, Cliona reclaimed her hand and with it she untucked her blouse from her skirt and began undoing buttons as he watched, slack-mouthed. When she had stepped out of her shoes and divested herself of blouse and skirt and slip and laid them neatly over the rail at the foot of the bed, he could remain still no longer. He sprang to cover the space between them. Rolly slid the gossamer straps of her brassiere off her shoulders. With a gasp, he cupped his hand around one of her small breasts and gave a strangled cry as he came all over himself. He mumbled an agonized apology but then saw Cliona had no idea what had happened so he knelt and removed the garters holding up her hose and then the hose themselves. This last made Cliona anxious as hose were hard to come by and she feared him snagging hers. Finally, he slipped her panties over her hips and down her long legs. A sob escaped him. Cliona patted his head and stepped away to fold down the blanket and top sheet and lie down on the bed.

He undressed hurriedly, turning his back to her to wipe himself with his undershirt. He already had a second erection by the time he wheeled to face her. She stared at his engorged member and would have liked to back out of the situation, out of his flat, out of London and this new adventure, but a retreat on the brink would have been cowardly and unsportsmanlike and unlike her.

As he entered her, Cliona cried out but stifled any more sounds of pain. Rolly was suffering too, by the sound of it.

Afterward, as he stroked her hair and kissed her cheek, she lay still and thoughtful. Cliona came to the conclusion that she didn't like sex. It was painful and awkward and messy and horribly smelly. If it were her flat, she would burn the sheets.

She was not distraught at having tried it—how else could she know what it was really like as it was quite unimaginable? That anyone would want to go through that nasty business twice was beyond imagining. She told her cameraman they wouldn't be doing any more of that.

By turns, he was distraught, penitent, and insistent. But none of it did him any good. After a month of entreaties, he was convinced that nothing he could do or say would get Cliona to accept either his hand in marriage or his hand anywhere on her willowy body again.

To expunge his passion, he had to turn her into a slut and a cock tease in his mind. And then, for corroboration, in the minds of others. Rolly's new coldness, his knowing leer, made Cliona's position in the studio much less pleasant. Then she stopped being called for bit parts, even for work as an extra. She imagined things were being said about her on and off set. And she was right.

It wasn't long after the atmosphere in the studio changed that Cliona discovered she was pregnant. "That . . . mess," she marveled, "the whole business lasting less than the time it took to undress—that's all it takes to make another person." She also marveled that it could happen the very first time; she'd assumed that the baby part took some skill or at least some practice. Of course she'd known of girls who had gotten pregnant when they didn't want to, but she had figured that the fetus had accrued, resulting from some magic number of accumulated experiences.

She was a bit simple perhaps, but she had grown up in the dark ages before World War II, was barely eighteen, and had come from a family that had worked to shelter her not just from harsh realities but from all reality. She didn't cling to fairy tales but had them tucked all around her, cushioned by well-meaning parents and older siblings who wanted to insulate her and indulge her. Her belief in Father Christmas outlasted all her baby teeth.

She might have declared herself uncertain about the institutions of the Church and of marriage, but as she considered her options, abortion was never one of them. Neither did it occur to her to consider giving the child up for adoption. Nor would she raise a bastard. Her only choice, as she saw it, was to provide a father for the child. But as she didn't intend to do the bold thing ever again let alone on anything like a regular basis, she decided to give the child a dead father.

This was not as difficult as it might seem. At first she thought about choosing a soldier who had been killed at the front, a hero a son could look up to and a daughter could use as a standard to judge other men by, but soon saw complications. She'd have to acquire and master details about the war and the dead man's record of service. And what about the War Widow's Pension everyone would be expecting her to receive? A dead soldier would be troublesome.

Instead, she chose a different casualty of war, one that had the added advantage of being neatly unencumbered by family relations. Arlen Jones died in a collapsed rooming house during one of the worst nights of bombing in the horrible blitz. He had no known relatives, people who could object to her naming him as father on the child's birth certificate, and the date of his demise would work nicely. The blitz could be blamed for her lack of their marriage certificate and all of his belongings, even for her having no photographs of her husband.

She had taken his name and scant biographical details from a roster of unclaimed bodies of victims. She wrote to her family back in Dublin of her marriage to an English baker a few months back and of her imminent return with the unborn child of their ill-starred union. She signed the letter Cliona Jones.

None doubted her. Not their child of grace made of butter. Headstrong Cliona had never lied to cover her tracks before. Rather, she had always seemed to enjoy defying convention. They saw no reason to suspect she had given up the practice. Besides, they were too busy with worrying about her future—a grieving widow not yet out of her teens about to embark on motherhood—and with forgiving her for her unforgivable marriage.

She gave notice at Ealing and left London before she started to show. The last thing she wanted was for Rolly to find out he was going to be a father. Then she'd never be quit of him.

The Rooney family welcomed her back like the prodigal she was. She had her choice among her parents' and two of her siblings' homes. She chose to bide with her parents. After her homecoming supper was cleared away and all the sisters and brothers had made their good nights, her parents bade her sit again at the table. Her mother clasped both Cliona's hands in her own as her father said, "I won't be bringin' it up but this one time: how is it you come to be wed to an Englishman?"

"Love, I guess, is the answer."

"'He was good to yeh?"

"Never an unkind word or gesture."

"If he was no two-headed monster, then why not bring him home and be married proper?" her father thundered. "Why in secret?"

"Da, you know I would have felt two-faced being wed in a church and you would have been mad as a box o' frogs to see me wed elsewhere. And then I thought you'd take to him being English a mite better if he were a fact rather than a threat."

Teddy Rooney grunted. He regretted what she had done but he could see the logic in it. "And why was this Arlen Jones not away in His Majesty's service?"

Cliona had wondered this, too, so she had an answer prepared. "His eyes," she said. "Bad vision." No one could fault her dead husband for that. "You should have seen the specs he wore, they were that thick."

Sheila Rooney released her daughter's hands and made the sign of the cross over herself as she asked, "How is it—thanks be to God—you happened not to be with your husband when the bombs hit?"

Cliona had almost rejected Arlen Jones as a candidate because of his occupation. The same night, a bank manager had been killed in the street when the portico of a hotel fell on him during the raid. She thought a bank-manager father would be more inspirational than a bread baker, but then she wouldn't be able to explain her lack of any inheritance. Now she had reason to be grateful for Jones's profession. "He was in bed hours before I got back. Our schedules coincided only on Sundays. He had to get up for work at three in the mornin' six days a week. We were filming late that night, and by the time I got there, the fires had been put out, but there was no building upstanding and no husband lying in bed."

Sheila started to cry softly, picturing her daughter standing in the ashes of her marriage. Cliona realized it would look well to shed a tear or two of her own, so she pretended to be in a movie. She imagined herself just coming back to Dublin and finding the rubble of London and the suffocating blackout shrouding her dear city.

True to his word, Ted Rooney never raised the subject of Arlen Jones again.

The night of May 30, 1941, Cliona's water broke and the midwife was sent for. Bridie had made a favorable impression on her antenatal visits. She was young and earnest and seemed quite knowledgeable. She talked to Cliona not just about what she should and shouldn't do but about the development of the fetus. On her first visit she told Cliona her baby was already the size of a plum. The next time she said, "Oh, you've got a turnip inside you now." Eventually she was told she was carrying a red cabbage, then a cauliflower, then a green cabbage, then a coconut, and finally a pumpkin.

Cliona had only once seen either a coconut or a pumpkin with her own eyes and both on the very same occasion, a wrap-up party for cast and crew on *Spare a Copper* in which she played two nonspeaking roles, a music shop customer and the bewigged and buttoned-down secretary to a German spy, both of which ended up on the cutting room floor. Still, she got paid and the party was fun and the exotic centerpiece was divvied up and the produce went home piecemeal with the guests, a bonus you could sink your teeth into during the privations of rationing. Perhaps because she was well liked, or perhaps out of sympathy for being erased from the picture, Cliona had been awarded the coconut, but she shuddered at the thing, all hard and hairy on the outside—but hairy *like it was balding*—and sloshy on the inside. She didn't know what to do with it. She traded her coconut for a small paper cone of hazelnuts, *real* nuts, she congratulated herself.

She didn't care to contemplate a turnip, or cabbages of any color, or a disgusting, hairy coconut growing inside her. She continued to think of the interloper as *the little plum* throughout her pregnancy.

Cliona was already in bed with regular pains when Bridie arrived. The midwife got right to work, opening her case. She felt around and listened through the Pinard Horn and frowned. With one hand on Cliona's belly, Bridie said something to Sheila Rooney during one of the contractions and the latter slipped out of the room. When she didn't return immediately, Cliona wished she hadn't begun this whole baby business. She thought, *I'm just a babby meself.* "I want me ma!" she wailed when another of the contractions came on.

When at last Sheila returned, she brought a strange woman into the bedroom, strange because she was not of the Rooneys' acquaintance and strange because one side of her face was drawn up toward her ear.

"This is Sister Martha," Bridie said. "She's come to help with the birthing."

"I'm a registered midwife," the newcomer said briskly. "A full year's training at Belfast's Union Infirmary. I was in a fire when I was eight," she added, turning her face toward the light for a full view. "But it didn't affect my hands or my brain, the parts of me needed this night. So let's have a look."

Cliona finally understood that something was wrong, that this Sister Martha had been sent for. "What's the matter with me babby? Why doesn't someone tell me? Ma? Is it dead?"

Bridie lifted her head from the wooden horn she had resting on Cliona's belly. "No, no, your baby's alive. The heartbeat is strong."

"Your baby is in the breech position," Martha said.

"What does that mean?"

"It's tryin' to come out arseways," her mother said.

"What?"

"Arse first instead of head first." Sheila was wringing her hands because she didn't know what else to do with them.

"That's bad, is it?"

Bridie stepped between the bed and Cliona's distraught mother. "Sister Martha is the best in Dublin when it comes to delivering a breech. Just do as Sister says and everything will be fine."

Martha spread her hands like wings and moved down Cliona's front and along her sides as if she were measuring her for a dress.

"Can you turn it?" Sheila Rooney asked. "I've heard how some can use their hands on the outside to turn the baby 'round on the inside. Have you ever done that?"

"I have done, but we'll be doing otherwise tonight."

"There's dangers of their own come from that," Bridie whispered.

"Your daughter," Martha turned to the mother, "is long and narrow on the inside as well as the outside. Turning is too risky for the baby. Now—Cliona, is it?—now, Cliona, I want you to get out of the bed and squat down. Bridie, you take this arm and, Missus, you take the other. Let's let gravity do some of the hard work."

For a moment it passed through Cliona's mind that this was the way Sister Martha took her revenge for what had happened to her face, the needless torture of the unscarred, but she was too sensible to hold such a thought for long. Cliona squatted as Bridie and her mother knelt on either side of her, keeping her upright.

"With the next contraction, push hard," Martha instructed.

"I have been that," Cliona said through gritted teeth.

"Harder, then," Martha corrected.

On the next contraction, Cliona grunted and groaned with the effort and the women on either side struggled to keep her from pitching forward.

"Harder still," said Martha.

"Shut your gob!" snapped Cliona. The outburst was so unlike her it startled both her mother and Bridie into laughter.

"Listen, Cliona," said Martha, "the baby's bottom is hanging out, but the legs are still tucked up. I need you to get them to follow on the next push. All right?"

Suddenly there was a loud whistling noise that sounded impossibly, horribly familiar to Cliona. "Ma, it's a bomb!" she cried.

"It can't—" started Sheila Rooney, but it could and it was. The whistling was followed by a horrendous thunderclap and a vibration that shook the house followed by another boom. Sheila got up from her knees and ran to the window. "Dear God in heaven!"

"Please get back to your daughter's side, Missus."

"But it *was* a bomb!" Mrs. Rooney protested.

"The baby doesn't care about bombs," Martha said. "And neither can we. No matter what happens out there, we have our work to do in here."

Cliona looked up at Sister Martha's resolute face and thought that, except for the puckering, she was really quite beautiful. Another contraction came. This one's for Sister Martha, she thought to her little plum as she strained forward. Cliona bore down until little blood vessels burst along her cheeks and forehead, like a sprinkling of purple freckles.

More whistling and more bombs hitting, explosions and the roar and rumble of brick and wood collapsing.

"You did it, Cliona! The legs are out. And you've got yourself a son."

Ted Rooney came running back from wherever he'd gone to escape the birthing. "We've got to get out o' here," he shouted as he burst through the door. "The DeVaneys' house is in splinters!" The DeVaneys' house had been next door.

"*You've* got to get out of here," Martha said with a gentle shove. "*We* have work to do."

Teddy would have given much to unsee the half-born baby dangling from between his daughter's thighs as he turned and fled down the stairs. He didn't leave the building, though. If the women could stand it, so could he. As he made his way toward the press where he kept the bottle of whiskey, it occurred to him to wonder if it weren't the Brits up there bombing in retaliation for the Republic maintaining its neutrality.

"Good girl," Martha said. "Now don't push. I'm going to reach up my finger and try to hook an arm and pull it down. If we get his arms down and deliver the shoulders, then his head can come."

Cliona thought there were too many variables to be left to chance. Too many *ifs* followed by too many *thens*. *If* Martha could hook each arm, *if* she could deliver the shoulders, *if* the head would come, *if* the bombing would stop, *if* their house would be left standing.

Bridie reported on the left arm descending. Martha again maneuvered. "It's going to be all right," she said as more bombs screamed and buildings imploded.

As the two women steadied her and Martha reached around and up inside her, Cliona shuddered with pain and the thought that not only had the War followed her home from London but it had deliberately chosen this very night to do so. What was the opposite of chance?

This was the proof she had needed of a higher power. The air strike could have happened anywhere at any time, but it was happening right here and now. On her street on the night she was to give birth. She vowed that if she and her child were spared, she would return to the Church. "God, forgive me," she said softly and then the head came out and, at last, she heard her son's cry.

In Cliona's mind, her notions of War and God's reckoning would forevermore be conflated if not interchangeable.

"Holy Mary, Mother of God, pray for us sinners, now and at the hour of our death," Sheila Rooney beseeched, concentrating on aspirating her H's and hoping that "now" and "the hour of our death" were not coincidental. Then she got up from her knees.

"Amen," Bridie said as Mrs. Rooney went downstairs to put the kettle on.

Bridie and Martha stayed the night. All agreed that while mother and child were resting well, it was still too dangerous for the midwives to be out on the streets, though none was foolish enough to think being indoors afforded any real protection.

The morning brought great sorrow. Neighbors had died or were in hospital. Not only was the DeVaney house demolished, but bombs had left craters in the next two houses on the other side. And in the house after that, the only thing left standing was a staircase to nowhere. There was no denying that God had chosen to preserve the Rooney house.

It was as if North Strand Road had been *the* target of the Luftwaffe. The air raid had killed dozens and destroyed seventy houses on Dublin's Northside. No one could understand why Ireland's neutrality had been violated. Germany declared it an error and promised reparations. Winston Churchill later admitted that the British had invented a device to distort Luftwaffe radio-guidance beams and that might have succeeded in throwing the planes off course that night. But Cliona continued to believe the attack divine in origin, not determined by anything man-made.

But the morning brought relief as well as grief. No member of the Rooney clan had been injured and, miraculously, Mrs. DeVaney was alive. She had been out back in the jacks when her house was hit. The body of her husband buried under the debris, she had been found sitting amid the rubble in shock, but she at least was safe.

Sheila Rooney fretted all this would cause Cliona to relive the night she lost Arlen Jones to the London Blitz. It was only diabolical that her poor daughter had to give birth during the bombing. New mothers were shaky enough without such horrors, past and present.

But there was joy as well. Everyone agreed Declan was a fine baby—already a dimple decorated his chin, marking him for great things. Serene Sister Martha pronounced him not only unimpaired by his perilous birth but uncommonly sturdy.

To the delight and amazement of her family, Cliona not only declared herself renewed in her Catholicism but she refused to delay the baby's baptism for even the customary month of confinement following the birth. She thought it unlikely there would be a repeat of the night's bombing now that she was returned to the Church, but she saw no point in taking chances with the little plum's soul.

For a time, the house on the North Strand Road was as crowded as it had been when Cliona was little. Joining her and Declan and Ted and Sheila Rooney was the newly widowed Mrs. DeVaney and Cliona's oldest sister and her brood, whose house had shattered as if it had been bone china. Miraculously, they had all been away visiting her mother-in-law in Wicklow.

Catherine Ann was a real war widow. Along with thousands

of his fellow soldiers, her husband had deserted from the Irish Army to join the British and fight Hitler. Catherine Ann's return to the Rooney house provided another set of hands and eyes on the new baby, and before long, Cliona was able to begin classes at the college run by the Dominicans, where she learned double-entry bookkeeping, by which she was able to support herself and her son even after her parents had passed and her sister remarried.

Declan had been a good son to her. Once he began working at The Abbey, he would purchase for his mother a ticket for every opening-night performance. Declan believed that the shock of the tragic death of his father and his own birth within a few months of each other had traumatized his young mother as well as forced her to give up her acting career. Though she seldom spoke of his father, she had quietly devoted herself to his memory. Some of Declan's mates and even his cousins referred to the house on the North Strand Road as The Convent as his mother led a nunlike existence there (and they enjoyed saying he worked at The Abbey and she lived in The Convent). Cliona made it clear to all comers—and there had been quite a few—that she was done with romance except for what she could view on the silver screen (where, thankfully, the lovers kept their clothes on).

Cliona enjoyed the performances at The Abbey as much for viewing the opening-night audience as for watching the plays. She still preferred films to theater. A measure of her preference was that for the forty-six days of Lent each year, Cliona gave up going to the movies. But she'd still attend an opening night at The Abbey during Lent as giving up the theater would have been no great sacrifice.

*   *   *

She arranged two cups and saucers on the tray along with the steeping teapot and a plate of toast and a pot of loganberry jam and returned to the front room, where Declan had remained, in a trance to all appearances.

"I didn't see you at Mass this morning," she said. She settled herself in the chair opposite and poured both cups.

"I went, though. To Our Lady Queen of Heaven. You know, the airport church."

She nodded. "Agnes phoned last night," she said as she handed him his tea.

He went from a slouch to bolt upright. "What did you tell her?"

She rearranged the items on the tray. She wanted to give him time to worry. "I told her you were out celebrating the Merrion Street mayhem and that you'd probably get back too late to ring her. What else would I be tellin' her?"

Declan slumped back into his chair.

"Agnes said she'd seen pictures of the battle with the gardai on the news in Bath and she was sure you'd been in the thick o' things. I said you were only in and out of the house with not a moment's breath to report on your participation, but that you looked well enough. 'No permanent harm done,' I said."

Declan shifted uncomfortably. "Did she say how the tour is going?"

"Standin' room only the last weekend in Bath."

"And where are they off to now?"

"They're off to Cardiff." She looked at her son. She never saw Rolly in him, thanks be to God. He was better looking, for one thing. She had always thought him kinder and more honorable too. She asked herself if she had thought that because he was hers and it pleased her to think so. Maybe he was like Rolly after all, and all the other men who had come sniffing around in the decades that followed. "But Agnes isn't going on with them. She's left the tour. She said to tell you that your wife is comin' home."

And Back

15.

Bleary-eyed, Betsy emerged from Customs at Mitchell Airport. She searched for a familiar face among those waiting beyond the mesh barrier and found none. Her gaze dropped to a pair of familiar brown leather huaraches. The woman wearing them was holding a hand-lettered sign in front of her face that read:

AMELIA
EARHART

Betsy tapped on the sign. "Really?" she said.

Gina lowered the cardboard and grinned. "It was beginning to feel like you were never coming back." Betsy put down her backpack and the sisters hugged.

"Careful," Betsy said. "I have a sore arm."

"My God," Gina scrunched up her nose as she pulled away. "You smell like . . . like a giant loaf of banana bread."

"I know. I know. There's a banana peel wrapped around my upper arm. I was hanging into the aisle half the flight to spare the poor man seated next to me." She shook her head. "Where are the twins?" She swiveled, expecting to see a pair of three-year-old boys pop up from behind a row of seats.

"They'd better be in bed. It's almost ten."

"Bed," Betsy yawned. "I want some of that."

"Sorry. No sleep for you. Not yet." She hoisted her sister's backpack and headed for the door. "I want to hear everything."

"You do realize it's like, I don't know, five in the morning for me?"

"Okay, then. Not everything. The banana peel compress can wait. Just some things."

"One thing. And then you'll leave me alone until morning?"

"Only if you give me the best you've got."

"That's easy." Betsy stopped and waited for her sister to turn back around and face her. "I'm in love." She enjoyed watching her sister's jaw drop.

Gina was practiced in the art of quick recovery. "Is he titled? Rolling in money? I wouldn't mind having a duke or an earl for a brother-in-law."

"He's wonderful and principled." She considered a moment. "Not conventionally handsome. More like ruggedly good looking in a burned-out super hero sort of way."

"Uh, oh. Sounds like he's probably insolvent. Is he employed at least?"

"He's a theater lighting technician."

"So semi-employed. I know those theater types. That's why I married a dentist. Is he interested in you or a green card?"

"I only wish he wanted to move here."

"Does this wonderful, principled theater guy have a name?"

"Yes, a wonderful name. Declan Jones. And he's not a theater type. He's an electrician."

"What kind of name is Declan?"

"Irish."

"And that makes him—?"

"Irish. Half Irish, to be precise. The Jones half is English."

"Oh. Now as to your options, either don't tell Mom or just refer to him as Mr. Jones. If you do decide to tell her he's Irish, promise me you'll wait until I'm there to watch."

*   *   *

Betsy stopped at her sister's bedroom door after she'd put her nephews to bed and announced, "I should tell you guys I'm embarking on my new career with a new name. Well, not new, I'm reclaiming my birth name."

Gina was puzzled. "But you already took back your birth name when you went through the divorce."

"Elizabeth. Shouldn't be any problem at the library—

they don't know me by any other name."

"But why? You've always been Betsy."

"Because I prefer it."

"Since when?"

"A long time, I guess. But I can tell you exactly when I decided to *do* something about it: the night I stayed at that creepy hotel at the port in Le Havre."

"The boys will still call you Betsy, you know," Gina said.

"Maybe. Our bedtime conversation tonight wasn't solely about steam engines and dump trucks. We had a nice chat about how I was Betsy when I went away and how I became Elizabeth while I was over there. They seemed to like the idea that I came back a different person. Anyway, when I left the room, they were already calling me Elizabeth. Well, Whizbeff, to be precise. If you like, you can call me Whizbeff too."

*　　*　　*

Each day when Elizabeth left work and returned to Gina and Matt's house, she sifted through the basket on the table by the front door that held incoming mail. And each day, not finding a letter, she asked Gina if there was "by chance" any other mail, and each day she was disappointed.

"Why don't you just write to him?" her sister finally asked.

"I would but I don't have his address. He has mine. And he's living at his mother's right now and I don't know her name or how she would be listed."

"You said he worked at the Abbey Theatre. You could write to him there."

"That feels desperate. Like I'm stalking him."

"He could have lost the scrap of paper with your address and right now be praying for you to get in touch."

"No. He couldn't have lost my address. It wasn't on a piece of paper. I wrote it in a book."

*　　*　　*

In the weeks since her return, she kept remembering, reliving, reveling, spending much more time thinking about Declan than they had spent together. Several times a day she heard him say she was a well-spoken lass and smiled to herself. Even more times a day she felt his mouth on hers and lifted her fingertips to her lips. She went to sleep with him each night and woke with him each morning. Their brief time together expanded inside her.

He had said he wasn't much of a letter writer—she remembered everything he'd said including that—but they both knew he would write to her. She worried that he had been caught up in another demonstration, that he had been arrested, that he was already isolated and wasting away in one of those wretched H blocks. At the library she sifted through international news sources for coverage of Dublin and found nothing specific to encourage or alarm her.

She worried he had been hit by a bus.

*   *   *

Elizabeth sat staring at the Scrabble board. "It's your turn," Gina prompted.

"Sorry."

"Your mind is definitely elsewhere," Matt said.

"Dublin," Gina nodded.

"Actually a lot closer to home." Elizabeth looked from one to the other. "Now that I'm feeling comfortable with the job and getting a regular paycheck, I think it's time I look for a place of my own."

"No!" said Gina.

"We would be happy if you'd think of this place as your home," Matt said.

"We thought you did," Gina sulked.

"I have," Elizabeth said. "You guys made that easy. Maybe too easy. I'm really grateful. You got me back on my feet. But it's time for those feet to do some walking. I'm going to look for someplace to rent on the East Side, closer to the library."

"What about the twins?" Gina threw out in desperation.

"How can you even think about abandoning them? They'll be broken-hearted."

"High drama," her sister lifted one eyebrow. "I gather this is a warm-up for your audition next week."

* * *

"God, I'm so tired," Elizabeth sighed as she came into the house. She looked enviously at her nephew Doug, who was snoring gently on the couch, and collapsed into the chair closest to the front door.

"Pssst. Dennis, remember?" Gina beckoned the other twin *sotto voce* from the kitchen doorway. "We've got a surprise that will make your Aunt Elizabeth really happy."

Dennis darted past his mother into the kitchen and returned with an envelope. "He-ah, Aunt Whizbeff," he said solemnly as he thrust the slim blue rectangle at his aunt.

Elizabeth had trouble making out the scrawl on the exterior of the envelope. She marveled at the Post Office's ability to discern its intended destination. The only thing she could tell for sure was the aerogramme's country of origin. She went into the kitchen to get a knife and, holding her breath, carefully sliced through the folds on the single sheet that served as both letter and envelope, all the while under Gina's intent gaze.

"It's not from Declan," she said, ending the suspense. "It's from Brian. The goofy young guy I told you about. The one I met on the boat going over from France. His handwriting is impossible. The nuns in Lisburn must have been way less persnickety than the nuns in Milwaukee." She shook her head. "I just remembered he's a Protestant. Not the nuns' fault." She bent over the paper, laughed, then read, then laughed again. "He's describing a ceremony his sister put the family through. A goodbye to his mother. His dead mother. Recently deceased." She laughed again.

"Hilarious," Gina said disapprovingly.

"They made these solemn speeches and released balloons into the air, a symbolic letting go of her soul, I guess. From what I can make out, it seems it started raining and all the balloons massed over Brian's head. You'll have to read it. You'll have to *try* to read it," she amended. "Not only is the writing difficult but it's minuscule. To fit it all onto the one page." Elizabeth returned her attention to the thin blue paper. "Oh, dear God. Oh, no. Poor Brian. His brother has been shot. In a riot in the North. He says by the I.R.A."

Gina was confused. "Not by—what did you call the police?—the Gardai?"

"Brian and his family are Protestant Northerners. Irish Brits, I guess, is another way of putting it. They'd be supporters of the Gardai." She looked down again. "Brian says his brother's in critical condition. He wrote this from the hospital." She stood up. "I'm going to the Post Office to buy a couple of these aerogrammes. I've decided to take your advice. I'm going to send a letter to Declan care of the theater."

*   *   *

Three weeks later another flimsy blue rectangle made its way into the incoming mail basket. This one was postmarked Dublin. Elizabeth's hand shook as she lifted it from the basket.

Dear Lizzie,

I was glad to get your letter and hear that you're settling in to your new job. Your sister and her husband sound like great sorts.

I've been meaning to write to you, but this is not the letter I thought I would be writing when I left you at the airport.

My wife returned to Dublin two days after you flew out and we decided to give our marriage another try. And I was failing badly. In bed and elsewhere. After I received your letter, I saw it was the guilt I was feeling that had built a wall between her and me. I told Agnes about you and about our night in the park. And after that, we started over.

I never meant to deceive you about being married. We had given up our flat four months before that day on Merrion Street. We had both agreed the split was permanent. Agnes left on tour—she's an actress—and I moved in with my mother. I didn't want to bring up the separation. As I recall, you didn't want to talk about your separation or divorce either.

Remember when I told you that contraception isn't legal in Ireland? Rubber sheaths aren't the only things you can't get here legally—there is also no divorce. If things went on as they were, I would never be free and I would no longer be wed. I'd be sitting on the sharp edge between the two. It all seemed final and yet endless. Like eternal damnation.

It wasn't my plan to make love to you. You reminded me of my wife in some ways, but different too. It was like having her back and having someone new, which is what I suppose most men dream of, gits that we are. And I was feeling happy for the first time in a long while. Despite the Troubles, despite my marriage. You seemed happy as well. I didn't want to spoil it all.

If Agnes hadn't come back, I would have written sooner and I would have written different. But she left the tour and came home and we are trying.

I won't ask you to forgive me and I won't blame you if you hate me. I promise that, no matter how things work out, I won't bother you again.

I wish you all the best. You deserve nothing less

Declan

Over the weeks since her return, she had continued to let herself fall more deeply in love even without any provocation from him. Now the falling was over. It was not bottomless. She had crashed. She felt a wave of nausea as she read and reread the words.

Gina came to the doorway expecting to see her sister beaming, not clutching her stomach. "What's the matter?" she said.

"I guess this is what they call lovesickness," Elizabeth said on her way to the bathroom.

When she returned, her sister was holding the letter and staring off into space.

"Gina, what are you thinking?"

Sheepishly, she confessed, "I was wondering how good an actress his Agnes is. And if she gave up much of a role in the show that was touring."

*   *   *

That night, when Elizabeth emerged from her room, she joined Gina and Matt at the kitchen table. Gina had just finished showing the letter from Declan to Matt. Elizabeth watched him watching a spot on the table.

"What is it?" she said. "What are you thinking, Matt?" She grabbed the edge of the table with both hands and leaned forward. "That I was a fool, right?"

"I was thinking about your whole trip," Matt said. "There you were, rejecting all these married men—there was the French businessman on the train, and then there was the American husband of the woman with the broken foot or ankle or whatever, and then there was the hotel owner on Lake Como. And the guy you fall for turns out to be another married man. It just seems so ironic."

"Why would you say that?" Gina demanded. "To upset her even more?"

Matt shook his head at his wife, who knew better. "Because she asked me what I was thinking. I didn't want her to believe I was sitting here thinking she's a fool. What I was thinking is that she has integrity even if the men she met didn't."

"Well, I'm glad you said it," Elizabeth slumped back in her chair. "First, because I do care what you think of me. And second, because you've made me realize I don't put Declan in the same category as the others, and that's some comfort."

*   *   *

Elizabeth complained that she was waking up tired.

Gina said, "I'm worried about you. You haven't been yourself since that letter from Declan. I wish you could just stop thinking about that rat."

"Not a rat," Elizabeth shrugged. "At worst, a mouse."

"You aren't angry?"

"I felt like he hadn't written because he didn't care. That I didn't mean anything to him. But everything makes sense now. You can't be really angry when everything makes sense."

"But he made love to you while he was still married and he told you he was single."

"Not exactly. He didn't say anything one way or the other and I didn't ask."

"That's not the point."

"You're thinking that I'm thinking that Declan is like Greg. Or like one of those other guys that I met over there. But I'm not. What I maybe didn't make clear when I told you about that night is that I went after him, not the other way around. He was . . . reluctant. I see it now, but I didn't then. Or didn't want to. I don't think he had any intention of having sex with me." Her eyes widened as she said, "I honestly think he just wanted to take me on a picnic."

"Come on."

"No, I'm serious. It's true he didn't tell me he was married, but he was separated and I was leaving the next day. I can see why he didn't think there was any reason to go into it all." She fell silent. Gina sat down on the floor to wait for her sister to harvest more thoughts.

"But more than all that," Elizabeth resumed after several minutes, "I really think his intentions were entirely honorable. And Declan is too gentlemanly to point out that I was the one who pursued him. I remember feeling annoyed that, after we picked up groceries, he stopped at his mother's and loaded up on all the other stuff he thought we might need, but he didn't include a condom. I felt disappointed that having sex with me was not on his agenda. Of course I didn't know that condoms weren't readily available. Can you believe contraception is still illegal in Ireland? In this day and age?" She shook off the digression. "Even though I didn't have to worry about getting pregnant, I was ticked off.

I even complained to him about it!" she marveled. "Anyway, he made up for it once I overcame his resistance. But I think it's fairer to say I had my way with him rather than he had his way with me. You know, I think he was still trying to be faithful to his vows." She was thinking that she didn't know how to explain to her sister that she was thankful that she hadn't allowed Declan to happen to her, that she had made a choice. And the opposite had been true for Declan.

Elizabeth shook her head as if to order the jumble of thoughts bouncing around in it. "I was so caught up in the intensity of the day. The last day of my trip. The flying bricks and bottles. The Gardai juggernaut. And my dashing Declan. Lord, it was exhilarating. Just try to imagine being swept up and carried to safety. By someone with that accent! And then indulged—Declan taking me to see where Oscar Wilde had lived. It was so sweet and silly and generous after everything that had happened. I think that's when I decided to love him. I honestly don't know what I would have done if he'd asked me to stay. Back in Archbishop Ryan Park I couldn't predict exactly what our future together would look like, but I was sure we would have some kind of future together." She shook her head again.

"Are you miserable?"

Elizabeth considered the question and was surprised by the answer. "Not anymore. I was a wreck right after his letter came. I felt stupid and . . . used. But I've had time to sort through it all and it's just nice to be able to remember what passed between us and appreciate it for what it was."

Gina said, "If I ever go through anything like what you've gone through, which I promise you I will not, you will be my role model. I've been afraid you were sinking into a depression. I was going to suggest you go back to that therapist. But if you're not brooding about Declan, I think you should see a doctor. Even Matt has said you seem to be dragging yourself around. I think you'd like our new G.P." She smiled wickedly. "The boys are terrified of her."

* * *

White-blond hair skinned back into a bun on the top of her head, steely gray eyes, and impressive girth, Gina and Matt's general practitioner studied Elizabeth's test results and then peered over her rimless glasses at her patient.

Determined not to be cowed, Elizabeth spoke up, "Do you think I might have hypothyroidism? I've done some research. That would account for a change in my metabolism which, in turn, could account for my weight gain and fatigue. According to the medical texts, I could also be looking forward to constipation, thinning hair, muscle weakness, heart disease, and impaired memory," she rattled off. "Hypothyroidism could even be the reason for my god-awful semi-annual menstrual periods. Maybe my traitorous thyroid is not putting out enough thyroxine."

"Your thyroid is fine." Dr. Genitis said.

"Are you sure?"

Dr. Genitis looked like one of those physicians who are sure of everything.

"I don't see how that can be. My symptoms keep getting worse. I can barely stay awake past six p.m. And none of my clothes fit. My metabolism is shot."

"We have your blood test results—the T4 and TSH both fall in the normal range. What does your OB-GYN say?"

"You think my problem is gynecological? God knows I've had gynecological problems since I started having—or rather, mostly not having—periods when I was a teenager. And once I did start menstruating, they've been crazy irregular ever since. So you think it's some kind of hormonal imbalance that's making me so tired and making me gain weight?"

"I've never thought of your condition in quite that way," the physician raised her precisely penciled eyebrows.

Elizabeth frowned. "My condition?" Then her eyes opened wide. "Oh! God. Are you saying I have an STD?" She was suddenly rethinking her perspective on her interlude with Declan.

"Sexually transmitted, definitely. Disease, absolutely not."

"What are you talking about?" Elizabeth realized she had raised her voice above an acceptable level when a nurse came down the hall and shut the office door.

"Your pregnancy," Dr. Genitis said.

"What?"

"Though I guess you could regard it as a hormonal imbalance."

"Are you saying you think I'm pregnant? That can't be."

"Your urine test says otherwise. When you had the blood drawn, we also ran a urinalysis, remember? You've got a positive result for pregnancy."

"That's not possible. Not. Possible. I'm infertile. For eight of our ten years together, I tried to conceive with my ex-husband."

"Well, that suggests that if there was an infertile partner in your marriage, it wasn't you."

Elizabeth sat open-mouthed.

"When was your last menses?"

"Trick question. I think about six months ago but, before you decide I'm an idiot, remember I've always been incredibly irregular. That's not the longest I've gone between periods. I didn't have a single period during the year I was sixteen."

"And when did you last have unprotected intercourse?"

"Seriously? The only time I've had sex in more than two years was four and a half months ago."

"Then I think we can safely say you are eighteen weeks pregnant. The weight gain, the fatigue, the nausea, every symptom you describe is attributable to your pregnancy. You're far enough along that a pelvic exam would be conclusive, but I think you're better off having that exam with an obstetrician. You need to be under the regular care of an O.B."

*   *   *

When Elizabeth arrived home, Gina met her at the door. She was flushed and fluttery.

"What is it?" Elizabeth asked. "Are the boys okay?"

Gina bobbled her head up and down.

"It's not another letter from Ireland?" Elizabeth asked warily. Wearily.

"I heard back from The Rep! I've got the lead! You're looking at Hedda Gabler."

"That's wonderful, Gina. Really, really wonderful."

The sisters hugged.

"I've got big news too."

"Yes?"

"I'm pregnant."

Gina took an involuntary step backwards. "You just had to go and top me, didn't you?"

* * *

Matt made popcorn. "Gina ate buckets of popcorn when she was pregnant with the boys," he said, pouring the popped corn into two equal bowls, keeping one for himself and Gina and handing the other to Elizabeth.

"This is all going to work out," Gina said. "You'll have to forget about moving out now. My play will be over before your due date so I'll be around to help when the baby comes. If you want me in the delivery room, just say the word. Oh! I could partner you for the birthing classes! This is going to be great."

"Have you picked out names too?" Elizabeth asked. "I think it does make sense for me to stay, if it's still okay with both of you, until after the baby is born. I'd like to wait until I'm on maternity leave to move."

"That will give me and the twins plenty of time to get you to change your mind," Gina said.

Matt and Elizabeth both rolled their eyes.

Undaunted, Gina continued, "Well, if you think you're tired now . . . You know, I can't wait to see Mom's face when she finds out her grandchild is going to be half Irish."

"Actually, a quarter Irish," Elizabeth corrected. "But she'll never know."

"What?" Gina squawked. "You're not going to tell her who the father is?"

"No."

"Well, I don't think you're going to get away with an Immaculate Conception. You'll have to tell her something."

"I've been researching artificial insemination the last couple weeks. I'm going to tell Mom and Dad and anyone who asks that the father is an anonymous sperm donor. It's not so far from the truth."

"Seriously?" Gina said. "Who is going to believe that?"

"After not getting pregnant for all those years, who is going to believe some kind of medical intervention wasn't required for me to conceive? Everyone knows I was trying to have a baby practically my entire marriage. No one we know is going to suspect that this is the result of a roll in the park with a virtual stranger."

"But you're not married. Artificial insemination wouldn't be legal. Who would treat you?"

"I'll say I found a sympathetic doctor whom I'll decline to name."

"I don't know. I just don't know. A turkey-baster baby might be harder for Mom and Dad to swallow than a roll in the park."

"I expect there will be more choking than swallowing at first. But when the baby arrives, they'll adjust. I mean, they'll just have to." She squelched the feeling of panic that threatened to undermine her determination. "I've decided to tell them and everybody else—except you two—that I planned my trip as a last fling before a last try at motherhood. I'll say that I had set up the appointment for my insemination to take place right after my return, and that I've firmly decided to 'spare everyone the technical details.' And I'll tell them I'm unshakeable in my resolve to protect the identity of the doctor who treated me. I'll also say that, given my gynecological history, I was waiting to share the joyous news until I was far enough along to feel reasonably secure in the pregnancy. Mom and Dad might not like it, but I think they'll believe it. It's slightly less improbable than a virgin birth."

"And Declan?" Matt asked.

"I knew that would be your first question, Matt. And, at first, I thought I'd have to tell him. That it was his right to know. But, really, why? He wouldn't want to be a father to this child. And, practically speaking, he can't be. You can't parent from across an ocean. Besides, he's back with his wife. None of us want our lives to intersect. But he's so . . . so Irish Catholic, who knows how he'd respond or what this would do to his marriage. This could ruin their lives, and his knowing would definitely complicate mine. I can't see that anything positive would come out of my telling him. Not for him or his wife or for me." She nodded her head slowly, still working through the idea as she spoke. "Or for this one," she cupped her hands over her belly. "This has to be my child, not our child."

Gina considered. "He didn't tell you about his wife, so you don't have to tell him about his child."

"It's not that. It's really not. But I don't think I owe Declan the truth. I don't think I owe him anything. Except maybe gratitude. For making it possible for me to have the one thing I've wanted for so long." She looked from one to the other, not sure what she read in their faces. "So, what do you think?" she said with a dry laugh, looking down at her midsection. "Fate? Or the luck of the Irish?" Somehow nothing about her trip seemed random now.

"What will you tell that one?" Matt asked, nodding toward her hands stretched across her abdomen.

"I had the ultrasound today. I'm going to tell my daughter the same thing I'll tell everyone else." She wondered if Matt still thought she had integrity, this person who was planning to lie to her child every day for the rest of her life. And she wondered if she could stick to the plan. "This much is true: I'll tell her I wanted her more than anything. More than other people's approval, more than being free."

"You've got that right," Gina said. "People are definitely not going to approve and you're going to have to kiss your freedom goodbye. It's a good thing you got all that adventuring out of your system because you're going to be pretty much stuck for the next couple decades."

"Some folks might say parenthood is the greatest adventure," Matt offered.

Gina snorted. "Some folks will say anything."

Though seated securely in a sturdy wingback chair, Elizabeth yielded to the familiar sensation of falling into the bottomless unknown.

About the Author

Margaret Hermes grew up in Chicago and lives in Saint Louis. Her short fiction collection, Relative Strangers, was the recipient of the Doris Bakwin Award. In addition to dozens of stories that have appeared in journals such as *Fiction International, The Laurel Review, Confrontation, River Styx,* and *The Literary Review,* and in anthologies such as *20 Over 40* and *Under the Arch,* her published and performed work includes a novel, *The Phoenix Nest,* and a stage adaptation of an Oscar Wilde fable. When not writing, she concentrates her energies on environmental issues.

Acknowledgments

The Opposite of Chance was written over the enormous stretch of three and a half decades. One of the chapters/stories was penned—I say "penned" because all my first drafts are written in longhand—in Ireland in 1982, and the final chapter written in the Midwest in 2018. The rest were undertaken irregularly, between other projects, so in development this work has been examined by an assortment of readers. For most segments, my first reader has been my dear partner, David Garin, whose indisputable preference for nonfiction helps me hone and pare. Several chapters were polished with the sound advice I received from the Three Rivers writing group in the 1980s, where I harvested lasting friendships as well as improved technique.

I am fortunate to number fine writers and astute readers among my acquaintance, and within my family. Librarian Arlene Sandler, water-colorist Shelly Helfman, and poet Jane O. Wayne were kind enough to review some of my fourth or fifth drafts of individual chapters. My daughters, Sarah Hermes Griesbach and Lucy HG Solomon, both being accomplished writers as well as immersed in the visual arts, lent their critical eyes to many of the chapters over the years and to a draft of the manuscript. From a distance of 2,000 miles, Lucy held my hand virtually through the process of revising.

Several of the chapters have appeared as short stories in different literary magazines. I am particularly grateful to Adam Davis, one of the editors of the *Green Hills Literary*

Lantern for his careful reading of "All Roads Lead to Mekka." His gentle questions and restrained comments led me to strengthen and clarify that chapter prior to its publication in story form in *GHLL*.

Despite abundant research, that chapter, with its pilgrimage, still needed vetting by Muslim readers. While having no Lebanese Muslims among my acquaintance, I am fortunate to have survivors of the war in Bosnia as friends. Elvir Mandzukic and Belma and Amir Kundalic read the Mekka story for transgressions. I am particularly indebted to Amir for pointing one out and for sharing his memory of their war torn homeland.

I am beholden to poet and memoirist Jason Sommers who took the time, twice, though facing his own deadlines, to scour through the chapters featuring Irish characters and what I hoped sounded like Irish speech. His seven years residence in Dublin and his acute ear made him my Hiberno-English language authority. His humor and encouragement make him my friend.

I owe a deep debt of gratitude to two dear friends who are gifted writers and discerning readers. Both read my finished manuscript in novel form. Jacquelyn Kelly advised me on tone—and persuaded me to tone down accents—and Linda Tucci bestowed upon me the gift of a careful line reading. Their comments and suggestions and encouragement were invaluable in making the disparate parts come together.

I was fortunate to have as my agent, Gail Hochman, who gave me the gift of sympathy when I was in need of it. Delphinium Books was the right home for this particular story with its unusual structure. Their editorial director Joseph Olshan gave my manuscript his careful attention and saved me —and you—from my excesses. I am so grateful to Delphinium's Nancy Green who saved me from some serious gaffes. "Copy editor" seems woefully inadequate. She should be given a title like Distinguished Wordsmith, or at least a crown.

Lastly, I owe this book, in the most fundamental way, to my mother, Ann Grace Hermes. It was she, following my divorce, which left me with two young children (unlike my protagonist) and no disposable income (like my protagonist), who telephoned one day to ask if I didn't want to go to Europe. She bought my plane ticket and supplied me with some travelers' checks (remember those?) and I set off with a borrowed backpack and great anxiety in the summer of 1982 (1981 was more tumultuous on the European continent, so that became the year of Betsy's journey). I am so grateful for that trip, which put distance between me and my divorce, and furnished me with material for stories, and provided the unprecedented gift at the end of my travels of time spent alone with my mother who died suddenly nine months later.